READY TO RIDE

JULIET KEANE

Copyright © 2024 by Juliet Keane

All rights reserved. This book or any portion thereof may not be reproduced or used in any manner whatsoever without the express written permission of the publisher except for the use of brief quotations in a book review.

This is a work of fiction. Names, characters, business, events and incidents are the products of the author's imagination. Any resemblance to actual persons, living or dead, or actual events is purely coincidental.

1

LILY

The sky was crystal blue and the asphalt was coal black. The contrast was made even more stark with the bright sunshine illuminating the sky. I had to squint against it to read the road sign announcing my arrival in Crestwood.

It had been a two-hour trip from the city and I was ready to be done driving. Part of the allure of living in a city was not needing to drive far to get anywhere. But I wasn't in the city anymore. I was in the middle of nowhere and completely out of my element.

The GPS was telling me to continue down the road for another mile before I would reach my destination. In that time, I would cross the complete distance of the town of Crestwood, population 14,235. For at least the hundredth time today, I wondered if I was making a huge mistake.

It was too late to turn back now. I had made a promise

to a friend – my best friend, Harper Sullivan – and I intended to keep that promise.

After parking my car between two huge trucks that had to be compensating for something, I took a deep breath before stepping into the stifling heat. Summer was nearly over, but it wasn't going out quietly. We had been dealing with the unseasonably warm temperatures for a couple of weeks and I couldn't wait for it to be over. There was nothing pleasant about sweat rolling down your back unless you were in the middle of a workout or an orgasm.

A sharp whistle made my head turn as I stepped onto the sidewalk.

"Can I help you?" I snapped at the man leaning over the hood of a truck. The brim of the hat pulled low over his eyes shielded most of his face, but not his cocky grin.

"I sure hope so," he replied with a deep drawl that was foreign to me. City boys didn't sound like that. "You got a name, beautiful?"

"I have one for you." I narrowed my eyes behind my sunglasses. "Starts with an A and ends with a hole."

The man slapped a hand over his heart. "I think I'm in love."

"Ronan, leave the woman alone and get to work." The second man stormed up behind him without looking at me.

"I was just trying to make a new friend," Ronan protested.

"If you think a woman like that would ever be your friend, you're even dumber than you look, Huntley."

"Ouch, Evan. That hurts." Ronan turned his attention back to me. "I'll see you around, beautiful."

"I damn well hope not," I replied, spinning on my heel. The two men grumbled at each other and I had only gotten a few steps away before I heard heavy footsteps behind me. "I'm not in the mood to be objectified," I said without turning around.

"Good to hear."

It wasn't the asshole who was following me, it was his friend. I sighed and turned to face him. "What do you want?"

"To apologize. On behalf of the idiot waiting by my truck." His smile was hesitant and crooked, lifting higher on the left side and revealing a dimple.

Damn. Perhaps I shouldn't have been so quick to turn away from him earlier. Beneath his dirty baseball hat, he had sparkling blue eyes and a delicate bone structure. That crooked smile softened the gruffness of his rough stubble. He was gorgeous.

"I'm Evan," he said, holding out a large hand.

"Lily." I intended to shake his hand, but he surprised me by bringing my hand to his lips and kissing the back of it.

"Welcome to Crestwood, Lily." Then he released my hand and stepped back before dipping his head in a slight bow. "I hope to see you again sometime."

Before I could process what had just happened or say anything, he was walking away.

"Damn," I muttered to myself as I stared at his perfect

ass in jeans that had no business looking that good. City boys never looked that good in a pair of jeans.

I forced myself to stop gawking and reminded myself why I was in Crestwood. I was here to help a friend, not to fantasize about sexy country boys.

A bell chimed as I stepped into the adorable bookstore. It was exactly what I had expected. It was modern, cozy, and inviting just like the owner.

"Lily!"

I was grinning as I raced forward to hug my best friend. It had been almost a year since we'd last seen each other. We both squealed and hopped up and down as we embraced.

"Harper Sullivan, you are so damn cute," I said, pulling back to check out her adorable dress. She had always been the trendiest girl in our friend group while my style was much more traditional. "And this store is perfection."

"Thank you." She looked around proudly. "We've been working hard."

"We?"

"My brothers have been helping with the heavy lifting." Harper gestured toward the far wall that was still bare. "All we have left is putting up some shelves over there. They just went out to grab some supplies."

"You are lucky that you have so many brothers to help out." I had always been a little jealous of her big family. Harper had five brothers while I was an only child.

"I appreciate them more now than I did when we were

growing up and they kept scaring away any boy who showed interest in me," she said with a laugh.

"Is it possible to scare away the cowboys in this town?" I asked, thinking about Ronan's blatant flirting.

"What could you possibly know about cowboys?" she said with a laugh. "Isn't this your first time out of a big city?"

"Hardly," I scoffed. But she wasn't exactly wrong. I'd traveled a lot in recent years, but never to a small town like this. "I ran into a couple of the locals on my way here."

Harper's eyes widened. "Of course you did. A pretty woman like you is bait to the men around here."

"Like me? What's so special about me?" I felt like I should be insulted at the implication that I was bait.

"I mean... look at you." Harper gestured up and down my body. "The women around her don't wear tight skirts like that. Or fancy knee-high boots with heels that pointy. Face it Lil, you look like a city girl. Something shiny and unattainable. And cowboys love a challenge. They'll all be lining up to take a turn roping you in."

"That is a terrifying metaphor." That was a lie. I was open to the right cowboy tying me up. Like maybe one with blue eyes and a crooked smile.

"Can you help me with these boxes?" Harper nudged one of them with her foot. A foot that was wearing a pretty pink cowboy boot. It might've looked childish on anyone else, but Harper could pull it off. "I want to get these out of the way before the boys get back."

"Yeah, sure. Put me to work." I clapped my hands once. "That's why I'm here, right?"

"Not exactly. I mean, you're here because I asked you for help, but I wasn't talking about manual labor. This is just some busy work until I can take you to the ranch later." Harper slapped a box knife into my hand. "That is when the real work will begin."

I was happy to help Harper with anything she needed. We had been friends since our very first day as roommates in college. In the following decade, she had stood by my side through everything and I counted her as family. Better than my real family because she'd never done anything to hurt me. That was why I had been so eager to accept her request for help with some legal and financial issues at her family ranch.

In the meantime, I was just as happy to help her stock the shelves in her new bookstore. She had been working on it for the last six months and I was so proud of her.

"That's the last box," she said as I bent down to slice open the packing tape.

The shop's door chimed again and two deep voices bickered back and forth from behind me. My entire body tensed as the bickering stopped abruptly and I heard a familiar whistle.

"I knew we'd be seeing each other again, but I wasn't expecting to see you like this, beautiful."

Ronan's familiar drawl made my breath hitch. With a loud sigh, I straightened and turned to glare at him. The glare lost some potency when I saw Evan standing next to him, mouth slightly agape as he stared at me.

"No!" Harper's command was sharp as she stomped across the room.

"No?" Ronan curved a teasing smile at her. "What's wrong, Harp? Are we not allowed to be friendly?"

"Not with my best friend, Huntley. You've already fucked every woman in this town. This one is off limits." She crossed her arms as she huffed.

"Your best friend?" Evan's eyes were still on me. "Lily... you're Lily Jameson."

I nodded uncertainly. "And should I know your last name?"

"Yeah." He exhaled hard, shaking his head. "It's Sullivan. I'm Harper's brother."

2

LILY

It figured that the gorgeous man I'd met earlier would be my best friend's brother. She had so many of them and Crestwood didn't have a huge population. Plus, the universe hated me and would have no problem putting me directly into the path of the one man I absolutely could not take to my bed.

"You two know each other?" Harper asked, glancing between me and Evan in confusion.

"Not exactly. We kind of bumped into each other outside."

"Ronan was being his usual self, harassing a pretty woman in a skirt," Evan explained.

"Of course." Harper stepped forward and slapped Ronan's arm. "You are too old to keep acting like such a dick. If I catch you hitting on Lily again I will castrate you, Huntley."

Ronan just laughed and caught her arm, pulling her

into a rough hug. "Come on, Harp. You know you find me utterly charming."

I glanced at Evan to see how he felt about this guy hugging his little sister, but Evan just shook his head and lifted the toolbox he was holding. "Let's go, Huntley. This is my day off and I don't want to spend it watching you annoy my sister and flirt with the city girl."

Ronan scrubbed a hand over Harper's head, messing up her hair. She put both hands flat on his chest and pushed him away. "Maybe I'll just flirt with your sister instead, Sullivan."

"I've got a few thousand acres where I can bury your body."

The threat was delivered so dryly that it made me laugh and when Evan looked at me in surprise, his crooked smile reappeared. "My sister clearly did a better job picking her best friend than I did."

"Lil, let's go grab some coffee and let the boys get to work. Ev, I'm going to lock up so you don't have to worry about any random customers popping in."

"Sure, Harp. It shouldn't take us too long to finish this up." Evan set the toolbox on the floor and flipped it open. My traitorous eyes were once again drawn to his ass.

"You feeling alright, beautiful?" Ronan winked knowingly as he stepped in front of me. "You're looking a little hot and bothered."

"Huntley, didn't I already tell you to leave her alone?" Evan said without looking up.

I took that as an invitation to sneak away without acknowledging Ronan's annoyingly astute commentary. I was definitely feeling warm in such close proximity to the man bent over in front of me.

"Sorry about that," Harper said after locking the door behind us. She looped an arm through mine and started down the sidewalk. "Ronan is harmless. Annoying, but harmless. He's mostly just a big flirt."

"He's Evan's friend?" I asked.

"Since they were little kids. Ronan basically grew up with the rest of us. He even helps out on the ranch. We can't seem to get rid of him. Like an invasive disease." She smiled playfully at me. "He seems to like you."

"He likes embarrassing me," I corrected her.

"That's pretty much the same thing to him." She hummed happily and squeezed my arm. "Evan will keep him in line. He's had years of practice."

"Your brother seems nice," I said as neutrally as possible. "Is he married?"

"None of my brothers are married." Harper frowned. "I think Dad is giving up hope on us settling down and popping out a bunch of babies. And he's seriously questioning his parenting skills now that none of his grown children have settled down and most of us are in our thirties."

"Sounds like the Sullivan clan has some serious commitment issues." I nudged Harper with my elbow. "I bet Ronan would put a baby in you if you asked nicely."

Harper gagged in the most unladylike way. "Just for that, I'm going to tell him that you think he's hot."

"He *is* hot," I said with a shrug. "So is Evan."

"No!" Harper flashed angry eyes at me. "None of my brothers are hot. Do you hear me? They are hideous."

"Whoa, chill. I'm not looking to hook up with any of your family members, Harp. I was just making an observation."

"Look, I love my brothers. They are flawed men, but they are good men. I just don't want you getting involved with any of them because when they inevitably fuck it up, I'm going to lose my best friend." She waved a hand to the coffee shop in front of us. "Let's get some coffee and chat about anything that isn't my family."

"Fair enough," I said with a laugh.

We stayed at the coffee shop for a couple of hours, drinking coffee and catching up on our lives. We used to talk every day on the phone, but both of our schedules had been crazy for the last couple of years. Harper had moved back to her hometown and opened the bookstore while I'd been focused on my career, helping lead a software startup to an impressive IPO. It wasn't until I'd been forced off the executive team and cashed in my equity that I'd finally had some time to breathe and focus on anything other than work.

"How is your dad doing?" I asked as we were heading back to the boutique.

"He's holding up alright. I know it's been hard for him to step away from the day-to-day work at the ranch, but it was time for him to think about retiring anyway." Harper had initially moved back to Crestwood when her father had suffered a stroke two years ago. It had almost killed him and he'd spent over a year doing rehabilitation to recover motor function. Once he'd gotten to the point where he could take care of himself again, Harper had decided to stay in town rather than move back to the city.

"I'm excited to see him again," I said.

Thomas Sullivan was a good man who had worked hard to run his ranch and raise his large family after his wife died twenty years ago. I knew from Harper's stories that he hadn't always been able to give his kids the time they needed, but he'd done the best he could. I met him a few times when he came to the city to see Harper and it had always been obvious how much he loved his kids.

"He is so grateful to you for agreeing to come help us out. When I told him I'd reached out to you, he said he couldn't imagine a better person for the job." Lily smiled proudly. "You're going to love the ranch."

"I'm sure I will." I was trying to remain optimistic. I had nothing against ranch life, but it was going to be completely foreign to me. "Have your brothers come around to having an outsider join the ranch business?"

"Eh." She shrugged noncommittally. "Don't worry about them. Once they see how smart you are, they'll be just as thrilled as Dad."

"I'm kind of surprised that Evan wasn't more hostile toward me," I admitted. From what Harper had told me before I arrived in town, her oldest brother had been the one most resistant to bringing me onto the team.

"Evan has a lot of strong opinions when it comes to the family business, but he's a good guy. A gentleman at his core. He would never be outwardly rude to you." She grimaced slightly. "I can't say the same about Brent and

Chase. Those two can be real dicks when they don't get their way."

"Looking forward to meeting them," I joked.

"You can handle them." Harper's confidence in me was rewarding. "You've dealt with guys a lot more dickish than my brothers."

"Businessmen can be challenging," I agreed.

She laughed. "I was talking about your ex-boyfriends."

"Touché."

Harper unlocked the door and pushed it open with a flourish. "You guys are amazing!" she sang out. "It looks perfect."

The guys were just putting the last shelf in place as we entered the store. Ronan fired a smirk over his shoulder. "Not the first time I've heard that from a woman."

"You dream a lot, do you?" I quipped without thinking.

Ronan laughed. "I'll certainly be having some dreams tonight, beautiful."

Evan punched Ronan hard in the arm. "We have rules against sexually harassing Sullivan Ranch employees."

"Oh, that's right. You're the new girl." Ronan raised a mischievous eyebrow. "The Sullivan boys have been real worked up about you, city girl. Your hairstyle does a great job at hiding your horns."

Harper gasped in horror and Evan looked like he was thinking about punching Ronan in the face this time. I tossed my hair over my shoulder and said, "Glad to hear that my stylist nailed the look."

"Ev, do you think you could lead Lily to the ranch? I was going to do it myself, but I forgot I told Dad that I would stop at the market to grab some stuff for dinner." Harper batted her eyes at Evan and he groaned.

"I'll do it," Ronan said, taking a step toward me.

"No." Evan pulled him back. "You finish cleaning up this mess and bring everything back in the truck. I'll ride with the city girl and make sure she doesn't get lost."

"I can just pull up the directions on my phone," I said.

Harper ignored me and hugged Evan. "You're my favorite brother," she said. "I'm putting you in charge until I get there. Make sure none of our siblings hit on Lily, okay?"

"Yeah right," Ronan scoffed. "There is no way to control those Sullivan hormones."

"I'll keep an eye on her," Evan promised, ignoring his friend.

"I don't actually need a babysitter," I protested.

Evan chuckled. "Think of me more like a bodyguard. When you meet the other Sullivans, you'll see what I mean."

"I'll be there as soon as possible," Harper promised, giving me a gentle shove. "You'll be in good hands with Evan."

I had to be the worst friend in the world because my mind immediately envisioned being in Evan's hands and what I was picturing was more than just good.

3

EVAN

"This is a nice car." I finished pushing the passenger seat as far back as it would go and clicked my seatbelt into place.

Lily glanced at me. "You're teasing me."

"No. It's...nice." I shrugged. "Not exactly the best car to have out on the ranch, but I'm sure it's perfect for city life."

"It gets good gas mileage." Lily kept her eyes straight ahead, her delicate nose tipped slightly upward. She finished backing out of the parking spot and asked, "Where am I going?"

"Head down the main road. I'll tell you when to turn."

I was a little annoyed at myself for agreeing to this favor for Harper. For the last three weeks, I'd been engaged in daily fights with my father for his decision to bring this woman to our ranch and now I was acting as her fucking tour guide.

Lily kept her hands firmly on the steering wheel, eyes

focused on the road. I stole a couple of glances in her direction against my better judgment. When I'd talked to her on the sidewalk before I'd known who she was, I'd briefly let myself appreciate her beauty. She had thick, wavy hair the color of caramel. High cheekbones and full pink lips. Her sunglasses shielded eyes that I knew were a hypnotizing hazel color.

"My sister has been raving about you," I said when I couldn't take the silence any longer. "She has a lot of faith in you."

"We don't have to do this," Lily said abruptly. "I know that you and your brothers don't want me here. No need to pretend."

"It's not personal." I should've felt bad that Lily knew she was unwanted, but I wasn't going to lie to her. "Our family has been running the ranch for decades without outside help. We're doing just fine."

"That doesn't mean you couldn't be doing better." She was annoyingly confident in her response.

"No offense, but what does a woman like you know about running a ranch?"

Her pouty lips pursed. "No comments are more offensive than the ones that begin with 'no offense'. I don't think your issue is women like me. I think your issue is that you don't want any woman involved period."

"You don't know shit about me, sweetheart." My molars were clenched hard.

"I always feel a lot of professional respect when men call me sweetheart." Her voice was laced with venom.

"You'll get my respect when you've earned it." I hadn't

meant to call her sweetheart. It had just slipped out. But I certainly wasn't going to apologize for it. "I have no problem with you being a woman. I have a problem with someone who has never stepped foot on a ranch coming into our incredibly successful business and telling us what we're doing wrong."

"You obviously don't know shit about me either, *sweetheart*." Her hands tapped the steering wheel. My eyes caught on her perfectly shaped nails. They weren't painted a flashy color, but their length and symmetry only further solidified my opinion that this woman wasn't accustomed to getting her hands dirty.

"The entrance to the ranch is just ahead on the right." I wanted to get out of that car before I said something hateful in the heat of the moment.

My anger over the situation had nothing to do with Lily and everything to do with feeling like a failure in my father's eyes. I was the oldest son, the one who had been running the ranch alongside my dad since I graduated college with a business degree. I had been running everything on my own for the last two years, losing a lot of sleep to late nights and stress. Then my father suddenly decided that I wasn't doing a good enough job and my sister was making a call to her college roommate. A woman who was barely thirty, had never ridden a horse in her life, and had a body that I would dream about seeing naked.

We drove under the large wooden arch shaped like a horseshoe announcing our arrival at Sullivan Ranch. Normally seeing that sign filled me with a sense of relief at being home, but my anxiety over sitting next to Lily was too strong.

"Where should I park?" she asked quietly.

"Up ahead by the main house. That is where you'll be staying tonight. Tomorrow I will show you the employee accommodation options." I couldn't wait to show her the bunkhouse. That should send her running back to the city in her stilettos.

"Is this where you live?" She sounded nervous for the first time as she put the car into park.

"No." I pushed out of the car like my seat was on fire.

Lily exited much slower, walking carefully in her fancy boots. I fought the urge to roll my eyes. "Is your stuff in the trunk?" I asked.

"I can get it later." She took a step toward the house.

"My parents raised me better than that. Pop the trunk, Lily." I would get my ass reamed by my dad if I let Lily carry her own bags into the house.

She grumbled something under her breath as she stomped back to the car. I was surprised to only see two suitcases. As far as I knew, Lily had been asked to move to the ranch for the foreseeable future. I assumed a woman like her would pack every piece of clothing that she owned and would need a suitcase just for makeup. But then again, taking a slightly closer look at Lily, I couldn't tell if she was even wearing makeup.

"What?" she demanded when she caught me staring. "If they are too heavy for you, I'll handle it."

"Sweetheart, I move cattle and lift hay bales for a

living. I can handle your suitcases." I winced when I realized I had yet again called her sweetheart.

This time she chose not to reprimand me and I was a little disappointed. I kind of liked her sassy attitude. I definitely liked her smart mouth.

There was no point trying to use the wheels on the luggage over the rocky path that led toward the house. Not to mention how dirty they would get. I tucked the smaller one under my arm and lifted the second by the handle, using my free arm to wave for Lily to move toward the house.

"Impressive," she said. "I like you better when you are keeping your mouth shut and using your muscles."

"Hm. Most women actually prefer it when I'm using my mouth." I stomped past her before she could think to trip me or kick my shins. If she was anything like my sister, those would be her go-to moves.

I climbed the porch steps and shoved open the front door without a backward glance, even though my manners were urging me to turn around and check on her. She was likely to break an ankle in those boots.

"I'll drop these in your room. You can wait in the living room for Harper to arrive."

"I think maybe I'll follow you. I wouldn't mind seeing where I'll be staying tonight."

I stifled a groan. "Of course." So much for getting away from her before I said something else offensive.

"This is a beautiful house. Is this where you were raised?" Lily's boots made sharp clicking sounds as she trailed after me.

"Yes." I wasn't in the mood for a trip down memory lane, but it would be rude not to answer her question. "This is our father's house. We all grew up here, but most of us have since built our own homes on the property. Harper has a place downtown, but she stays over a lot to spend time with Dad."

"Well, it's nice of your father to let me stay here tonight."

"I hope it will be up to your standards." I eyed her expensive shoes as we stopped in front of a closed door on the first floor and felt my eyes trailing up her calves.

"I'm sure you know a lot about not meeting a woman's standards." She reached past me to open the door and her arm brushed against my stomach. Both of us flinched.

After she walked into the room, I stepped inside and placed her luggage just inside the door. "Make yourself at home," I said and added under my breath, "but don't get too comfortable."

She dropped onto the bed, bouncing once on that tight ass of hers. "It's so sweet of you to be worried about my comfort."

When I looked at her sitting on that bed, head tilted playfully and a devilish smile on her lips, all I could think about was how much fun it would be to have her squirming beneath me in delicious discomfort.

I closed the door behind me a little too hard. As I made my way down the hallway, I heard voices coming from the communal part of the house. My dad and brother stopped talking abruptly when I entered the kitchen.

"She's here," I muttered, heading to the fridge to grab a beer. Truthfully, I would've liked something stronger. Something that would make me stop thinking about Lily's damn perfect pink mouth.

"And? Does she have horns? Or claws? Claws could be fun." Chase shared a smirk with our dad. He was the Sullivan brother with no filter. "Is she hot?"

I twisted the top off my beer bottle and took a long pull. "She's a city girl," I said with a shrug.

"Your mom was a city girl." Tom Sullivan fixed me with a level look. "As long as Lily is working for us, you will treat her with the same respect as all of our other employees."

"Oh yeah. We'll respect the hell out of her." Chase lifted his own beer and feigned a toast toward me. "Right, brother?"

Tom smacked the back of Chase's head. "I'm not fucking around, son. I asked that woman to come help us out. She's doing us a big favor being here and we all need to act grateful. Be the gentlemen I raised you to be." His eyes darted between us. "And keep your dicks in your pants while you're at it."

"That won't be a problem." I took another long sip. Lily might be a beautiful woman, but it would take a lot more than a pretty face to get me to sleep with the enemy.

"Did you invite her to family dinner?" Tom asked.

My eyes narrowed. "She's not family."

"She is staying in my house and that makes her our guest. Treat her like one." Tom headed outside to start pulling meat from the deep freezer in the garage. Chase turned to me sporting a wicked grin.

"Is she hot?"

"Yeah," I said through a deep exhale. "Hot as fuck."

"Nice." He slapped a hand on my shoulder. "At least we'll have something pretty to look at while she's here. This place could use a little more eye candy."

"She won't be staying long," I said, picking at the label on the bottle.

Chase regarded me with a skeptical look. "Would it be so bad if she did? I know you don't like the idea of bringing an outsider into the family business, but she's been Harper's best friend for over a decade. If Harp trusts her and Dad trusts her, maybe she's the right person for the job."

"For what job? The job that I've been doing for fifteen fucking years?" I snapped. "I don't need some bitchy princess from the city telling me how to run my own fucking business!"

Chase's eyes widened as he looked past me and cleared his throat. "I assume you are the princess? Am I supposed to curtsey?" he said, cocking an eyebrow.

Even before I turned around I could feel the heat of Lily's glare scorching the back of my neck. I hadn't meant to raise my voice like that and I felt like a dick for what I'd said about her.

"I'm Lily Jameson," she said in a cold voice. "The bitchy princess from the city."

I turned with an apology on my lips, but Chase moved faster. He stepped forward with an outstretched hand.

"Chase Sullivan. The asshole snarky middle Sullivan son. It's nice to meet you, Lily."

She lifted his hand to place it on top of her head. "I'm assuming you've been dying to check for horns."

Chase barked out a laugh. "I like you already, Lily Jameson. Can I get you a beer? Or I think we've got some wine around here."

"Beer is fine." Her eyes followed him as he walked away. "You're the brother who handles the guest ranch, correct?"

"That's me." He pulled two beers from the fridge and popped off the lids before turning back to her. "I hear that we'll be working closely together over the coming weeks."

"Much to your delight, I'm sure." She nodded her head in thanks as she took the bottle he offered to her. "If you have some time this week, I'd love to meet with you to start discussing the financials for your part of the business."

He offered her a tight smile. "Sure. That sounds like fun."

Lily was quiet for a long moment, alternating introspective scans of the two of us. "I'm not the bitch you both seem to think I am. I'm only here because Harper asked me to be here. She said your dad needs help and I happen to like and respect Tom Sullivan. I'm not asking you to blindly hand over control of your family business, but I am asking you to at least give me a fair chance to do what I came here to do. What your father has asked me to do for your family."

There was another long moment of silence and then I

nodded. It was a fair request and I'd been nothing but an irrational dick to her for no reason. "Okay. We won't go out of our way to make your life difficult on the ranch. We're on the same team."

"I think that makes you a Sullivan now, city girl." Chase winked at her. "That means you can't bang me or any of my brothers."

"I'm devastated." She rolled her eyes in a way that I found utterly charming. "But Ronan's not off the table, right?" My hand tightened hard enough around the beer bottle that my knuckles turned white.

"Oh shit. You met that asshole?" Chase chuckled as he looked at me. The backdoor opened with a creak. "What the hell were you thinking introducing her to Crestwood's local Lothario?"

"Let's just say that Ronan introduced himself."

"That boy needs to learn to keep his dick in his pants," Tom grumbled before dropping a stack of meat on the counter.

Chase cleared his throat and nodded toward Lily. "Our guest has made an appearance."

When Tom saw her, a smile lit up his face in a way that I hadn't seen in a long time. I had forgotten that he and Lily already knew each other.

"Lily-billy! Welcome to the ranch. Get over here and give this grumpy old man a hug." He opened his arms wide and Lily laughed as she stepped into them.

"You're not grumpy, Tom. Your son already has the market on that." She smiled at me over Tom's shoulder. "Thanks for letting me stay with you."

"Oh please. We're the ones who owe you a big thanks. I can't wait to see what you are going to do around here." He stepped back and gestured toward the bar stools at the island. "Pull up a seat and tell me all about your life. What have you been up to?"

"Most recently?" She took a seat and crossed one toned leg over the other. "Dealing with country boys whose egos are bigger than their trucks."

"So you've met my sons." Tom shot a glare at both of us. "Don't worry. They will be on their best behaviors while you are here."

Those damn lips of hers curled into a perfect smile and she looked at me as she said, "Don't take all the fun out of it, Tom. I like a challenge."

4

LILY

"You're up early."

I nodded at Evan and headed straight toward the coffee maker. The sun wasn't up yet and I'd been hoping to sip some coffee on the back deck and watch the sunrise before dealing with the Sullivan male egos.

"Don't you live somewhere else?" I grumbled.

He leaned against the countertop a few feet away, sipping from a large mug. "I'm here for you."

"Huh?" I must have misunderstood him.

"If you're going to work at the ranch, you need to know how this place runs. Days start early around here. Pour some coffee and I'll take you on a tour."

He was behaving much differently since I'd caught him calling me a bitch to his brother in that same kitchen. Dinner last night had even been enjoyable, but that might've been because Harper and Tom did most of the talking. Chase had spent most of the time on his phone while Evan had sat quietly, mostly watching me with assessing eyes.

"Huh," I said, giving him a quick once-over. He was dressed for ranch work. Worn jeans, dirty boots, and a t-shirt that had no business looking so damn good on him.

"What?" His hands gripped the countertop as he braced for my response.

"I just didn't expect you to be a morning person." I opened the cabinet in front of me in search of a mug.

"Owning a ranch doesn't give me much of a choice." He pushed the cabinet door shut and opened the one next to it. "Here."

When he handed me a mug that said "crabby 'til I drink my coffee" with a large red crab on it, I laughed. "Nice of you to share your mug with me."

"I gave that to my brother Brent a few years ago." Evan smiled. "If you think I'm crabby, you'll be impressed when you meet him."

"I don't actually think you are crabby." I focused on filling the mug with heavenly-smelling coffee. "I think you are rude."

"That's fair. I was rude to you. I'm sorry."

I froze, unsure what to say. I hadn't expected an apology. "Thank you for apologizing."

"If you're ready to go, we can take our coffee with us. I'd like to show you around before the ranch gets too busy."

I glanced down at the jeans and boots that Harper had lent me. "Do I look like a country girl?"

"You look good, Lily." His eyes widened and a flush

crept up his neck. "I mean, your outfit is appropriate. For work. On the ranch."

If I was a better person, I would've ignored his obvious embarrassment. But I couldn't resist smiling. "You're cute when you blush, Evan Sullivan."

He recovered quickly. "I'm always cute, actually. Let's go."

The first step onto the back deck nearly took my breath away. The view before us was stunning. Rolling green grass, mountains in the distance, and vibrant pink and orange streaks across the blue sky. "Wow," I breathed. "That's incredible."

"I reckon we have the best sunrises in the entire state." His hand touched my elbow. "Come on. Let's go to the stables."

This was my first time really seeing the ranch. Our arrival yesterday had ended before any of the real ranch began. I could see dozens of barns and buildings scattered in the distance and Evan led me toward the nearest one.

"We have about 50,000 acres of land for the ranch side of the business. On the other side of the main road, we have another 10,000 acres that we use for the guest ranch business. Chase handles all of that, though, so you'll have to schedule a tour with him."

"Harper told me that Tom started the guest ranch for your mom." After dinner, I'd spent a couple of hours peppering Harper with questions about the ranch and her family.

"Mom was a city girl like you. But she got a big kick out of this life and she loved bringing people out here who'd never been on a ranch. She'd get them up on a horse or fishing in one of the ponds..." Evan smiled wistfully. "Mom loved to see other people have fun. Ranch work isn't glamorous, but it's important work. Mom wanted to reach as many people as possible so they could appreciate what we do here."

"She sounds wonderful." I knew that the Sullivans had lost their matriarch a long time ago, but Evan's grief was still raw. It was right there on the surface. "You don't help with that part of the business?"

"I don't have the time. Running the working ranch is more than a full-time job. When Chase started showing interest in that part of the business a few years ago, I was happy to hand it over to him."

"What about your other brothers? Are they involved in the business?" I was surprised at how open he was being with me. It was almost like I was talking to a different man than I had yesterday.

"Just Nate. He works for me. I've tried to get him involved in the management aspects of the business, but he's happy to just keep his head down and do the grunt work." Evan waved a hand at the ground. "Be careful. There's a good chance you're going to step into some horse shit."

"That's alright. These are Harper's boots." I followed Evan toward a fence and watched as he placed his mug on a post before hoisting himself onto the horizontal beam and swinging a leg over so that he was straddling it.

"Need help?" he asked.

I handed him my mug and climbed up next to him,

not quite as gracefully. Once I was mirroring his posture, I said, "You walked me out here so we could drink our coffee closer to the horse shit?"

"I thought you might want to see the horses, smart ass." He smirked as he handed me my coffee. "They'll gradually be let into this pasture."

Now that we were facing each other, I got my first good look at Evan in the morning light. He was gorgeous. I'd never seen eyes as blue as his. "Do you ever get used to the smell?" I asked, wrinkling my nose.

"Honestly, not really." His chuckle was deep and sexy. "I don't notice it much while I'm working, but sometimes a breeze comes through when I'm sitting on my porch and... it can make your eyes water."

"It is quite pungent," I agreed.

He chuckled again and I felt a small surge of pride at being the one who made him laugh. He struck me as someone who didn't laugh a lot.

"Do you ride?" he asked as the first horse trotted into the pasture.

"Never," I admitted, waiting for him to make some comment about me being a rich city girl. When he said nothing, I added, "But I've always wanted to learn how."

His eyes stayed on the horse as he took a sip of coffee. "You've come to the right place, sweetheart. I'll teach you myself."

He used that term of endearment the way some Southerners call everyone darlin'. I tried not to read too much into it.

I had the sudden urge to hear Evan laugh again. I

waited until he was sipping his coffee before I asked, "Would you say it's easier to learn how to ride a horse or a cowboy?"

He choked, spitting a mouthful of coffee on the ground. He wiped his mouth with the back of his hand and gave me a purposeful look. "I've never ridden one of those, so I can't answer that. But if you stick around here long enough, maybe *you* can tell *me*."

"Not planning to tell you about my sex life, Sullivan." I sat up a little straighter as the horse approached us. "Is it... do we need to move?"

"Nah. This one is docile. We're sending her over to the guest ranch because she's an easy ride."

"I see. Guess that means I'll be staying on this ranch." I flashed him one of my best smiles and he returned it reluctantly.

"I thought you weren't going to tell me about your sex life."

I shrugged. "I lied. I like the sound of your laugh."

"Don't get too used to it." He rubbed the back of his neck. "I know I apologized for being rude to you, but I want to apologize for the way I spoke about you yesterday. There was no excuse. Those words I used were unacceptable, for you or any woman."

"It's fine. I've been called much worse, Evan." If only I had a dollar for every time a man had called me a bitch.

"It's not fine." His eyes flashed in the sunlight. "No one should speak about you like that, Lily. And they damn well better never do it in front of me."

"I don't care if people think I'm a bitch. It's a badge of

honor for women in the corporate world. Men only call women that when they are threatened. When they think they are about to lose some power or control." I knew that was exactly why Evan had used that word to describe me. "If you are good at your job like I am, you make just as many enemies as friends."

"Which one am I?" he asked with a curious tilt of his head.

"That's entirely up to you, cowboy."

5

EVAN

"How's the city girl doing?" Chase hadn't been surprised at all when I'd shown up in his office across the street. He was busy scheduling his employees' shifts for the next month and barely even glanced at me. "Is she wearing come-fuck-me boots again today?"

"No. She's wearing Harper's old boots. And tight denim." I grit my teeth at the memory of her ass sticking out in those jeans as she climbed the fence next to me.

"I know you're determined to hate Lily, but I think I kind of like her. She's spunky. Nice to look at. And she doesn't take any shit from you." He looked up. "Even when you are eye-fucking her."

"She's my employee." I was technically the head boss for every employee on the Sullivan Ranch payroll, including Chase.

Chase chewed on the end of his pen. "You know, city

girls tend to do more grooming than country girls. Down there..."

"Stop. Right now." This was not a conversation we were going to have. "I gave Lily a quick tour around the ranch this morning. I'd like her to get the same treatment over here. Can I trust you to give her a tour without saying horribly inappropriate things to her?"

"Like call her bitchy?" He raised a challenging eyebrow. "I'm not the loose cannon in the family these days."

"I've apologized to her. I'd like you to do the same."

"Fine. Send her over. I'll show her around."

I looked at the calendar on the wall, full of reservations. "It might be good to have her help with one of these corporate bookings. That's pretty much her wheelhouse."

"Fine with me. I hate those events." Chase shrugged and turned back to his scheduling. "We're going to need to hire a few more people with the teenage workers going back to school. Our calendar is booked through the end of the year."

"Talk to Lily about it. She's our finance girl now."

"She's not a girl, you know." His words were quiet but forceful. "I know we've been joking around, but Lily is a professional woman. She has a master's degree in finance and a law degree. She knows her shit. I think maybe we should try to show her the same respect we would show to a fifty-year-old man in the same role."

It wasn't often that my younger brother was able to put me in my place. "Yeah, I think you're right. So you probably need to stop undressing her with your eyes, Chase."

"I will if you will, brother," he quipped back.

"She's my employee," I repeated.

"She's beautiful." He scribbled something on the calendar. "And you haven't had sex in a long time. I give it three months before the two of you are fucking."

"I'll take that bet, brother."

After leaving his office, I headed back to my domain. We had a fence down on the east side of the property and I had a few men already out there, but I wanted to see for myself that it was being repaired properly. It wasn't glamorous work, but it was necessary to keep the ranch running smoothly.

I was still several yards away when I heard a light, feminine laugh. We had a few women working around the farm, but I hadn't sent any of them out here today.

"Nice, Lil. You're a natural at this."

I recognized Nate's voice instantly. He had the deepest baritone of all the Sullivan men. It took me a moment longer to recognize Lily's lithe frame leaned against a fence pole. She was holding a pair of wire cutters in one hand.

"What the hell do you think you are doing?" I demanded, dropping from my saddle.

"Fixing a fence," Lily said with a proud smile.

"Lil laid this whole section," Nate said, gesturing to the wire fence next to him. He dropped a hand on her bare shoulder and something in my gut twisted. "She's a quick learner."

"Check my work, Boss." She lifted her chin in a challenge. "See if the city girl has what it takes."

I tied my horse to the fence and then stepped closer to Lily. Despite a layer of sweat glistening on her skin, she looked beautiful. The fence looked good, but I knew it would. Nate never would have let her do it wrong.

"Not bad," I said, testing the tension. "If only you could get the rest of my men to be so focused on their work." I glared down the line at where they were gawking at us. I had a feeling they'd all been staring at Lily this whole time. When they saw my glare, they hurried to make themselves busy.

"They've been working hard," she said. "Marv had to haul away that giant tree limb that took out the fence and Peter dug out the rotten posts." She gestured vaguely at the fence. "Plus, it's hot as hell out here."

Nate grinned at me. "The guys kind of love her."

"I'm very lovable." She peered at me over the top of her sunglasses. "Wouldn't you agree, Boss?"

"You're going to get sunburned." My eyes trailed over her pink-tipped nose and along the curve of her shoulders.

She pulled a small tube from her back pocket. "I need to reapply. The guys were all sweet enough to offer me assistance if I need it. Isn't that sweet?"

"They're a bunch of sweethearts." I glared again at them even though they were all diligently avoiding looking in our direction.

"We need to get this woman a proper hat." Nate tipped the brim of his at her.

"I'd look good in a Stetson," she stated with complete confidence.

"Damn good," Nate agreed.

If it had been any of my other men, I'd have reprimanded him for flirting with her. But Nate wasn't that type of guy. He had no idea how to flirt with a woman or how easily they responded to his mere presence. I didn't want Lily to end up being one of those victims.

"I need to steal away the cowgirl," I told him. "Chase is going to show her around the playground."

"The playground?" She looked at me in confusion.

"That's what we call the guest ranch sometimes," Nate explained. The real name of the guest ranch was Lucky Charm Ranch, a name that Dad had crafted to honor my mother, a woman he had always affectionately called Lucky. "Because people come there to play pretend cowboy. The real work happens over here."

"Clever." She did not sound like she meant it. "Well, Nathaniel, it's been great working with you. You're my favorite cowboy so far."

"Nice." He held up a hand and she smacked it with her own. "You did good work, kid."

"Didn't we establish that I'm only two years younger than you?" she asked with a shake of her head.

"Yeah, but you're friends with my little sister and she's definitely still a kid." He winked at her. "You better go. The boss is glaring at us."

Lily turned to me. "Should I just meet you back at the main house or..."

"No, we'll ride." I started walking toward my horse.

"But I walked down here."

I nodded. "I figured as much since you don't know

how to ride a horse. We'll double up. It's not the most comfortable way to ride, but we aren't going far."

Her earlier confidence was gone as we stopped next to the horse. "How do I..."

"Stirrup." I pointed to it. "Put your right foot in there, throw your left leg over." I put my hands on her hips and lined her up. "I'll help boost you up."

"Are you sure about this?" She chewed nervously at her lower lip.

"I'm not going to let you fall, sweetheart."

"Okay." She slowly lifted her foot and took a moment to get it safely situated in the stirrup. When she pushed off, I lifted her up and made sure her leg cleared the saddle. We both ignored the way my hand grazed over her ass.

"You good?" I asked.

She smiled down at me. "Yeah. This is fun."

I'd been riding horses since almost before I could walk and took the ride for granted. It was nice to see someone excited about something that I did every day. I quickly untied the horse and nudged her boot from the stirrup.

"Scoot as far forward in the saddle as you can go," I said.

She inched forward and then I moved into position behind her, doing my best not to completely invade her personal space. There wasn't much I could do about our bodies pressing together, though. Her ass was basically perched on my dick.

"Cozy," she said with an awkward laugh.

"Do you want to wave goodbye to your fans?" I

couldn't even blame my men for staring. They had never seen me share a saddle with anyone.

Lily waved happily to them before jerking in shock when I moved the horse into a trot. "Oh god. I'm going to die," she breathed.

"Hardly." I laughed and took her hand, placing it on the saddle. "You can hold on here." Then I shifted the reins and took her other hand, placing that one on my leg. "Or hold onto me. Either way, I'm not going to let you fall, sweetheart."

"Do you call all your employees that?" Her fingers pressed hard into my thigh.

"I don't want to get punched in the face." I regretted suggesting she hold onto me. That kind of grip on my thigh wasn't taking my thoughts anywhere pure or professional. "Actually, I don't think I've ever called anyone that."

"I think you do it to piss me off," she said. "It sounds very patronizing."

"Do you want me to stop?"

Her head turned slowly until her eyes connected with mine. "I didn't say that."

6

LILY

"This is quite the operation you've got going." I watched as several horses pranced past, saddles full of giggling riders.

Chase had spent the last couple of hours walking me around the playground. It turned out that Evan and Nate hadn't just been jesting with that nickname. Chase and the other employees also called it that. Once I saw how much fun the visitors were having, I decided it was an appropriate name.

"When I took over operations from Evan, our profit margins weren't great. He didn't have the time to devote to making it successful. But we've come a long way over the last ten years. And we've still got plenty of room to expand operations."

"The profit margin still isn't great." I hadn't spent a lot of time with the guest ranch's financial records, but I knew that much was true.

"Any ranch is expensive to run, even ones just for amusement like this. Especially since most of our business is seasonal."

I nodded, dozens of ideas already swirling in my brain. "Maybe we can do something about that."

"I have a proposal on that, but it's hard to justify the expense of keeping this place running through the winter months. It gets pretty brutal in the valley and I can't see a lot of tourists wanting to camp out here in a blizzard." Chase bent down to pick up a piece of trash. He crumpled the soda can and tossed it into the nearest garbage bin. "It can be a hard sell. Ev would prefer to put more money back into the working ranch and I can't really argue with that. We make most of our money over there."

"You've got to invest money to make money."

"I guess you would know about that. You turned that tiny little startup into one of the most profitable IPOs in the last decade."

I gaped at him. Sure, my professional history wasn't exactly a secret. It was easily found on the internet if one was inclined to look. I just hadn't expected Chase to be one of those people.

"What? You think a country boy can't pay attention to what's happening on Wall Street?" He gave me a knowing look. "A lot of people make assumptions about ranchers. They think our life is the land. Did you know that Evan and I both have business degrees? We didn't want to just step into these roles simply because our dad owned the place. We wanted to be good at our jobs. Hundreds of people depend on the ranch being successful for their own livelihoods. That's not a responsibility we take lightly."

He was right that I had made some assumptions about him, but I had never assumed that he nor Evan weren't qualified for their jobs or that they didn't take their responsibilities seriously.

I turned away, studying the open land in front of me that was dotted with horse stables and fishing holes. "When I started at Tethered, there were ten employees. I was 25, fresh out of law school. I'm not sure why anyone thought I could do the job, but I became both the company lawyer and the CFO before shifting into a business expansion role. Three years after I started there, we began shopping around our 1,000-employee company to investors. Two years after that, our IPO had us valued at 5 billion dollars." I turned back to him. "I understand the pressure of having people depend on you to make the right decisions. Your job isn't easy, Chase. You and Evan are good at what you do, but so am I."

He nodded slowly as he regarded me. "You're an impressive woman, Lily Jameson. I think I could learn a lot from you."

"I've already learned a lot from you. Want to show me the cabins now?"

"Let's do it."

The guest ranch was more than I had expected. It was a picturesque place to spend a few days fishing, riding horses, roasting marshmallows over campfires, and sleeping in cute cabins. Every guest that we passed was smiling and so were the employees. I was almost a little sad to cross back to the working ranch. And I was more than a little tired.

I had walked miles around the two ranches and Harper's boots were functional, but a little too tight. I was going to have some blisters for sure.

"Lil!"

I watched as Evan bounded down the front steps of Tom's house, wearing a smile that was far too appealing. It was remarkable how fast his attitude toward me had changed.

"Hey," I said, trying not to let my exhaustion show.

"You definitely got some sun today." He pressed a finger to my pink shoulder. "I think you might need a stronger SPF."

"I'm working on my cowgirl glow."

"How did it go with Chase?" He looked a little nervous.

"Good. It's a different vibe over there, but it was fun." I didn't think it was fair how Evan didn't look tired at all even though he'd worked much harder than me all day.

"I thought I could show you where you'll be staying if you're up for it. Dad won't mind if you stay in his house, but I figured you might want some privacy."

"Yeah, okay. Should I go grab my bags?"

"Let's walk over and then I'll drive you back to get your luggage." He swung an arm in front of him. "Ladies first."

"But I have no idea where we are going," I laughed.

"Just head down that way." His hand pressed lightly to my lower back as he guided me forward. "What did you think of your first day on the ranch?"

"It was a lot different than I thought it would be. I sort of just assumed that being out in the country would be slower-paced, but there was a lot going on today."

"Organized chaos," he said with a chuckle. "The days are busy, but things mellow out about now every day."

I nodded, noting how much quieter it seemed already. "You seem to have mellowed out a lot too."

"Believe it or not, this is actually my default mode. I'm not usually a crabby prick." He walked with his hands shoved deep in his pockets, eyes on the dirt road we were walking. "I was dealing with some family shit over the weekend and I was in a pissy mood."

"It happens to the best of us." I nudged him with my elbow. "Sounds like maybe you just need to get laid."

"You shouldn't say shit like that to your boss." He smirked reluctantly. "But you're not wrong."

"I hear ya." Evan was right that I shouldn't be hinting that I could use an orgasm, but I'd never had much of a filter. I'd spent the last five years working mostly with men, most of whom had no problem talking about their itchy balls, disdain for condoms, and preferences in female pubic hair.

"You're not very shy, are you?" Evan's look was either disdain or intrigue. I couldn't tell the difference.

"It depends who I'm talking to. I guess I feel comfortable around you. Might have to do with that semi-erotic horseback ride earlier."

"There was nothing erotic about that ride," he protested.

"Oh please. Your arms wrapped around me, holding

me against your chest. My hand digging into your muscular thigh. Both of us breathing hard." I rolled my eyes. "I know you're not that naïve, Evan."

"Sounds like you are easily stimulated, sweetheart."

"You have no idea," I muttered.

Evan cleared his throat, a surefire sign that he was uncomfortable. "What's your plan for tomorrow? More fence fixing with Nate? Or back to the playground with Chase?"

"I notice *you* aren't volunteering to spend more time with me," I said wryly. "But no. I'm actually spending the morning with Tom. He's going to walk through the financials with me. I think he said he was going to invite you to join us. And then in the afternoon, Nate mentioned something about breaking some new horses, whatever that means."

Evan nodded. "Yeah, our trainer will be getting started on the new riding horses. Basically getting them used to life on the ranch. Saddling, grooming, riding. Our trainer is really skilled. I think you'll like watching them work."

"Huh." I laughed. "That's kind of what you're doing with me. Breaking me. Getting me used to life on the ranch."

That deep, husky chuckle was back. It did something squishy to my insides. "Preparing you to be ridden?" he added with another laugh.

"Ugh. You really shouldn't say things like that to your employee," I joked.

"Yes, I'm clearly the inappropriate party." He kicked a

rock away with his worn cowboy boots. "Why did you agree to do this? It's a big change from your old job."

"That's kind of the whole point." I wasn't ready to tell a man I barely knew about the circumstances that had led me to Crestwood. As we rounded the curve in the road, two homes loomed in the distance. One was small, more like a cabin or a rustic cottage. The other was farther away and larger. "I was born in a town like Crestwood."

Evan had a terrible poker face. "Really?"

"Why is that so hard to believe?" His shock felt like an insult.

"I don't know. It's just hard to look at you and see a small-town girl."

"It was a long time ago," I conceded. "And I didn't grow up on a multi-million-dollar ranch."

"Most people don't." His shoulders pulled up. "When I was a kid, I had no idea that my family had money. Everyone always worked so hard that it felt like we were working class. Our parents didn't spoil us. We always had chores around the ranch and we had to earn spending money." He rubbed the back of his neck. "It wasn't until I was in middle school that I realized a lot of kids would never have spending money. Some of them couldn't even afford to eat. I felt like such a jackass for being so oblivious."

"It's not a bad thing to come from a family that has money. Especially one that works as hard as yours."

Evan had stopped in front of the cottage and he was staring at it when he said, "Ronan was one of those kids. One of the ones that couldn't afford to eat."

"Is that why he turned into such a smartass? To give his mouth something else to do?" I felt bad as soon as I made the joke, but Evan laughed.

"I never thought of it like that. Maybe." He nodded toward the cottage. "This is where you'll be staying. It's not fancy, but I think you'll like it."

"It's adorable." I loved the robin's egg blue door and the yellow shutters. It had a matching yellow rocking chair on the small porch. "Who usually lives here?"

"No one these days. This was actually my mom's house. She had this built after Nate was born. Said she needed a place where she could escape for a few hours where the bathroom floors weren't covered in piss." He shook his head at the memory. "I can't say I blame her on that. Four boys in six years is a lot."

"She sounds like a fun woman."

"She was the best." Evan slipped a key from his pocket. "Come on. I'll show you the inside."

The cottage was overflowing with femininity. No rustic wood ceilings or leather furniture. No dead animal heads on the walls or dark paint. Everything was white or bright. The paint on the walls, the tiles on the kitchen backsplash, and the linens on the bed. The cottage was just one large room, each corner serving a different purpose. One had a small kitchenette with pale yellow cabinets. Another corner had a white sofa and two full bookshelves. The third corner was the sleeping area holding a large bed covered in pillows and blankets. The last corner held the only door in the cottage.

"That's your bathroom," Evan said when he caught me

staring at it. "There's no closet, but you can use the armoire."

I took a slow lap around the room, smiling when I noticed all the details. A few framed photographs on the bookshelves showed a pretty woman surrounded by young boys. "Is this one you?" I asked, tapping the picture of a boy with dark brown waves and beautiful blue eyes who had wiry arms wrapped tightly around the woman's waist.

"Yeah." Evan coughed once. "If you'd rather stay at Dad's, that's fine. He would be happy to have you there."

"No," I answered immediately. I was completely charmed by the cottage. The fact that Evan was willing to let me stay in a place that had meant so much to his mother was overwhelming. My eyes were a little misty when I looked at him. "This place is perfect. Thank you."

He looked away quickly. "Let's head down to my place and grab the truck so we can pick up your things."

It was a quick walk to his place and I found that comforting. Living so far from civilization could be a daunting prospect, but I felt better knowing that Evan would be so close.

"Do you like living out here?" I asked. "Don't you get lonely?"

"Lonely?" He laughed and shook his head. "My kids would never let that happen."

Somehow I hadn't noticed the bikes in the yard until he said that. And the baseball glove resting on the porch steps. A random pink tennis shoe on the welcome mat. "You have kids?"

"Twins. They recently turned twelve. Somehow. Feels like they were screaming babies just yesterday." He must have noticed the confused look on my face because he added, "They're with their mom this week. We share custody. One week on the ranch, then one week at her house."

"So you aren't together?" I felt like a big snoop digging into his personal life.

"Never were." He laughed again, this time awkwardly. "A one-night stand that turned into a life sentence. That's what Ronan always says about my situation."

"But you share custody. Seems like you don't hate the sentence."

He nodded, eye lighting up in a way that was breathtaking. "I love my kids. Couldn't imagine my life without them."

"Still. Probably would've been cheaper to just use a condom."

"Definitely would have been cheaper," he agreed, a relieved smile appearing. It was like he had expected me to react poorly to the news of his fatherhood. "I'll introduce you to them when they get back. You'll like them. Everyone always likes them more than they like me."

"Huh." I tilted my head and pretended to consider that information. "They must be special then because I already like you a lot, Evan Sullivan."

7

EVAN

"Good morning." Lily eyed me skeptically from behind the blue cottage door she was using to shield her body. "Can I help you?"

"Coffee." I held out a mug. "I figured you wouldn't have had time to pick any up since you just moved in last night."

"Oh. That's...sweet." She looked like she was half-asleep. Her hair was messed and her eyes were still glazed with sleep. Probably because I'd stopped by at the crack of dawn like a total idiot. Just because my days started early on the ranch it didn't mean that hers had to. "Do you want to come in?"

I could tell she was only asking to be polite. She was clearly still dressed in whatever she had worn to bed and my dirty mind immediately pictured something scandalous.

"No, just dropping off the caffeine. I'm heading out to

check on the cattle, but I'll see you up at the main house in a bit."

"Okay. Thanks." She tipped the mug at me and took a sip. "You make good coffee, Sullivan."

"I'm good at a lot of things, sweetheart." I winked at her. "You'll see."

As I was walking away, I berated myself yet again for being so damn flirty with her. I didn't want to be the creepy older boss hitting on his hot, female employee. Especially one who was eight years younger and best friends with my little sister. That was never going to end well for me, or her.

I remembered her face twisting in surprise when I mentioned the kids. But she had recovered quickly, taking the news in stride. A lot of women made snap judgments about me when they found out I'd fathered twins after one night of too much alcohol. In my past, that was where a lot of women had lost interest in me. I actually didn't mind. It was a quick way to weed out any woman who would never be able to accept my kids as a constant in my life. I was never going to push them aside in favor of a romantic entanglement. They were my whole world and always would be.

I took my usual tour around the land. Checked the cattle and the fences, stopped by the stables. Directed workers where extra help was needed. Some ranch owners weren't as involved in the day-to-day logistics. It would be easy to hand that off to someone else, but I didn't like the idea of being locked away in an office somewhere. I liked getting my hands dirty.

"I like Lily," Nate announced out of nowhere as we were taking a break to watch our trainer work the new horses. "She's smart. Funny. And a hard worker."

"And?" I cocked an eyebrow at him.

"And she has a nice smile," he finished in typical Nate fashion. Where Chase would've made some comment about Lily's ass, Nate would never even think to make a comment like that. I wouldn't be surprised if he hadn't even noticed that Lily had a great ass. If I hadn't seen him hooking up with women a few too many times, I might even think he was gay. But no, my little brother was just a gentleman. It was admirable, really.

"Yeah, she does," I agreed with a sigh, picturing that perfect smile.

"You seem a little smitten, bro." Nate gave me a knowing look. "She's not the devil you thought she'd be, is she?"

I couldn't help myself. "I haven't checked thoroughly enough for those horns."

"Our sister will castrate you if you make a move on her best friend." Nate frowned and kicked a toe at the fence post. "Don't be a fucking idiot, Evan. Don't mix business and pleasure."

"I said nothing about any pleasure with Lily," I protested even though I had been thinking about exactly that when I jerked off in the shower this morning.

"Who is Lily?"

We had somehow missed the loud stomping of our uncle as he approached the fence. Uncle Rick didn't make an appearance on the ranch unless he was visiting our dad up at the house, and that only happened a few times per year.

"Lily Jameson," I said. "Dad's most recent hire."

"The lawyer from the city?" Rick didn't even try to hide his disgust. "That's the last thing this ranch needs. We are doing just fine without interference from some outsider who couldn't tell a bull from a cow."

"Nah, she could tell the difference." Nate smirked at me. "Speaking of the outsider, aren't you supposed to be meeting with her right now?"

I glanced at my watch. "Shit. I'm late. Can you send a team out to expand that fence near the hill? We need to get the new cattle moved next week."

"No problem." Nate was nothing if not dependable. "When you're done with Lily, send her my way."

I glared at him before realizing he wasn't trying to be an asshole. He threw up both hands. "Whoa, whoa, whoa. Not like that. I meant because of the fence. She's good with a wire cutter." He looked genuinely alarmed by my reaction.

Rick didn't miss anything about our exchange. "Seems like you think she might be good at some other things, son," he said clapping a hand on my shoulder. "Just don't let those thoughts fuck with our business."

Rick and I headed up to the house together. Apparently, my dad had invited him to the meeting. That made sense since Rick handled the thoroughbred part of the business. That was the newest part of our business portfolio and over the last couple of decades, we had produced several world-class racehorses. One of them almost won the Triple Crown.

That part of the business had never interested me. Rick mostly attended fancy parties and shook a lot of hands. He passed around a lot of paper, but the actual breeding work was done by his employees. Still, it was incredibly profitable and I couldn't deny that he was getting results.

Dad had a nice office on the ground floor of his house, but we held our meeting at the same place we held our family dinners. Lily was already there at the dining room table, laptop open in front of her with a tall stack of papers next to it. She stood when we entered the room.

"Hey." She smiled at me before turning her attention to Rick. "Wow. You look just like your brother," she said with an awkward laugh.

"I hear that happens with brothers." Rick held out a hand and shook hers politely. I often forgot that Dad and Rick looked practically like twins because though their looks were similar, their personalities and styles were completely different. Rick was wearing a suit and cowboy boots that were designed for style and not function. His hands didn't have a single callous and his nails were almost as tidy as Lily's.

"Have you seen Dad?"

She waved a hand toward the kitchen. "He insisted on getting me coffee. I explained that you had already taken care of me, but you know how he is."

"Yeah, I do." I decided to take the seat across from her. Sitting right next to her felt too presumptuous.

"Rick, it's great to finally meet you. I must admit I'm a little overwhelmed by the amount of charming Sullivan men I've encountered over the last few days." She had such a beautiful, genuine smile that I had to assume everyone was just as charmed by her as me.

"Well, I assume a woman like you could have your pick." Rick was quick to return the charm. He was a notorious bachelor and a big flirt. He was almost sixty-five now, but that never stopped him from creeping on young women. I could still remember him making gross comments to my high school girlfriends. "Any chance you have a thing for older men?"

"Older men, sure." She glanced at me and then gave Rick the look that I knew meant she was about to put him in his place. "*Old* men, not so much."

"Touché." He said the word through tight lips.

Dad came into the room wearing a scowl that said he'd overheard their exchange. He put a full coffee mug in front of Lily before turning his ire to Rick.

"Lily is practically a daughter to me. Keep her out of your dirty fucking mind." Tom Sullivan was not one to mince words.

"You might want to say the same to your son," Rick looked at me as his upper lip curled into a snarl. "We both know there is no way he'd be sitting here right now if he wasn't trying to fuck the woman sitting across from him."

My chair creaked loudly as I leaned forward, barely holding myself back from lunging at my uncle. I didn't give a shit what he said about me, but I didn't like the way he was treating Lily. She didn't deserve his bullshit.

"Actually, I invited Evan to this meeting. Seeing as how he handles the largest and oldest part of the business, it made sense for him to be involved. Your assistant already sent over the files I requested regarding the portfolio that you handle, Rick. If you plan to make shitty comments throughout this meeting rather than be useful, I request that you just leave now." Lily didn't look at any of us as she thoroughly scolded my uncle into submission. She was looking at something on her computer with a bored expression.

"You have a lot of nerve speaking to me like that, girl," Rick said.

"Her name is Lily." My words sounded strangled which was exactly what I felt like doing to Rick.

"Rick, keep your mouth shut or leave," Dad said firmly. "Lily, let's get started. I believe you were asking me about last year's profit and loss statement."

We spent the next two hours answering Lily's questions. Rick only spoke when he was asked a direct question and I think we all preferred it that way. Lily spent a lot of time flipping through the paperwork and making notes, her brow furrowed as she nibbled on her lower lip. I spent a lot of my time watching her and picturing those lips around my cock. Then I would spend several minutes sucking in deep breaths through my nose and willing away a boner.

Chase stopped by as the meeting was winding down. Lily had a few questions for him about the expenses at the playground and then it was over. The meeting I had been dreading for weeks had been completely painless. Lily clearly wasn't trying to pick apart our business. She was just trying to understand it.

"I've got what I need," she said, making another note on a contract. "You guys can get back to your jobs." She glanced at Rick. "Or being an asshole. Whatever."

I choked on a laugh while Chase didn't bother hiding his. Even Dad huffed out a laugh. "I think you might be the best thing to happen to this ranch in a long time, Lilybilly," he said, patting her shoulder as he stood. "Rick, I'll show you out."

"I shouldn't have said that," Lily said when they were gone.

"Like hell. That old asshole needs to be knocked down a few pegs," Chase said. "In fact, that earned you a night on the town. Drinks are on me."

"Drinks?" Lily didn't look thrilled by that offer.

Chase pointed at me. "You in? Eagle's Nest with the boys. And Lily."

"It could be fun," I said hesitantly. It wasn't rare to go out drinking with the guy on a random night when I didn't have the kids, but for some reason it didn't sound appealing to me now unless Lily also agreed to go. "If you're going to be a real country girl, you need to drink cheap beer at the Nest, Lil."

"Fine. Okay. Sounds fun." She smiled hesitantly. "I've always wanted to party with a bunch of cowboys."

8

LILY

"You're the new girl," Chase said, looking at me over the front seat. He rode shotgun in Evan's truck while I was camped out in the backseat next to Nate. "And you are prettier and shinier than a lot of the local girls. Guys are going to be hitting on you all night."

"And?" I couldn't understand why he was trying to scare me.

"If anyone gets out of line, flag down a Sullivan brother. We'll handle it."

Nate nodded. "Gladly."

"Is this what it's like to have brothers?" I asked. "Harper is a lucky girl."

"I doubt she'd agree with that," Evan said with a laugh. "She used to get so pissed when we'd scare off her boyfriends."

"She felt the same way about me when I scared off drunk fraternity guys in college." I had always felt protective of Harper, but I hadn't realized just how accustomed she was to having other people protect her.

"I knew I liked you, Lily Jameson." Chase punched Evan's arm. "Not as much as this guy, though."

"Fuck off," Evan muttered.

"More advice," Chase continued easily. "The beer is cheap and tastes like it. But it won't get you as fucked up as the absinthe and moonshine, so it's what I strongly recommend you drink."

"This place is located in our time period, right? We don't have to travel to the Old West to reach it?" I had never been to an establishment that sold actual moonshine.

"He's fucking with you, sweetheart," Evan said, winking at me when he caught my eye in the rearview mirror.

Maybe it was the excitement of having a night out, or maybe it was the thrill of being in such close quarters with three sexy cowboys, but my thighs clenched together as heat laced through my core. All of the brothers looked good tonight, but there was nothing quite as hot as Evan's sexy wink.

"We're here." Nate was out of the truck before Evan had even put it into Park.

It took me a moment to release my seatbelt and Evan had already opened my door before I could do it. He held out a hand and I took it without thinking.

"You might want to stick close to us for a bit," Evan suggested, keeping his hand around mine even after I was safely out of the truck. "If people see that you are here with us, they'll be more likely to mind their manners."

"What if I don't want them to do that?" I said, slightly squeezing his hand. "What if I'm looking to find a cowboy to take home with me tonight?"

"You've already found one." His crooked smile nearly knocked me off my feet. "But if you decide to slum it with some loser, that's entirely your prerogative."

He dropped my hand only to put his on my lower back as he led me from the parking lot to the bar. Evan Sullivan's manners were impeccable.

The Eagle's Nest was exactly what I hoped it would be. A basic county bar filled with relaxed country folk. Old, scuffed tables and chairs were spread throughout the main room. There was a long bar across from the door lined with beer taps. In a second room, people were milling around a dance floor. Chase had mentioned something about dancing, but it looked like it was too early in the evening for that.

"I'll get the first round," Evan said.

"I'll help you carry." Nate headed straight toward the bar.

"Go with Chase and grab us a table." Evan nudged me toward Chase even though it looked like he wanted to do the exact opposite.

Chase picked a table near the large window at the front of the bar. I dropped into the seat across from him and looked around the room again before my eyes settled on Evan's broad back and narrowly tapered waist. I just barely stopped myself from staring at his ass.

"What's going on with you and my brother?" Chase asked bluntly.

"Nate?"

"Fuck no." Chase laughed. "With the brother you can't stop staring at."

Heat flushed my cheeks as I turned to him. "You're insane. There's nothing going on with me and Evan."

"Bullshit." He pointed to his brother. "That man was determined to hate you right up until he met you. Now, he goes out of his way to bring you coffee and open doors for you. He likes you."

"And? I like him too. I like Nate. I even like you, most of the time." I wasn't going to let Chase embarrass me.

He rolled his eyes. "Fine. You like me and Nate. But you want to get naked with Evan."

Okay, he had a point. Not that I was going to concede that point out loud. "Evan is my boss. Our relationship is purely professional."

"If you say so." He didn't believe a single word that left my mouth.

"Isn't Harper supposed to be meeting us here?" I was eager to have someone at our table who wasn't an insanely attractive male.

"She's on her way," Evan confirmed, placing a frothy beer on the table in front of me. He sank into the chair next to mine, bending his long legs to fit beneath the table. His knee brushed against mine.

Nate took the chair across from him. "You feeling okay, Lil? Your cheeks look a little flushed."

"It's warm in here." I reached for the beer, hoping it might cool me off.

"Wait until the dancing starts." He grimaced slightly.

"You're all single, right?" I said, looking at each of them. They nodded. "So is this really your plan? Sit at this table and ignore women all night? Because that is an excellent way to remain single."

"We're not ignoring women," Chase said, dipping his head at me. "We're choosing to focus on one woman."

"Which is a good way to assure that *you* remain single," Nate said with a laugh. "Feel free to tell us to fuck off."

"Oh please. If I was going to hook up with a cowboy, I'd pick one of you." Three sips of beer and I was already saying shit I shouldn't be saying.

Evan shifted in his seat while Nate and Chase laughed. "I think we all know which one of us you would pick," Chase said. His bluntness was something to be both admired and feared.

Nate decided to save me by pointing to the television screen mounted behind the bar. "Looks like little bro might get to pitch tonight."

Noah Sullivan was the youngest of the Sullivan siblings. He was the only one I had known before arriving at the ranch because he was a star MLB pitcher. Harper was always updating me on his season or his recovery from injury. Noah was almost as good at getting hurt as he was at throwing a curveball.

The boys all got swept up in baseball talk which I didn't mind. I actually enjoyed baseball and I thought it was sweet how proud they were of their brother. It also meant that the attention wasn't on me anymore.

"He has a home stretch next week. We should go to a game," Chase said.

"I've got the kids." There was no disappointment or frustration in Evan's tone.

"Dad will watch them," Chase said with a dismissive wave of his hand.

Evan sighed. "It's not about that. I like spending time with my kids."

Damn. That was almost as sexy as his wink. I blamed my body's physical response to his paternal devotion on my own daddy issues.

"Heads up," Nate muttered. "Macalister incoming."

The tension that descended on our table was stifling. All three sets of male shoulders were straining against their shirts.

"Who–" I started to ask who was causing that reaction, but it was too late.

"Didn't expect to see you here." The man who stood next to our table could only be described as cold. Cold gray eyes, icy stare, and frozen smirk on his lips. His attention was focused on Evan. "Must be Naomi's week with the twins."

"How are your kids, Jimmy?" Nate blinked once, betraying nothing about how he felt about the man standing a little too close to my chair. "Oh that's right. You don't claim them."

"Fuck you, Sullivan."

The words were laced with anger and I found myself

leaning away from him, moving closer to Evan. That slight movement brought Jimmy's eyes to me.

"Which one of these assholes do you belong to?" he asked.

"Jimmy, kindly fuck all the way off." Evan's arm dropped over the back of my chair as if he could sense my discomfort.

"I see." The smile that touched his face was just as cold as his stare. "Does my sister know you're working on a stepmom for the twins?"

"I'd tell you to ask her yourself, but I know she kicked you out of her life years ago." Evan's fingers brushed lightly over my shoulder and I couldn't tell if it was intentional until he repeated the motion.

Jimmy stared blankly for a long moment and then smirked. "How's your sister? Heard she moved back to town. I've been planning to reach out to her."

"Do it and I'll cut off your fucking hand," Evan said without hesitating.

"No you won't." Jimmy took a step back. "You Sullivans are all talk and empty threats. The only one of you worth anything is Harper, and even she is only good for one thing. And frankly, I've had much better."

All three men were ready to pounce, but none of them were as quick as me. I was out of my chair before they could move and my punch landed with perfect aim. Jimmy screamed as his nose cracked, hands flying up and leaving the rest of him vulnerable. I swung my knee between his legs and connected solidly with his balls.

"Fuck!" He dropped to his knees as he screamed in pain.

"Don't talk about Harper like that." I knelt down, grabbing his head by his hair to force him to look at me. Blood dripped down his face. "In fact, keep her name out of your mouth altogether."

I shoved his head away and stood, clenching and unclenching my aching fist before looking at the Sullivans. They were all on their feet. Nate stared at me with wide eyes and Chase was laughing.

"I think I'm in love," he said, placing a hand over his heart.

Evan was scanning me carefully. "Are you okay?" he asked, eyes resting on my hand.

"Am I supposed to be able to bend my fingers?" I asked, grimacing as the pain intensified. Jimmy was still growling behind me while slowly getting to his feet.

"We should go," Nate said, springing into action. He stepped around the others and started pushing me toward the door. Every eye in the bar watched us leave.

Evan took over once we were outside. He tossed his keys to Chase. "You drive," he said and then he raced ahead to open the back door for me.

"Careful," he said as I slid inside and then he surprised me by sliding in right beside me. Everyone's doors slammed shut and Chase revved the engine to life.

"Let me see your hand, Lil." Evan was sitting so close to me that we were sharing a seat.

"Seatbelt," I breathed.

"Oh, right." He shook his head to clear it and then

reached across me to grab the seatbelt. Once it was clicked into place, he secured his own and then held out his hand again.

I reluctantly placed my hand in his open palm. It was hurting so bad that I was scared to have someone touch it.

"Try wiggling your fingers," he said.

"Lily Jameson, that was the coolest fucking thing I've ever seen," Chase declared proudly as he pulled onto the highway. "That punch... perfection!"

"Someone needs to call Harper and tell her not to go to the bar," I said, watching as my fingers slowly began to move. All of them except my pointer finger.

"Already texted her. She asked if any of us thought to take a picture of Jimmy crying on the ground. I told her of course I did." Nate turned in his seat. "Chase is right. That was a seriously impressive punch, Lil."

Evan was running the pads of his fingers slowly over my knuckles and not saying anything. I got the feeling that he wasn't as impressed as his brothers.

"I shouldn't have done it," I said, letting my head fall back against the headrest. "But I know all about his history with Harper. I just couldn't let him say shit like that about her and not do something about it."

"We would've handled it," Evan said quietly. "You didn't need to break your hand."

"Yes, I did." I gave him a pointed look. "If I'd let the three of you handle it, it would've gone way too far. At least one of you would've ended up in handcuffs."

"He could still go to the police," Evan countered. "Is it any better if you're the one who gets arrested?"

I laughed. "He's not going to do that. Men like Jimmy Macalister would never want anyone to know they got beaten up by a girl in a bar. Besides, I'm a lawyer. Let him try to sue me. I'll fucking win."

"Lily…" Evan's voice was filled with caution.

"Ev, it couldn't be you who did it," I said quietly. "He's your kids' uncle, right?"

Evan nodded without looking at me. "Yes, but Naomi is estranged from her family."

"Still. Your kids don't need to hear that their dad beat up their uncle. It's better that the crazy city girl did it."

That earned me a small smile. "I think you've got at least one broken bone, sweetheart. We need to visit the emergency room."

"Road trip!" Chase sang out happily.

"No, no. That's not necessary. Let's just go home and I can see a doctor tomorrow." I wasn't sure how I'd ever be able to sleep while I was in so much pain, but there was no reason to ruin everyone's night. Especially when they all had to work early in the morning.

"Not a chance, city girl," Chase said.

Nate nodded his agreement. "Sullivans don't leave anyone behind. You took one for the team. The least we can do is get you patched up."

I wanted to protest, but Evan was still softly stroking my hand. It didn't seem possible that a man who was so strong and masculine could have such a soft and gentle touch. "Dad would never forgive us if we didn't get you medical attention," he said. "And Harper would probably pull a Lily and break our noses."

"Fine," I agreed reluctantly. "Let's go to the hospital."

Crestwood wasn't big enough for its own hospital, so it was a thirty-minute drive to the nearest one. We got lucky and there wasn't much of a wait. An x-ray confirmed two broken bones and I was given a temporary cast, painkillers, and a referral to an orthopedist. The guys stayed in the waiting room for the two hours I was receiving treatment and they all cheered when I finally joined them.

"There's our little Rocky!" Nate said, squeezing me against his side in a rough hug.

"Yeah, yeah." I was too exhausted to push him away.

Surprisingly, Chase still had the keys and he drove us back to the ranch with Evan again sitting beside me in the backseat. We were all tired now and our adrenaline had crashed. With the radio playing softly, I found myself drifting off.

A gentle hand squeezed my leg. "We're home," Evan said.

My eyes fluttered open and I was horrified to find that I'd been sleeping with my head on his shoulder. Chase drove the truck beneath the ranch's arched entryway and his eyes landed on my gaze in the rearview mirror. His lips tipped up in a knowing smirk and we both knew there was a reason why I still hadn't lifted my head or otherwise moved away from Evan.

9

EVAN

I was generally a morning person. My whole life I'd been waking up before sunrise and I did so without complaint. But not this morning. I had only slept for a few minutes after returning from the hospital. I kept replaying what had happened in that bar, how Lily had reacted before I could. I kept hearing the noise when her hand connected, knowing that I hadn't just heard Jimmy's nose breaking. The sound had been too loud, too indicative of multiple broken bones.

Lily had a broken hand because I had hesitated. She had stepped up and defended my sister while I had sat and watched. I froze.

After I finally forced myself out of bed, I went through the same steps I went through every morning. Making coffee, getting dressed, and most recently, staring obsessively at the cottage near my home for any sign that Lily was awake. I wanted to take her a coffee and see how she was feeling. I wanted to touch her soft skin again and feel her breathing. I wasn't sure I'd ever felt more relaxed than I had last night when she fell asleep on my shoulder.

The lights were off in the cottage, so I resisted the urge to stop and started in the other direction.

"Ignoring me so blatantly? Rude!"

I was smiling as I turned. "I didn't see you there." I wasn't sure how I had missed her sitting on the porch. Probably because it was still mostly dark out. "You should be sleeping."

"I'm waiting for my coffee, Sullivan."

"Give me a second." I headed back into my house and was glad that I had made extra coffee instinctively. Almost like I knew I was going to need it. When I approached the cottage, Lily slipped off the rocking chair and came to take the mug from me.

"Are you hurrying off to work or do you have some time?" she asked.

"For you? I've got time, sweetheart."

She took a seat on the top step and patted the space next to her lightly with her plastic splint. "Did you get enough sleep?"

"Never." I decided that it was alright for me to sit close to her since the morning air was a little chilly and she was only wearing shorts and a T-shirt. "I haven't gotten enough sleep since the twins were born."

"Being a parent sounds amazing," she joked.

"Sometimes it is." I nudged her arm. "How is your hand, Rocky?"

"Still broken. The painkillers helped knock me out, though." She kept her eyes on her coffee as she said, "I'm sorry I used you as a pillow last night."

"Please. Women have used me for much worse."

"Do tell, Sullivan." The rising sun was casting everything in an inviting golden glow, including Lily's beautiful face.

"That's not a wound I'm willing to reopen." I looked out across the field in front of us. "It's been a long time since I've had someone to share a sunrise with."

"Hm." She glanced at me. "I think you're my first."

Both my heart and my cock reacted to that. "I'm glad you saved yourself for me, city girl."

"There you go again with the inappropriate comments, Boss."

"What's on your agenda today? More uncles to tell off? Or assholes to punch in the face?" If I hadn't been so worried about Lily's hand, I would have been impressed by her absolute fierceness. I'd been wanting to punch Jimmy Macalister in the face for years.

"Calling the orthopedist first thing. Then I'll probably spend some time walking around and moping about the fact that I can't answer emails with a broken hand."

"Sounds fun," I joked. "If you want some company, you could ride around with me for the day."

"Like we did yesterday?" she asked with wide eyes.

"No. That wouldn't be comfortable for us or the horse. We can take one of the ATVs." I preferred a horse, but I was willing to change my ways for the woman sitting next to me. It was the least I could do considering she had a broken hand because I hadn't been competent enough to prevent an altercation.

"Okay. That sounds like it could be fun. And we can cover a lot of ground. I still want to see the bunkhouse and machinery barns."

"You do?" I stared at her in disbelief. "Why? Those are two of the least interesting places on the ranch."

She shrugged. "I want to see everything. If we're going to start restructuring our finances and make changes to operations, I have to know how all of it works. Even the non-interesting stuff."

I didn't miss how easily she was referring to the ranch like she was part of it. It was no longer an abstract thing or a job assignment to her. "Did you get what you needed in the meeting yesterday? I know Rick wasn't making your job easy."

"Meh." She waved a dismissive hand in front of her. "I'm used to men making my life harder. Especially at work. I just didn't like how he talked to you."

"You mean the part where he said I wanted to fuck you?" I wouldn't normally be so blunt, but Lily was adorable with flushed cheeks.

"He only said it to embarrass you."

"Or because it was partly true." I laughed as her mouth dropped open. "I wasn't in the meeting because of that, but you're a beautiful woman, Lil. If we had met under different circumstances, I definitely would have hit on you."

"You *did* hit on me." Her body leaned slightly closer to

mine. "Saving me from Ronan's shit and kissing my hand? You were flirting, Mr. Sullivan."

"Maybe I was," I admitted. "But then I was also a complete asshole to you."

"No, you weren't. You were mostly polite to me. Yeah, you said something cruel to your brother about me. But you didn't know I was going to overhear that and you needed to vent to someone."

I still cringed every time I remembered what I had said about her in Dad's kitchen. "That morning I found out that I'm not going to have the kids for Christmas. Naomi's family isn't big on the holiday and she always lets me have the kids that week and then she takes them the following week, but this year she wants to take them to see their grandparents." I could feel Lily watching me. "I know that Christmas is months away and I'm sounding a bit unhinged, but that's my favorite time with the kids. So I was in a shitty mood and I took it out on you."

"Damn." I heard her exhale slowly. "I would've given almost anything for one of my parents to care that much about spending time with me."

"Shitty parents?" I grimaced. What a stupid thing to say. But I had no idea how to pry into her past without sounding like an idiot. My social skills left a lot to be desired.

"That's putting it mildly." Her response was final and didn't leave room for me to pry further.

"Well, I'm not sure if it helps but... *I* care about spending time with you."

She looked more embarrassed by that admission than she had about my comment about wanting to fuck her. Lily was so damn cute.

"I already have a best friend, Evan. Not looking for another one."

"That's good because I don't think best friends usually want to fuck each other."

She jabbed her elbow hard into my side. "That desire is not reciprocated, Boss."

I couldn't understand the way she was looking at me. Lily had a way of staring at me that made me question everything I'd ever said to her. "Hey, you know I'm just joking around, right? Am I making you uncomfortable?"

"No. I mean, yes. But not because of those silly jokes you make." She twirled a strand of caramel hair around her finger. "This whole experience has been unsettling."

"In a bad way?"

She let out a breathy laugh that was unbelievably sexy. "No. In an incredible way."

"We can do better," I said confidently. "Finish your coffee. It's almost time to get to work."

Riding around on an ATV wasn't quite as fun as having Lily in front of me on a saddle, but it was a more efficient way for us to move around the ranch together. Our first stop was at the edge of the property where we were expanding our fence line. I had a team of ten working on the project to hopefully get it completed quickly. Every single one of those men watched us approach.

"There she is! The undefeated lightweight champion!" Nate grinned at Lily and the men all started clapping.

Lily popped out of her seat and performed a dramatic bow. "Watch who you are calling a lightweight, Sullivan," she joked.

"Whoa. Don't hit me!" Nate threw his hands up in exaggerated fear.

"Have you guys been working today or just standing around gossiping?" I knew I should probably run the ranch with a firmer hand, but I liked my employees and I wanted them to like working for me.

"Hey, it's not their fault my reputation precedes me." Lily didn't seem bothered by the staring the men were doing. The same could not be said for me.

"Macalister had it coming. We've all wanted to punch that guy at least once," Marv said. He had been working for my family for years. He and Dad had been friends since before I was even born and he ran the ranch whenever I needed a day off. Marv was more of an uncle to me than Rick. He was also an excellent judge of character. "Good for you for actually doing it, kid."

"Honestly, kicking him in the balls was the more enjoyable part." Every man winced slightly and that made Lily laugh. "Don't worry, boys. If you don't piss me off, your boys will be fine."

As Lily walked away to pet the horses, Marv strolled over. "I'm not worried about my balls, but how long as she had yours in her pocket?"

"What the fuck, old man? What are you implying?" I

had always liked Marv, but he sure knew how to push my buttons.

"Last week you were bitching about your daddy hiring someone to help run the ranch. Now you're her personal tour guide and you're taking her to the Nest for drinks?" Marv clucked his tongue. "You've got a crush on that girl."

"Lily is an employee. A good one. She already found ways for us to save a quarter of a million dollars in overhead costs and she's only been working for us for four days." I wasn't sure why I felt the need to defend Lily to anyone, let alone Marv. He was a good man and he was only giving me shit because that was how our relationship worked.

Marv leaned against the ATV. "So she's smart. Competent. Cares about the ranch. Can hold her own in a bar brawl. And looks good in tight jeans." He nodded his head toward her. "I think you just found your soulmate, son."

"I mentioned that she's been here for *four* days, right?"

"And you haven't shown interest in a woman in years. Isn't your hand getting tired?"

Did I mention that Marv was a pain in my ass? "We can't all be lucky enough to find our soulmate at eighteen, Marv."

His relationship with his wife, Nellie, was the stuff of fairy tales. They started dating in their last year of high school. Got married the day after their graduation and started popping out babies nine months later. Marv had six daughters and thirteen grandkids.

"Get your head out of your ass, son." Marv was still looking at Lily. "The universe just put an incredible woman on your ranch. A woman who is so far out of your damn league that you should never have crossed paths. But here we are. And that same woman keeps looking over here at you like she would rather ride you than a horse. You've been handed a gift, Evan. Don't fuck it up."

10

LILY

"Thanks for letting me spend the day with you." I strolled next to Evan on the dirt path that led to our homes, enjoying the gentle breeze cooling my sunburnt skin. It seemed that no matter how much sunblock I applied, I was destined to have pink shoulders.

"No problem. I enjoyed the company." Evan had been quieter than usual since our coffee chat on my porch.

"You don't have to worry about babysitting me tomorrow. Tom wants to spend some more time going over the financials." I felt guilty for how much time I'd taken from Evan when he clearly didn't have time to spare.

He nodded somewhat absently as we stopped in front of the cottage. "Do you... what are your plans for dinner?" His blue eyes were locked onto mine.

"Actually, Harper wants me to meet her downtown." I looked down, unable to maintain eye contact after feeling like I'd just rejected him.

"That'll be nice for you." Evan's feet shuffled in the dirt. "I'll take off then. Have fun tonight and tell my sister not to take you to the Nest unless she has money for bail."

I laughed and climbed the first two porch steps before whirling around. "Hey, Ev? I'm free tomorrow night. Would you like to get dinner with me?"

His eyes widened. "Uh, yeah. Okay. Dinner." Then the shock wore off and he smiled. "Actually, how about I make you dinner at my place?"

"Okay. That sounds nice." I had never had a man ask to make me dinner. "I'll see you then."

"Good night, Lily." He gave me a little wave before sauntering away. I stayed on the porch and watched him for far longer than was acceptable. His ass had hypnotic properties.

I didn't have time to worry about the fact that I'd just asked my boss on a date and he'd just offered to make me dinner. I was due to meet his sister for dinner. Even worse than asking out my boss was the fact that he was my best friend's older brother and I had to sit across from her all night and not mention any of this.

"The boys are being nice to you?" Harper pressed over plates of pasta. Crestwood didn't have a lot of dining establishments, but one of her friends from high school had opened an adorable Italian restaurant just a couple of blocks away from Harper's store.

"Yeah, they are. We had a bit of a rocky start, but now they are being really sweet and helpful." I sipped my wine and tried to think of another topic to discuss.

Harper was way ahead of me. "Sweet, huh? You're talking about Nate."

"Nate is sweet, yes. But Chase and Evan aren't complete barbarians."

"Let's be honest. Chase can be an asshole. He doesn't mean to be, but he has no filter and no one has ever put him in his place. Nate likes to put on a front so everyone thinks he's sweet, but he only does that to hide the trauma he's carrying around from his time in the military. Evan, on the other hand...he might be the real sweet brother. He's the loyal type and he does everything he can for our family. When he found out about the twins, he stepped up. He is great with them and they adore their father." Harper was smiling as she talked about her brothers. "Evan has a hard time asking for help, though. That's why he had such a bad reaction when he heard that Dad had hired you."

I wasn't comfortable talking about Evan with her. I was sure that I wouldn't be able to hide the feelings I was having toward him. "What about your other brothers? Do they visit the ranch often?"

"Noah lives there during the off-season. He doesn't have time to visit during the season, but he loves the ranch. Brent...not so much." Harper's smile wavered for the first time. "I don't know what happened with him, but once he left Crestwood, he never looked back. We see him at Christmas and that's it."

"That's too bad. I'm sure Tom wishes he would visit more." I couldn't imagine having a dad like Tom Sullivan and not wanting to see him.

"Brent was always kind of the black sheep in the family. He never liked working the ranch and he was a total nerd in the best way possible. The intellectual of the family." Harper tilted her wine glass at me. "Actually, he kind of reminds me of you. Maybe I should set you up with him."

"Oh, no. That's not a good idea." My cheeks flushed. "You don't want me dating one of your brothers."

"I don't?" She pursed her lips. "I've been thinking about that, and I'm not sure I feel that way anymore. You're my best friend. I love my brothers. I love you. If you ended up with one of them, we'd be sisters. What's bad about that?"

It was such a Harper way to look at the world. "You're assuming it would work out. What if I dated one of them and we had a nasty breakup? You would have to choose your brother, Harper. And then I would lose my best friend."

"Huh. It sounds like you've actually been thinking about this." Her mischievous smile appeared. "Which one?"

"Which one what?" I quickly shoveled pasta into my mouth to hide my embarrassment.

"Which brother have you been thinking about dating?"

I pretended to be too busy chewing to answer. That didn't deter my friend.

"It's not Chase. You would get so sick of his stupid mouth. Nate?" She quickly considered that and shook her head. "He's too easy. Too outwardly likable. You need a challenge." She snapped her fingers. "It's Evan. Of course. The responsible one with a heart of gold who clearly needs someone to sand down his rough edges. It's perfect."

I finished chewing and swallowed down the pasta with a gulp of wine. "I'm not looking to smooth down anyone's edges."

"But you didn't deny that you want to date Evan!" Harper reached for the bottle of wine and quickly refilled my glass.

"Harp, Evan and I are just friends. He's helping me learn the ropes around the ranch. That's it."

"Liar." Harper knew me too damn well.

"He has two kids. He's a lot older than me. We're in different places in our lives. When Evan looks at me, I'm sure all he sees is an obnoxious city girl."

"If you think that, you don't know my brother. He's the one who tried to convince me not to move back here after Dad's stroke. He encouraged me to keep my life in the city. Evan doesn't look down on people from the city."

"Why *did* you stay, Harp?" I couldn't believe that I hadn't thought to ask my best friend why she had been so quick to give up everything to move back to Crestwood.

"Because I was tired of staying away." The answer came easy to her. "After what happened with Jimmy, I didn't feel like I belonged here. I was always worried about running into him somewhere and I didn't want to spend my life looking over my shoulder." Her perfectly manicured nails tapped her wine glass. "But then Dad almost died and I regretted those years that I'd spent away from my family. Jimmy had already taken so much from me and I wasn't going to spend another minute letting him affect the rest of my life. I wanted to be in Crestwood, so I stayed."

I should have known that Jimmy Macalister was part of her decision. He'd been controlling Harper for years. I remembered the first time she told me about him. It was our freshman year in college and we'd been roommates for several months. I had used a fake ID to buy some cheap booze and we got drunk in our dorm room. Somehow, we'd gotten on the topic of our first times.

Harper's story had been brutal. When she was seventeen, an older man had taken an interest in her. He had pursued her aggressively until she finally agreed to go on a date with him. It wasn't long before she thought they were in love. After three months of dating, Harper had finally had sex with him. The next day, everyone in town was talking about it. The asshole had recorded the encounter and circulated it to all his friends. That asshole was Jimmy Macalister.

"You shouldn't have broken your hand defending me," Harper said quietly, looking at the splint resting on the table.

"It was totally worth it, Harp. He deserves worse."

"I never told you that the reason Jimmy targeted me was because of Evan getting Naomi pregnant. Jimmy always hated my brothers because everyone loved them. Sleeping with me and humiliating me was Jimmy's way of getting payback."

"That fucker. I should've cut off his dick," I said, my hand closing over the butter knife.

"That was why I made my brothers promise they wouldn't go after Jimmy. I didn't want my niece and nephew to ever find out that they were pawns in Jimmy's sick game. I didn't want Evan to have a strained relationship with their mother and her family because of me."

"You are a better person than me," I said definitively. "I would've sicced all five brothers on that shithead."

"I'm not supposed to know, but Ronan stole Jimmy's truck and took it out to his cousin's junkyard. He stripped it for parts and crushed it." Harper giggled. "He recorded the whole thing and anonymously sent it to Jimmy. Said that if Jimmy came anywhere near me again, he'd be the one getting crushed."

"Damn. That's impressive." Now I understood why Harper put up with Ronan's flirtations. "I wish I'd had some brothers to threaten the boys who messed with me in high school."

"After what you did last night, you're going to be just as protected as me. All of my brothers are fiercely loyal and you are family now."

"What's the deal with the Macalister family? Evan mentioned that Naomi and Jimmy are estranged from each other." I was trying not to sound nosy and I was failing miserably.

"That happened after the twins were born. James Macalister Senior was not happy that his grand-babies had the Sullivan family name." She rolled her eyes. "They own a rival ranch out in Brixburg. Our families have always had a bit of a competition, but it got worse when Dad allowed Uncle Rick to grow the thoroughbred part of the business. And then Evan knocked up the Macalister princess." She shook her head at the memory. "That damn family disowned Naomi and the twins. Kicked her off the ranch. Evan gave her a down payment for a house and her maternal grandparents stepped up to help out, too. That's the only family she has left now."

"That's terrible. But... why didn't Evan have her move in with him?" More prying questions. I couldn't seem to stop.

"They were never together. Or, after that one night anyway. When they found out about the pregnancy, they both agreed that it didn't make sense to try to force a relationship when neither of them was interested. Evan was happy to take care of Naomi because he cared about her as a friend and as the mother of his children. If they had lived together, it could have complicated things. And Naomi found a man a couple of years later and she's happily married with two more children."

"And Evan never found anyone to pop out more babies with?" I blamed the wine for my inability to stop prying.

Harper could read me like a book. "Maybe he just did."

"No!" I wagged a finger at her. "I'm not looking to be anyone's baby mama."

"I know he's making you dinner tomorrow night," Harper said smugly. "He texted me to find out your favorite meal."

"Well, that's just... kind of sweet." I wanted to be mad that he'd spilled our business to his sister, but I was too touched by why he'd done it. "So you've known about this all night?"

"Lil, I've known you liked my brother since I saw you check out his ass as he walked away after kissing your hand in front of my bookshop."

"I did no such thing!" I was mortified. I had no idea that Harper had witnessed that exchange and even less idea that I'd been so obvious about my admiration of Evan's derriere.

"I've overheard him calling you sweetheart," she continued. "He doesn't do that, you know. Some of the men around here like to call women darling or honey. A small-town quirk or whatever. But Evan has never done that with anyone but you. I don't know what that means, but I think it means *something*."

"We're just having dinner as friends," I insisted, ignoring all evidence to the contrary.

"If you say so." She finished her wine in one big swig. "Just be careful, Lil. Based on history, Evan isn't good at using a condom."

11

EVAN

"Let me get this straight. You finally got the balls to ask a woman on a date and the best you came up with was cooking for her?" Ronan shook his head like he'd never been more disappointed in anyone in his life.

"Funny, I don't remember asking you for your opinion."

"Make sure you jerk off before she gets here. It's been so long since you've had sex that you're likely to blow in your pants halfway through the meal."

"Ronan, I already helped you load the hay onto your trailer. You can leave." I kept my focus on the steaks I was preparing.

"Exactly how long has it been, man?" he continued. "I know there were a few women after Naomi, but you haven't been with anyone in a long time."

I sighed and clenched my jaw. "Three years," I grunted.

"Fuck. I don't know how you do it. Or why. Plenty of women in this town would happily help you relieve some tension."

I didn't bother telling him that I'd never been a fan of casual sex. That night with Naomi had been an anomaly and I'd ended up with two kids. Even though I loved my kids, I had no desire to repeat that night. I had tried dating a few women, but it was hard to find anyone in Crestwood that wasn't interested in me because of our successful family business. Marrying a Sullivan would be a quick ride to the easy life. That's not to say that all women were only interested in men for their money, but the women who showed interest in me always fit that stereotype.

"Here." Ronan tossed something into the air and I caught it reflexively.

"Seriously?" I glared at the box of condoms in my hand.

"Lily deserves better than an unplanned pregnancy on a first date. Wrap it up this time, Sullivan."

"I wrapped it up that time too, asshole." It wasn't my fault the condom broke and I had been too drunk to notice.

Ronan took a sip from the beer that he had stolen from my fridge. "From everything I've heard, Lily sounds like the real deal. The fact that she had no problem breaking Macalister's nose makes her damn near perfect in my book. I like her for you. Don't fuck it up."

"Why does everyone keep telling me that?" I growled. First Marv, then Harper, and now Ronan.

"Because you have a history of avoiding anything that might make you happy and from the looks of it, Lily Jameson makes you very happy." He gestured to my outfit. "I mean, look what you are wearing."

"What about it?"

"Jeans without any holes and a blue button down?" His eyes flicked upward. "Fresh shave and styled hair? You're already whipped."

"I'm having a friend over for dinner and I don't want to sit around in my dirty work clothes. Fuck off."

"And the cologne?" he pressed with a knowing smirk.

"To cover the stench from your boots." I was still pissed that Ronan had stomped through my house in his work boots after I'd specifically told him not to. I didn't want my house smelling like horseshit.

"Fine. I can take a hint." He chugged the rest of the beer and left the bottle next to the box of condoms I'd thrown there. "Just remember, city girls are a little crazy but that only makes them all the more fun in the sack."

"Out." I pointed a knife toward the front door.

Once Ronan was gone, I still wasn't able to focus. Truth be told, I was nervous. It had been a long time since I'd been on a first date and I'd never had one in my own home. When most of the food was prepped, I slid on a pair of nice leather boots and grabbed the flowers I'd picked in the field earlier. They were nicer than anything I could've bought from a florist and Lily didn't strike me as the kind of woman who would be upset that I hadn't spent money on them.

She wasn't due at my house for ten more minutes and it took far less time than that to walk next door to her cottage. I found it curious that my hands were clammy. I had never felt this way before a date. I had walked this same path just a few hours ago when I dropped off Lily's morning coffee, but this trip felt different.

I knocked twice on the blue door and took a deep breath.

"What are you doing here?" she asked by way of greeting.

"We have a date tonight. I'm picking you up." I held out the bouquet. "These are for you."

"Lilies?" She took them from me with a smile. "Cute."

"I am." I took a long moment to drink in her appearance.

Tight black jeans and an even tighter black tank top with hints of gold sparkles throughout. The neckline was just low enough to hint at her cleavage without being obvious. That didn't stop me from staring for a beat before moving onto the rest of her. Caramel hair styled in soft waves hanging past her shoulders. Flawless skin now tinged with pink from the sun. As far as I could tell, she wasn't wearing any makeup.

"You're a vision, Lily," I said, pushing aside the naughty thoughts that had become second nature when I was around her.

"You clean up good, Sullivan." She squeezed my arm. "I'll put these in water and then we can go."

"Mom always had fresh cut flowers in here. You should be able to find a vase in one of those cabinets," I said, gesturing. I would've gotten it myself, but that felt a little too much like I was invading her privacy.

"These are from the field, aren't they?" she said, grabbing a clear vase and filling it in the sink.

"Yeah. Mom planted them years ago and even though no one has been maintaining the field, they just keep coming back."

Lily placed the flowers in the vase and tweaked a few of the stems. "They are beautiful. It's probably a bit narcissistic, but lilies have always been my favorite flower."

"Mine too," I admitted.

She smiled and crossed the room. "So you've got a thing for lilies, huh?" Her teasing smile was just as sexy as the rest of her. She nudged me gently through the door and closed it behind us. "Lucky me."

"Sweetheart, you haven't gotten lucky yet."

I expected an eyeroll or snarky comment. Instead, she slid a hand down my arm before slipping her fingers through mine. "I'm not so sure about that."

"Harper told me that I have to be on my best behavior tonight, so prepare to be charmed." I wasn't sure what had possessed me to tell my sister about this date. Maybe I had been testing the waters to see how she would feel about me taking an interest in her best friend. I hadn't expected Harper to be so encouraging of the date.

"I think she has ulterior motives."

"Like what?"

Lily laughed. "Like getting her best friend to move to Crestwood permanently."

"Oh. Because if we started dating, you'd have a reason to stay?"

"Something like that."

I hadn't even thought about the fact that Lily might not stay. Her job on the ranch didn't have a firm end-date, but it was understood that she probably wouldn't be staying beyond a year or so.

"You're planning to move back to the city when you're done here?" I asked as casually as possible. Our first date was not the time to ask about long-term habitation plans.

"Of course. That's where my life is. I own a place there. All of my friends except Harper live there. And I'll need another job once I'm done here. Going back to the city is the only logical choice."

"Maybe..." I wasn't sure how inappropriate it was for me to weigh in.

"Or..." she prodded.

"Or maybe for once you could choose to do something illogical," I said, releasing her hand to open the front door to my house.

"Oh, Evan. If you only knew just how often I've fucked up my life by being illogical." She patted my chest as she stepped past and damn if I didn't feel that touch in every nerve in my body. Ronan was right that it had been far too long since I'd had sex. "It smells good in here."

"Harper said you are a meat and potatoes type of girl. Hopefully she wasn't setting me up for failure."

"She wasn't," Lily assured me. She was taking in my house as subtly as possible. "Your home is nice. Not entirely what I expected."

"Which was what?"

"I don't know. You're a busy guy and you've got two kids. I guess I wasn't expecting it to be so clean." She eyed the throw pillows on the couch. "Or so color coordinated."

I laughed. "That's Harper's touch. I built the house, she helped me with the décor."

"You built this house?"

"With the help of family and friends. I had been living at the main house with Dad when I learned about the twins. Some of my siblings were also still living there at the time and I thought it was important to have my own place. Everyone pitched in and helped get this built. The babies needed their mom that first year, so I usually only had them for a few hours at a time. But once they were done nursing, I moved into this house with them."

"I think it's pretty great that you and Naomi have been able to co-parent so beautifully. You both stepped up in a big way and made sure your kids were the priority. Not all parents would do that."

"Then they aren't really parents." I had never doubted my decisions even once. Yes, it had been hard. Yes, it would've been easier to write a check to Naomi every month and go on with my life. But that was never an option for me. I loved my kids before they were even born. "Can I grab you a drink?"

"Sure. Whatever you're having." Lily wasn't quite as relaxed and smiley as she had been a few minutes ago.

I grabbed two beers and popped them open. "I need to throw the steaks on the grill. Want to follow me outside?"

"I'd follow you anywhere with the promise of food."

"In that case, there are appetizers in my bedroom." As soon as the comment left my mouth I wanted to take it back. That was way too forward and I wasn't even entirely joking.

Lily didn't pick up on the undercurrent of longing in my voice and she laughed loudly while slapping my arm. "You weren't lying about that charm, Sullivan."

I handed her the beers and grabbed the platter of steaks. The grill was right outside on the back deck and I had already started it before I went to Lily's house. All I had to do was add the steaks. Lily leaned against the porch railing and watched me.

"Do you cook a lot?" she asked.

"Whenever I have the kids. I try not to fill them with fast food. On the off weeks, I don't cook very much." I shut the grill lid and took my beer from her. "It's not as much fun cooking dinner for yourself."

"I hear ya. The pizza delivery man was my best friend back in the city."

I mirrored her posture, leaning next to her close enough that our arms were touching. "You're nothing like I thought you were going to be."

"You were really hoping for horns, weren't you? Is that some kind of fetish?"

Well, fuck. Now it was.

"I, uh, thought you would hate it out here. Complain about the smell and lack of a Starbucks. Wear your fancy clothes and be afraid of getting them dirty." I twirled the beer bottle in my hand. "I thought for sure you'd have no interest in getting to know a guy like me."

"You probably thought I'd have a terrible right hook too." She looked down at her broken hand and then up at me, hazel eyes twinkling beneath long lashes. Lily was tall, but I still had several inches on her and I enjoyed the visual of her looking up at me. It wasn't too dissimilar from how she would look on her knees with my cock in her mouth.

I swallowed hard and pushed that thought away. "I made some bad assumptions based on the little information I knew about you. I was hoping that tonight you'll let me get to know you better."

"Knowing as in the biblical sense?" she teased.

"Not on a first date." I pretended to be appalled by the suggestion of something I'd been wanting all week. "Tell me about your childhood. Where did you grow up? Do you have any siblings?"

"Here it comes. My favorite part of a first date where the man asks personal questions that I try to dodge." She took so long sipping her beer that I assumed she was dodging me, but then she said, "I was born in a small town in Nebraska. My family was dirt poor. We lived in a trailer that was about the size of the cottage I'm staying in now. Dad was a gambler and an alcoholic. Mom preferred meth. They fought all the time. Dad left to buy more booze one night and he just never came back."

She spoke so matter-of-factly, like she was telling a story and not pouring out her childhood trauma to me. "Mom ended up fucking one of her dealers and invited him to live with us. He actually made pretty good money and things were a little better because we at least had some food in the house. But then he got a little too comfortable. He was always a little handsy." She turned to face away from the house, looking at the sun setting in the distance. "I was twelve when he finally crawled into my bed."

The air became oppressively hot and every muscle in my body coiled tight. "Lily, you don't have to–"

"Don't worry. I'm not going to tell you the disgusting details."

That was the least of my concerns. I was much more concerned about Lily and what it might do to her to relive her past.

"I think that he thought I would just let it happen. There had probably been other girls who had been too afraid to fight. If I'd had anything worth living for at the time, maybe I would've reacted differently. But I had no one and no fear. I fought back. Got him right in the head with Mom's ashtray. I don't know what that thing was made of, but it knocked him out cold. Then I threw some things in a bag and left. Mom had one sister who I had only met twice, but I knew where she lived. I walked there, told her what happened, and she told me I was going to stay with her from then on. And that's what I did."

She fought. Of course she did. Lily was a fighter. "Your parents sound like total assholes. And the guy who touched you... if he's still alive, I would be happy to kill him for you."

"Honestly, I have no idea what happened to him. Once I moved in with my aunt, I never talked to my mom again and she never tried to contact me. Eventually, that stopped bothering me. My aunt is amazing. She made sure I got through high school and into college. She even helped pay for some of it even though she didn't have a lot of money. When I got my big equity payout last year, the first thing I did was buy her a house." Lily smiled proudly. "When I told her about this job, she was the one who encouraged me to do it. She was convinced I'd come out here and fall in love with this place."

"Then I think I owe your aunt a huge favor because I'm really glad you are here."

"Me too." She surprised me by leaning across the inches separating us and pressing her lips lightly against my cheek. "I'm glad I met you, Evan."

"Obviously. I'm pretty amazing." I couldn't take my eyes off those perfect lips.

"Hm. I think I'll reserve judgment until after I taste your cooking."

"Shit. The steaks." I'd been so enraptured by her that I had completely forgotten I was in the middle of grilling our dinner.

Lily giggled as she watched me scramble to check on them before breathing a sigh of relief that I hadn't overcooked them. Our intense moment had effectively been ruined, but that was probably for the best. Lily looked like she was ready to move on.

After saving the steaks, we headed back inside to eat. Lily helped me set the table and bring over the food. We ate at a leisurely pace and she insisted that it was her turn to ask prying questions about my life. That mostly just led to me revealing embarrassing stories about the trouble I'd gotten into with my brothers when we were kids.

Things were going well until I made the mistake of asking her about her last job, the one that had made her millions of dollars and a headhunter's dream.

"Why did you leave? That wasn't part of the equity deal, was it?" I asked. After Chase's monologue about Lily's impressive background, I'd done some research. It was truly an impressive story.

"No. It was...complicated." She made a big show of checking the time on her phone. "You've got an early morning. I should head home soon."

"They teach you how to dodge questions in law school?" I joked.

"No, I actually learned that when I got arrested." Her expression was way too unreadable for me to tell if she was joking. She pushed back her chair. "I'll help you clean up before I go."

"Not a chance." I stood and caught her arm as she reached for the dishes. "You're not cleaning on our first date."

She gave me the glare I loved best. The one that I would kill to see while I was tossing her onto my bed. "You did all the cooking. You have to let me do the dishes or something."

"Next time," I said dismissively. "I'll walk you home."

"You're joking, right? My house is right there." She pointed in the direction of the cottage. "I'm pretty sure I can find it."

"I'm sure you can," I said with a chuckle. "But I'm

going to make sure you find it safely. This might not be the big, scary city, but we do have wild animals out here."

That cut off any further protest and she nodded. "Fine. But it sure feels like this is your way of trying to get invited in."

Shit. She was right. "I'm not. I wouldn't do that. I –"

"I was teasing, Ev." Her eyes sparkled with mischief. "You've been nothing but the perfect gentleman all week. I expect more from you than a cheesy attempt to get laid."

"You're faith in me is heartwarming." I wasn't completely kidding. I liked that she didn't think I fit the mold of a stereotypical single man. I liked being held to a higher standard.

We had only taken a few steps outside before she asked, "What kind of wild animals are out here?"

"Nothing too scary. Coyotes, foxes, an occasional wolf." I was starting to feel like I'd made a bad decision using wild animals as an excuse to walk her home. I just hadn't been ready to say goodnight to her yet. "They mostly stay away because of all the activity around the ranch, but as long as we have cattle we will have something trying to sneak in for a snack."

"And here I thought *you* were the snack." Her wink was perfectly exaggerated and I found myself laughing yet again. Lily had a knack for making me laugh.

We were already at the cottage. It truly was close to my house, something I hadn't accounted for when I'd told Dad I was going to set Lily up there. It had just seemed like the logical choice at the time, but now I had to admit that I liked having her so close.

"Thanks for making me dinner, Evan. It was delicious." We were standing in front of the blue door, glancing awkwardly at one another. It had been a long time since my last first date and I had no idea how this was supposed to end.

"It was nice to have some adult company for once." I loved my kids, but they didn't always appreciate a nice home-cooked meal and our dinner chats weren't super stimulating. "Do you have plans for the weekend?"

"I promised Harper I would help her with some stuff at the shop. What about you?"

"I've got the kids starting after work tomorrow. That means I'll be spending the next week cleaning, cooking, driving them to all their glamorous life events, and generally pulling out my hair and wondering how I ended up here."

"You love it," she said confidently.

"Yeah, I do." I rubbed the back of my neck. "I should give you my number. I might not be around a lot, but you can call me if you need anything."

She slid her phone from her pocket with a small smile. "Smooth, Sullivan."

"Shut up," I grumbled.

Lily entered the number I gave her and then looked up. "Aren't you going to ask me for my number?"

"I don't need to, sweetheart." Before I could talk myself out of it, I leaned down and pressed my lips to the spot just in front of her ear. "We both know you're going to call me."

"You are way too cocky," she said in a breathless whisper that made my cock harden.

I tilted my head. "What was that? Did you just complain about my cock being too big?"

"You are ridiculous." She put a hand on my chest and shoved me back. "Go home, Boss."

"Good night, Lily." I turned and tossed a wave over my shoulder. "I look forward to your call."

12

LILY

Evan stopped by in the morning with coffee, but he only said a quick good morning and then headed out to work the ranch. I spent the morning working with Tom on financial projections for the next two years and we formalized a strong plan that would allow us to expand the business without sacrificing the current portfolio.

Tom had never been to college, but he was smarter than anyone I had worked with in the corporate world. He understood his business and the challenges and opportunities in front of us. He was also open to my suggestions around expanding Chase's part of the business while being more careful in the thoroughbred investments.

I ran into Nate when I was leaving the main house and he talked me into joining him for a visit to the stables. One of the mares had delivered a new foal a couple of nights ago and it was fun watching the little guy hobble around on knobby legs.

"That might be the cutest thing I've ever seen," I said when the mare rubbed its head down the foal's back.

"Have you seen me?" Nate protested.

"Yes, yes, you are adorable." I shook my head with a smile.

Nate leaned forward on the fence, resting his elbows in a casual stance that made him look like a cowboy posing for a calendar photo spread. I made a mental note to add a hot cowboy calendar to our business portfolio.

"It's almost the weekend. Got a big date lined up?" I asked.

He shot me a knowing look. "Subtle, Mom."

"Ew. Don't do that." I shuddered. Maybe I was almost thirty, but I wasn't looking to be anyone's mom. "I'm just trying to be friendly. Maybe find out why a guy as charming as you doesn't have a girlfriend."

"I'm not gay," he said quickly.

I flinched. "Oh. I wasn't trying to imply..." But then I stopped because he had read me perfectly. I had been implying that. "I'm sorry. That was rude."

"No, it's fine. A lot of people make that same assumption." He chuckled and fidgeted with the brim of his hat. "My best buddy from high school came out about ten years ago. If I was gay, I wouldn't still be single. I'd be with him. He's a total catch." He grinned at me. "Honestly, that would make my life so much easier because I understand men. I *do not* understand women."

"We aren't some alien species, Nate. Women aren't as

complex as you seem to think." I found it impossible to believe that Nate wasn't good with women.

"That's easy for you to say. You are one of them." He switched his positioning so that his back was pressed to the fence. "I spent eight years in the military, mostly surrounded by men. I suffer from a bit of an arrested development when it comes to women. Sure, I can get them into my bed without much effort. I can make them scream my name just as easy. But anything more than that..." He tossed up his hands. "I don't have a clue what I'm doing."

"You do just fine talking to me."

"Yeah, because there's obviously never going to be anything sexual or romantic between us," he said with complete certainty.

I wanted to be offended by that, but he was right. Almost from the second I first met Nate, I had known that we would only ever be friends. "So you are afraid of women who make you want something more? Why?"

"Because for that to happen, I'd have to let someone in. And there's a lot of shit I'm carrying around that I don't ever want anyone to see." His usual spark of humor had vanished from his gray eyes. In the time I had spent with Nate, he had always put on a front of being relaxed and content. He was always quick with a smile and a joke. The man beside me now looked nothing like that other Nate.

"Believe it or not, I can completely understand that feeling," I said, squeezing his bicep. It was like squeezing a rock. "For a long time, I kept everyone out too. But that hasn't really been working for me, so I'm trying something new."

"What's that? Riding cowboys?" He raised an eyebrow. "Word on the ranch is that you went home with my brother last night."

"What? No! I mean, well kind of. Evan invited me over for dinner." I crossed my arms and tapped a foot. "I did not *go home* with him."

"A woman who doesn't put out on the first date. I can respect that." He laughed when I punched his arm. "I have to admit I'm a little surprised. Getting involved with the boss can be a risky move."

"What do you mean?" My heart thudded in my chest. Had Harper told him about my past? Had she told Evan, too? Maybe that was why he'd started showing interest in me.

Nate shrugged. "If it doesn't work out, would you be able to keep doing this job? I have to imagine that would be an awkward situation for both of you."

"Yeah, probably." Awkward was putting it mildly. I knew for a fact that I wouldn't stick around if I got involved with Evan and we later broke up.

By the time I got back to the cottage, I was exhausted. My days started early on the ranch and I'd been getting a lot more fresh air and exercise than I was used to. I'd been so busy that I hadn't even finished unpacking my two suitcases. I decided to take care of that first before letting myself relax. I was afraid that once I sat down, I wouldn't want to get up.

Since I hadn't brought much, I didn't take long to get

everything organized. Then I went to the kitchen and made a quick sandwich. I'd grabbed a few supplies at the local market when I was downtown visiting Harper, but I was planning to make a trip to a bigger town for a more thorough grocery haul.

It was amazing how much simpler my life was in the cottage. The place was small enough that it took very little effort to keep it clean. I didn't have the immediate urge to pull out my laptop and start working because I didn't have a demanding boss or needy coworkers bothering me. In fact, I hadn't even heard from Evan today after he dropped off coffee. He seemed perfectly content to let me do whatever I needed to do without micromanaging me.

"Now what?" I wondered out loud, looking around. There was no television or internet which really limited my evening entertainment. I settled for reading since Evan's mother had left the bookshelves fully stocked. I used to love reading before I'd gotten so busy with my career that I never had time. Most of the books were romances which was probably the last thing I needed to read as a single, perpetually horny woman.

My reading selection ended up not mattering because once I snuggled into bed with the book, I only read about ten pages before falling sleep.

Even though Harper wasn't expecting me until midday, I found myself waking before sunrise after an incredible night of sleep. Since Evan was busy with his kids, I didn't wait around for coffee. Instead, I pulled on a running set and shoes and headed outside for a jog.

It was nice to be able to run down the middle of the

dirt road and take up as much space as I wanted without having to worry about traffic or other pedestrians. It was even nicer to have trees, rolling fields, and the distant mountains as my scenery. Running in the city could be frustrating and I usually got bored quickly, but not out here. I wanted to keep running to see as much of the ranch as possible.

The morning had started chilly, but it heated up quickly once the sun made an appearance. But the time I was headed back to the cottage, I was covered in sweat. Unfortunately, I hadn't thought that far ahead when I chose my running path and now I would have to pass Evan's house looking like a sweaty beast.

I slowed to a brisk walk as I crested the hill and swore under my breath when I heard Evan's voice. Of course he was outside. The universe obviously hated me. But then his house came into view and I was staring directly at his ass in perfectly fitting sweatpants. He was bent into the hood of his truck, fiddling with something. When he twisted slightly to the side, his naked torso was exposed.

"Fuck," I breathed, completely enraptured. There was no doubt in my mind that Evan had an incredible body and now I was dying to see it. My footsteps quickened along with my pulse. I was about to call out a comment about this view being the best part of waking up when his front door flew open.

"Dad! My cleats aren't in my room." The dark-haired girl standing on the porch spotted me instantly. "Who's that?"

Evan stepped back and turned. A smile lit up his face

and he waved. "That's our new neighbor, Em. Lily, come over and meet my daughter."

Emma's resemblance to Evan was uncanny. She had his dark waves and blue eyes. She was tall for her age and very slender, but her cheeks were still round with youth. She eyed me curiously as I approached.

"Emma, this is Lily Jameson. She's staying in Grandma's cottage." Evan was wiping his hands on an oil-stained towel and it took all of my will power not to openly gawk. His body was just as incredible as I had imagined. I wanted to get lost in the curves and dips of his muscles, all the way down the narrow expanse between his hips.

"Hi, Emma. It's nice to meet you." I felt awkward standing there in my sweaty clothes with Evan just a few feet away, looking like an absolute sex god. I was just glad that Emma couldn't read my mind.

"Are you dating one of my uncles?" she asked bluntly.

"What?" I gaped at her.

"I mean, why else are you staying in Grandma Penny's cottage?"

Evan was quick to explain since I clearly had no capacity for communicating with a tween. "Lily is Aunt Harper's best friend. They went to college together. Lily has been working as a lawyer and CFO for a company in the city and Grandpa hired her to come work for the ranch."

It was cute listening to Evan hype up my resume to his daughter. She wasn't impressed. "Why would you want to move *here*?" she asked.

Ready to Ride

I didn't think a joke about riding hot cowboys would be the best course of action. I decided to go with the truth. "Because Harper can convince anyone to do anything if she puts her mind to it."

"Em, your cleats are in the mudroom. Right where you left them. And wake your brother up for me." Evan spoke with a perfected dad-voice that I somehow found just as sexy as the voice he used when he was flirting with me.

"Fine." Emma put a hand on her hip. "I'm glad you're here, Lily. This place could use more girls."

"I agree. I'll see you around, Emma." We both watched her skip into the house. "Well you don't need a paternity test for that one. She looks just like you and acts just like Harper."

Evan laughed. "Much to my dismay. The teenage attitude is coming on strong in that one. Did you want some coffee? I would've brought some earlier but I thought you were sleeping in."

"No, thanks. I'm heading downtown soon so I'll grab some there." I should've already picked up a bag of coffee grounds, but I hadn't wanted to give Evan a reason to stop visiting. "I'll let you get back to whatever you were doing."

"Just checking the fluids," he said, tapping the hood. His eyes left my face, traveling slowly downward. "I..."

"Yes?" I pursed my lips to keep from laughing. He was obviously checking me out and doing a terrible job of hiding it. Not that I was doing much better. I had been staring long enough to count all eight of his abs and commit them to memory.

"My phone service has been spotty," he said abruptly,

playfulness dancing across his beautiful face. "In case you tried to call me."

"I did not." I shook my head and started to walk away. "That wasn't subtle at all, Sullivan."

"Neither are those clothes," he called back to me.

HARPER AND I had been through a lot together. There was almost no aspect of our lives that we hadn't shared. But despite her incessant prying, I couldn't bring myself to share the details of my date with Evan.

"It was a nice date, Harp. That's all you need to know," I said firmly, shelving an antique Jane Austen novel.

"That means you totally had sex with my brother." She shuddered. "Which, ew. Absolutely gross. But...was it good enough for a second date?"

"We are not talking about this." I should just deny her claim, but I was hoping she'd be less likely to ask more questions if she thought it might lead to me discussing sexy times with her brother. "I think Evan is a really nice guy and we have fun together. That's all you need to know."

"Mhmm. Fun." She raised a skeptical eyebrow. "I think we're done with everything here. Let's grab a coffee before we leave for the game."

"What game?"

"The twins have a baseball game in an hour. Didn't Evan tell you?"

My whole body tensed. "No. Why would he do that?

We've been working together for a week and had one dinner together."

"Relax. I'm not implying that you should be the twins' stepmom." Harper rolled her eyes at my dramatics. "It's just a fun thing the whole family does every Saturday. There's not a lot to do in this town and it's a good excuse for us to all get together. It's not going to look like anything if you show up. Promise."

"I don't know." I had never dated a man with kids and I had no idea what the proper protocol would be. But Evan was the one who'd eagerly introduced me to Emma, so it wasn't like he was trying to keep me a secret. "If I go, you have to sit right next to me so everyone knows I'm there with you."

"Whoa. Like a date?" Harper grinned wickedly. "Damn, you are working your way through the Sullivans fast. I should warn Nate and Chase."

This would my second trip to Amelia's Cafe after stopping there in the morning. The woman at the register smiled broadly at us. She was the same person who had waited on me earlier. "Harp, where are you been?"

"Sorry, Amelia. I've been so swamped at the shop and I haven't gotten around to hiring any help yet." Harper gestured to me. "This is my friend, Lily. She's working for my dad up at the ranch."

"Oh lucky girl! So many cowboys, so little time." She winked at me and grabbed two cups. "What can I get you?"

We placed our orders and Amelia got to work on them while Harper finished introductions. "Amelia and I went to high school together, but she's a couple of years younger than us. She opened this place a couple of years ago and I've been addicted to her lattes ever since."

"No, you're addicted to the friend-of-the-owner discount," Amelia said.

"Maybe." Harper tossed a handful of dollars into the tip jar. "We need to schedule our next girls' night. It's been too long."

"How about next weekend? We can hit up the Eagle's Nest and flirt with the new bartender. He's a total dreamboat." Amelia handed us our drinks.

"He's 22, Amelia. We're too old to ogle a man that young."

"You might be too old, Sullivan, but I'm only 27," Amelia said. "I'm sure I could teach him a few things."

"I'm sure you could," Harper agreed with a laugh. "I'll text you to solidify plans, but keep your Saturday night free."

Amelia sighed dramatically. "Fine, I'll clear my busy schedule of knitting and watching true crime documentaries."

That didn't sound like a bad Saturday night to me, but maybe I'd just been single for too long. Regardless, I liked Amelia. She reminded me of the other girls Harper and I were friends with in college.

Harper had been at the ranch this morning having breakfast with Tom, so she'd driven me downtown. Knowing that I was stuck with her as my ride made me feel slightly less uncomfortable about tagging along for the baseball game.

"Their little league team is really good. They almost made it to the World Series over the summer," Harper explained. "Next year is the last year the twins will be eligible to play and this is their league's all-star game."

"Wow, that's impressive. And both of them play?"

"Yeah. Emma could've played softball instead, but she prefers baseball. And she's actually their top pitcher. Not a bad hitter either." Harper parked her car next to Evan's truck. "Tommy plays shortstop and leads the team in RBIs. Our brother Noah always says they got their skills from him, but Evan was actually an incredible player back in the day."

Before I could ask any follow-up questions, Harper was out of the car and heading toward the bleachers. I hurried to catch up because it would be too embarrassing to look like I had shown up there on my own.

Tom and Chase were seated next to Evan. I was surprised to see Marv sitting on the other side of Tom but then again, it made sense. He was practically part of the family.

"There they are!" Tom said as if it had been a foregone conclusion that I would be at the game. "Come on, girls. The game is about to start."

I felt Evan watching me as I climbed the bleachers. When I reached his row, he stood. "We can scoot down," he said.

"No way. I'm not sitting by myself." Harper grabbed my hand and climbed up another row, pulling me into the seats behind the men. I found myself staring at the back of Evan's head until he twisted to look at me.

"I was hoping Harper would bring you. I forgot to mention the game earlier and someone still hasn't given me her number." His hand closed around my calf in a gentle squeeze. I was surprised that he was touching me like that right in front of his family.

"Where's Nate?" I asked as heat rushed up my neck.

"He's the coach," Harper said, pointing at the man talking to the umpire.

"Ooh. A man in baseball pants. Hot." I yelped and squirmed as Evan squeezed my leg harder. "Watch it, Sullivan."

"You're the one running your mouth, sweetheart."

We hadn't been talking loudly, but Tom's head swiveled slightly toward us. I nodded my head in his direction to warn Evan that his dad was eavesdropping on us.

"Don't worry. He's old. His hearing is shit," Evan said loudly.

"Not shit enough to miss you dropping endearments, son," Tom replied without turning away from the field. "Now shut up. The game is starting."

Evan gave me another smile and a wink before turning back around.

Harper had been right about the game being a fun time. Dozens of people had shown up and everyone was cheering loudly. We were only able to converse between innings and even then Evan and I had to censor our words. Tom was clearly suspicious that there was something going on and he wasn't subtle about it.

"Emma is amazing," I said after she struck out the

side. We were headed into the last inning and it was a tied score.

"She's got an arm like her daddy," Tom said proudly.

"She's better than I was at that age," Evan countered.

"She's a lot prettier too," Harper joked.

Tom clapped his hands. "She's batting first this inning and Tommy is up third. Let's see if the Sullivan twins can pull out a win for the team."

The other team had switched to a new pitcher. He was a lot larger than the other kids and his warmup pitches were scarily fast. As Emma approached the batter's box with her dark braid trailing from her helmet, I bit my lip and leaned forward. She looked so delicate compared to the catcher in all his protective gear.

When I felt Evan's fingers brush over my hand, I looked down in surprise. I hadn't even realized that I had rested my hands on his shoulders. Evan lifted my non-splinted hand and pressed a quick kiss to my fingers before putting it back on his shoulder. The whole exchange was so familiar and intimate that it took my breath away.

But then the pitcher curled into his windup and threw a pitch that sailed directly at Emma. She spun away from it and took the hit squarely on her back. I was on my feet, yelling various obscenities while the Sullivan family all stared at me like I'd lost my mind. Evan had jumped to his feet too, but only to see if Emma was okay. When she hopped to her feet and trotted to first base, he glanced at me and laughed.

"Easy, killer. She's alright."

But I had already turned my attention to the woman standing a few rows down the bleachers. She hadn't taken her eyes off Emma and she was biting hard on her lower lip.

"That's Naomi," Harper said after I'd fallen back onto the metal seat.

"Of course." I don't know why it hadn't occurred to me that she would be there. She was the twins' mother. It made perfect sense. It also made perfect sense that she was stunning. Emma had gotten her tall and slender stature from her mom. But Naomi had pretty blond hair and curves that made me envious.

Evan didn't notice my blatant staring, but Chase happened to look over and his lips tipped up. I knew he was about to say something that would embarrass me, but the crowd interrupted with a roar as the next batter got a base hit. Emma was the go-ahead run on second.

"Let's go, Tommy!" Evan yelled.

I had yet to meet his son, but it was striking to see him walk to the plate with the same confident stride as his father. It was the type of thing that couldn't be taught or learned. He swung at the first pitch and drove a line drive to center field. Emma had read the hit perfectly and flew toward third. Nate waved an arm frantically, sending her home.

We all jumped to our feet to watch Emma slide as the catcher swung his glove down to apply the tag. The ump threw both arms straight out and we all lost it. We screamed and clapped and traded high-fives.

Emma must have heard us because she looked our

way and shook her head like we were the world's greatest embarrassment. Chase proceeded to yell even louder, specifically emphasizing her name.

The inning ended with their team up by just that one run. Emma returned to the mound to close out the game and when she struck out the last batter, we yelled even louder than we had before. Evan turned around. "You might be a good luck charm, Lil."

"Is she one of those charms that you have to rub to get the good luck?" Chase said.

"Charles Sullivan!" Tom barked. "We do not talk about women like that."

My jaw dropped. "Charles?" I said, looking at Evan for confirmation.

"Yeah, we used to call him Chucky, but he insisted on going by Chase when he was ten and some girl told him that Chucky was a creepy name and he would never get a girlfriend." Evan flinched when Chase landed a punch on his arm.

"I don't know. I think the name of a creepy, psychotic doll is perfect for him." I smiled extra sweetly at Chase. "You even have those soulless eyes."

"You're on my list," he said, pointing at me with a threatening look. "I was coming around to you, but you just ruined my goodwill."

"Don't worry about it. I've been on his list since I drove an ATV into his car on accident when I was fifteen. Nothing happens on his list." Harper reached across me to flick the brim of Chase's hat. He quickly slapped her hand away.

"My god. In their thirties and still acting like toddlers," Tom huffed. "I raised you kids to behave better than this. You turned into such smartasses."

For someone who had grown up alone and always wished for siblings, I was enthralled by these small teasing actions and taunts. No matter what was being said, it was obvious the Sullivans all deeply cared for each other.

"Dad, where do you think we learned how to be a smartass?" Chase asked with a laugh. "Between you and Marv, we learned every trick in the book."

The older men exchanged a look and Marv shrugged. "Kid's not wrong."

Evan cleared his throat. "I'm going to check in with the twins. Lil, I'll give you a ride home."

"Oh, that's not–" I instinctively was going to reject his offer. But then I remembered that Harper had no reason to go back to the ranch and driving me there would be completely out of her way.

She must've agreed because she quickly accepted on my behalf. "That would be great, Ev. Thanks."

Evan just nodded slightly, looking annoyed that I had tried to reject his offer. As he descended the bleachers, my eyes stayed with him. He was quite possibly even more attractive when he was in motion. Despite his large frame, his steps on the metal bleachers were light. He held himself like an athlete, with strong shoulders and confident strides. I was enthralled by him.

"You've got some drool, Lil," Chase muttered.

"Shut up, Chucky." I flicked his hat the same way Harper had done.

"Nah, I don't think I will, *sweetheart*," he said with a taunting lift of his eyebrow.

Tom shoved his arm. "Knock it off and start walking, son."

After we left the bleachers, I waited awkwardly behind everyone as they took turns congratulating the twins. Tom hugged Naomi and there was no sense of awkwardness in their interaction. Evan also didn't look uncomfortable standing next to her, laughing at something his dad said. I was dreading the moment where Naomi would notice me and we would be forced into an introduction. I wasn't ready for that, not while I didn't know what was happening between me and Evan.

My phone suddenly became the most interesting thing in the world as I strolled a few feet away to check the messages that had been building for the last week. Most of them were from my old job, from clients who hadn't heard that I no longer worked for the company. A couple were from friends who were wondering what the hell had happened to me. That was understandable. I had disappeared quite suddenly from my old life without any explanation.

The most recent message, one that I had received while I was at Evan's place, was the one I had been struggling to resist. I didn't want to hear Drew's voice, but part of me was desperate to know why he had called. We hadn't spoken in six months and I had finally accepted that I was better off without him.

"Hey, Lil. It's me." There was a long pause. "I just wanted to see how you are doing. I am in New York and yesterday I walked past that little Italian diner that you loved. It made me think of you. I miss you." Another pause was punctuated by his hard exhale. "I'm so sorry for how things ended. I never wanted that to happen. Take care of yourself. Maybe call me back if you are willing to give me a chance to apologize to you directly. Bye, babe."

I kept the phone pressed to my ear long after his message had ended. Of all the things I'd expected him to say, I hadn't expected an apology. Drew Nelson never apologized to anyone.

"Lily." A hand on my shoulder snapped me out of my daze and when I turned around, Evan was staring at me with concern. "Everything okay?"

I nodded, not trusting myself to speak.

"You ready to go?" He gestured vaguely toward his truck. The twins were already throwing their gear into the back. "Harper already left so you are stuck with me."

"I'm alright with that," I said quietly.

"You sure everything is okay?" Evan frowned slightly.

I nodded and forced a smile while giving his hand a quick squeeze. "I'm good. Promise."

I didn't sound very convincing, but Evan was tactful enough not to press me on it. He put a hand lightly on my lower back as he guided me across the parking lot. His quiet way of supporting me was a foreign experience. I was used to men being pushy, forcing their opinions and feelings onto me until they became mine. I was used to them leaving if I tried to resist their pressure.

Evan just opened the passenger door for me and gave me a sweet smile. He introduced me to Tommy before turning the key and then we drove back to the ranch with the three of them replaying the game, laughing, and teasing one another. I felt like I didn't belong there, but I also couldn't imagine being anywhere else. I wanted to sit there forever, basking in the warmth of a family who loved and supported one another.

Evan parked in front of his house and gave the kids orders to get their dirty uniforms in the laundry room before he let them exit the truck. They both responded with rolled eyes, but I knew they would do what he said. They respected their father and I did too. He adored his kids, but he wasn't afraid to parent them.

"Thanks for coming today," he said as he walked me home, again at his insistence. I doubted he was worried about a wild animal attack while it was still light out, but I didn't mind the time alone with him.

"It was fun. The twins are both so talented. You must be proud of them."

"I am. For a lot of reasons." His hands were shoved into his pockets like he was afraid of touching me. "Lily, are we okay? I'm picking up on some weird vibes from you. Did I do something wrong?"

"No," I said instantly. "You've been great, Ev. Really. I'm just... working through some stuff from my past."

"An ex?" he guessed correctly.

I nodded, not wanting to lie to him. "He called me and left a message that I wasn't expecting. We've been over for a while and I wasn't looking to revisit that part of my life.

But that message was like having an old scar ripped open."

"You still have feelings for him?" There was no judgment or anger in his words, just resignation. It was like he'd been expecting me to walk away from whatever was happening between us.

"Feelings, yes. Good feelings, not so much." I ran a hand through my hair, letting my fingers tangle in the windblown tresses. "Drew kind of fucked me up. He made it hard for me to trust people, including myself."

"What did he do?" Now there was an undercurrent of anger in his voice.

I finally dared to look at him. "That's kind of a long story. Do you need to get back to the kids?"

"They'll be fine for a little bit."

"Okay. I'll grab some beer. Wait here." I didn't want to tell him this story inside the cottage. I didn't want to bring my past into the place that had become my sanctuary.

When I returned with two beers in hand, Evan was already seated on the porch steps. I handed him one of the bottles and sat next to him. "Did Harper tell you anything about why I left my old company?"

"No, I never asked." He laughed dryly. "Probably not the best move from a hiring perspective."

"I started working there while I was still in law school. I had a degree in finance and they needed help getting their pricing strategy sorted as well as managing their long-term partnerships. The CEO was a guy I went to college with. Drew Nelson. We had been friends for years and I liked working with him. When he asked me to stay on after I had my law degree, it was an easy decision." I wondered if that decision would have been so easy if I hadn't been half in love with Drew at the time.

"It was a hectic life. We were always traveling to visit our clients or prospects. The team was small, so everyone pitched in to make a sale. We were growing the company at a ridiculous pace and we were succeeding. I loved it. But it was also my whole life. I worked from the moment I got up until I went to bed and my social circle was pretty much limited to the people I was surrounded by at work." It had been fun in the beginning. It was like going to work every day surrounded by friends.

"There was a lot of stress and people had coping mechanisms for dealing with that stress. A lot of people turned to partying, but that was never my scene." I took a long swig of beer and briefly closed my eyes. "I turned to Drew. It was intense and toxic and I was addicted." That was the only way I could think to describe our relationship. It certainly hadn't been love. "It was on and off for about three years. Neither of us had time for an actual relationship, so it was convenient to be able to turn to each other."

Evan wasn't reacting to anything I said and that was the only reason I was able to pour out the whole story. "Drew had a lot of demons. He drank, did hard drugs, and was occasionally out of control. He would throw things in meetings like a child. Scream at employees, including me. But then he would turn around and make some grand apology and make you feel special. I was so deep into it at the time that I didn't even realize how fucked up it was.

And then we reached the point where we were ready for the IPO."

This was the part that I hated to relive the most. It was the part that had so thoroughly destroyed me. "The board had caught wind of Drew's shitty behavior. There were a bunch of meetings about how to mitigate risk and somehow, it was determined that the biggest risk was me."

"What?" Evan barked out. "How the fuck?"

I laughed because that had been my exact response at the time. "They thought that I had too much dirt on Drew. They were worried I would use our sexual relationship as ammunition to bleed money from the company. As if I wasn't already going to get a huge payout once I cashed out equity as part of the IPO. And I honestly could've handled that insult if Drew had come to my defense. If he had said just one thing to support me." I swallowed hard as I remembered staring at him across the conference table, silently begging him to say something.

"We were friends for years. Colleagues for longer. Lovers or whatever... I just thought he would have my back. But he was the one to slide over the letter of termination."

"Shit." Evan scrubbed a hand over his chin. "I'm so sorry, Lil. You didn't deserve to be treated like you were expendable."

"But I was. The IPO went through and the company is more successful now than it ever was." That was probably the part that stung the most. No one had even missed me when I was gone. "I'm completely replaceable."

Evan grabbed my arm. "You don't really think that, do

you?" His look was pleading. "Look, I know that we haven't known each other long at all and we're only starting to get to really know each other, but I've never met anyone like you. You're not replaceable, you're one of a kind. If that Drew asshole couldn't see that, then he didn't deserve a single moment that you gave to him."

"You're one of the good ones, Evan Sullivan." I put my hand on top of his. "I feel like I'm always unleashing my baggage on you."

"I like my women a little damaged," he joked. "Besides, we all have some sort of baggage. Mine just happens to be two kids."

"You should probably get back to them. Celebrate the big win." I hated to send him away, but I knew he loved spending time with them.

"You can celebrate with us. Do you want to join us for dinner?"

"You're sweet, but I think it's probably better if I don't." I was still feeling a strong pull toward Evan, but it felt like things were moving way too fast.

"Better for who?" he asked.

"Everyone." I leaned over and kissed his cheek, catching a whiff of pine and sandalwood. Evan smelled exactly how I thought a cowboy should smell. "I'm in my head right now and I need some time to process."

He nodded and pushed to his feet, holding out a hand to help me up. "Take whatever time you need. I'm not going anywhere."

13

EVAN

When Lily said that she needed some time, I thought she meant a couple of days. I didn't expect for us to go a whole month where we barely talked or saw each other except for a few minutes each morning when I stopped by with coffee or during our awkward interactions at Sunday dinners. I couldn't tell if she was purposefully avoiding me or if she was just busy.

Dad told me that Lily had come up with some complicated plans to expand the Lucky Charm Ranch business that was requiring her to spend a lot of time over there with Chase. I knew it was insane to be jealous of my own brother, but I missed being the one she followed around. I missed watching her strut around in her tight jeans. I spent most of my nights picturing her tight ass while I jerked off. I was so far gone for that woman and we hadn't even kissed.

"You're being extra mopey tonight, Sullivan." Ronan

tossed his wadded-up napkin at my head. "Did you break up with your girl?"

"We were never together." I wasn't in the mood for this. When Ronan had suggested dinner and drinks at the Nest, I assumed we would talk about work or Noah's chances at making it to the World Series. I wasn't expecting to be grilled about Lily.

"Good to know. I assume you won't give a shit if I shoot my shot with her then." His eyes narrowed at something over my shoulder. "Because city girl is looking damn fine tonight."

I would like to think that I would play it cool, but suave had gone out the window a long time ago when it came to Lily. I had no chill about whirling to find her in the crowded bar. She and Harper were laughing about something as they weaved between the tables to reach the bar. Neither of them noticed the heads that swiveled to follow their progress.

"Did you know they were going to be here?" I asked through gritted teeth.

"Harp may have mentioned it." Ronan kicked my foot under the table. "Are you going to stare at her all night or find the balls to go talk to her?"

They greeted another woman at the bar who I recognized as one of Harper's old friends. All three of them were dressed for a night out and quickly swallowed the shots the bartender placed in front of them.

"They are clearly doing a girls' night thing. They don't want us bothering them." I turned back around and finished my beer.

"Bullshit. They are dressed to draw male attention. That male might as well be you." Ronan pushed back his chair. "I need to take a piss. Make yourself useful and grab the next round."

I grunted my annoyance and considered just leaving while he was in the bathroom. It seemed preferable to putting up with his bullshit. But I had come out with him because I didn't want to sit at home alone while the kids were with their mom. In this case, bad company was preferable to no company. Even if it meant that I was now skulking toward the far end of the bar and trying to remain as inconspicuous as possible.

While I waited for the bartender to notice me, I dared a glance down the blemished wooden bar and felt my breath catch in my lungs at the sight of Lily with her head thrown back, laughing with abandon. Her hair was pulled back, revealing every curve of her perfect face.

"I'd ask what I can get you, but it's pretty clear what you want," the bartender said.

I snapped my eyes away from Lily. "Two drafts." Then, before I could stop myself, I added, "And another round of shots for the ladies at the end of the bar."

"Sure thing." The bartender barely even looked my way as he slammed down two pints of beer and turned to pour the shots. I kept my eyes on him until he had slid them in front of the girls. He nodded his head toward me and three sets of eyes flashed my way.

I lifted a beer at them in a silent toast, doing my best to keep from staring at Lily. It was really hard to keep my eyes off her when she looked so damn good. Especially when she put her lips on that shot glass and caught my eye before tipping her head back. My eyes were on her throat as she swallowed and blood rushed to my cock. The image of Lily with her head tilted back, swallowing hard, had been one of my favorite fantasies for a month now.

"If you don't fuck that woman, I will." Ronan snatched up the second pint and shoved my shoulder. "Go."

Harper lifted a hand to wave us over. If I ignored them now, I would look like a total dick. I told myself that it wasn't a big deal to stroll over and say hi. If they didn't want company, they wouldn't have come to the busiest bar in town. I felt slightly more encouraged when they all smiled as I approached.

"You ladies should be careful. There are some creepy guys here tonight." I hooked a thumb at where Ronan was hovering behind me.

"Thanks for the shots, bro!" Harper was speaking in her pitchy drunk voice.

"Oh no. How many shots have you had?" I asked warily. My sister was a notorious lightweight,

She held up a finger and then slowly added another. "Just two. But we had some drinks at dinner too."

"We'll keep an eye on her," Amelia promised.

Harper's face screwed up in annoyance. "I'm not a child. I can booze my hold. Shit. Hold my booze."

Ronan chuckled and held out a hand to her. "Come on, Harp. Let's dance."

"Yes!" Harper snatched his hand and stumbled into him when she took a step forward. Ronan caught her easily and held her slightly away from his body. I wouldn't trust many men with my drunk sister, but I knew Ronan would watch out for her. He always had. Amelia snatched her drink from the bar and turned to Lily. "I'm going with them. You in?"

"Oh, um..." Lily glanced at me. "Maybe in a bit. I think I need a little more liquid courage first."

"Atta girl. If you don't join us soon, I'm coming back for you." Amelia wagged a finger at me. "I'm counting on you, Sullivan. Get our girl nice and drunk."

"Yeah, I don't think so." Not only did I refuse to make someone else drink too much, but I also had no desire to put Lily in a vulnerable position while we were surrounded by a bunch of drunk men.

Lily finally looked at me after avoiding me during the entire conversation. "I didn't know you were going to be here," she said.

"It was Ronan's idea." I hoped she didn't think that I had known they were coming and made my plans accordingly. "I haven't seen you around the ranch much lately. Keeping busy?"

"Yeah, I have a bunch of ideas for next year. Tom is eager to flesh out the financials, so I've been focused on that." She held up her hand and wiggled her fingers. "And I started physical therapy this week because I finally got my cast off."

"That's great news, Lil." I had completely forgotten about her broken hand. "Now you can get back to answering those emails and give your life purpose again."

"Ha ha." She slapped my arm and we both froze. It was our first physical contact in weeks. "Sorry."

"No, don't be." I did what I always did when I was nervous. I rubbed the back of my neck. "Hey, in the interest of sounding like an insecure weirdo, have I done something wrong? It feels like you've been avoiding me."

"You haven't done anything wrong, Evan." She was looking at anything but me.

I was trying to be mature, but I had spent the last month lusting after a woman who couldn't even look at me. "Did you return his call? Is that what this is about? Are you going back to that asshole? Please tell me you're not that stupid."

"I'm sorry? What gave you the impression that you can talk to me like that?" The fire I hadn't seen since her first day in town had returned to her eyes.

"You're right. I'm sorry. That didn't come out the way I intended." I didn't feel bad about calling her ex an asshole, but I did feel bad for accusing her of being stupid. Lily Jameson was the exact opposite of stupid. "I've just missed you."

"I didn't call Drew back. I have nothing to say to him." Lily leaned across the bar and called for the bartender to bring more shots. "I didn't get dressed up to come out tonight and mope about my past." She snatched the shot glasses and shoved one at me. "I came to drink, dance, and maybe kiss a hot guy. You in?"

"I'm not really into hot guys," I joked, taking the shot from her.

"Then we'll stick with the drinking and dancing." She tapped her glass to mine and we both downed the shots quickly. Lily gestured to the doorway leading to the dance floor. "Are you any good at that?"

"If we do another round of shots, maybe it won't matter."

I didn't miss the fact that Lily hadn't told me why she had pulled away after our talk on her porch. But I did notice her contagious laugh after we did another shot and the way she leaned into me as I led us to the dance floor.

The band was playing a popular song that I knew I had heard on the radio but otherwise meant nothing to me except that it gave Lily a reason to smile at me.

"I'm going to be terrible," she said as I led her toward the edge of the dancers. They were all moving in time to the music.

"You ever two-stepped?" I took her hand and pulled her closer.

She shook her head and her teeth sank into her lower lip. "I can't even one-step."

"That's not a thing," I said with a laugh. I put my other hand on her waist and moved her into position. "Just follow my lead, sweetheart."

Lily was hesitant during the first song. She kept looking down at our feet. By the second song, she started to move more comfortably. "This is fun," she said. "I honestly didn't expect you to be a good dancer."

"Your faith in me is flattering." I pressed my fingers more firmly against her waist. "You never answered my question about why you've been avoiding me."

"I told you I've been busy." She kept her eyes focused over my shoulder. "Chase has me planning this corporate event coming up soon and I've had to spend a lot of time really understanding how the guest ranch works. Did you know there is only lodging for twenty people? With the amount of business we hope to do next year, we need to triple that number."

"You stopped answering the door when I brought your coffee." This had been the hardest thing to accept. I had enjoyed those morning chats with her. Up until the last few days when she'd stopped answering her door, it had seemed as though she liked those morning chats, too.

"I've been getting an early start to my days."

"Earlier than mine?" I asked doubtfully. My days already started before dawn.

The band switched to a slower tune and the people around us shifted easily into softer embraces. Lily remained tense in my arms.

"We don't have to stay," I said, even though I wasn't ready to let her go yet.

She surprised me by stepping forward and shifting her hand from my shoulder to my neck. "I like this song," she said softly.

I slid my hand to her lower back and pulled her close. "I like *you*, Lily."

"I haven't been avoiding you, I've been punishing myself," she said. "I like you, Evan. You're a great guy and you make me laugh. But you're still technically my boss and I remember very clearly how badly this could end for me."

"I would never pull the kind of shit with you that your ex did."

"I'm enjoying my time on the ranch," she continued as if I hadn't spoken. "I like my job, the workers, the animals, and the cottage. I didn't expect to like any of those things, but they've become some of my favorite things. If we got involved and things didn't end well, I'd have to leave. I'd lose my job, my new friends, my home, and I'd probably lose Harper, too. I just don't think I'm willing to put all that on the line."

"For me," I added. "You're not willing to put it on the line for me."

"For anyone," she corrected me. "I already did that once for Drew and it shattered my world. I don't think I could do it again."

"You wouldn't have to. Lil, if we got together there wouldn't be a shattered ending. I would never let that happen. And if you decided to dump my ass, I would never expect you to quit your job or move away. Harper would never cut you out of her life."

I hated that some other man had so thoroughly broken her heart that she couldn't even envision a happy ending for us.

"You don't know what would really happen," she said, shaking her head.

"Neither do you." I tightened my arm behind her back. "Lily, you're writing me off before you've even given me a chance to let you down. Which I'm not going to do. Do you keep missing the part where I tell you that I like you?"

She was still unconvinced, but I felt her shoulders relax. "I don't trust people easily, Evan. It's not really about you."

"Okay, then I'll earn your trust." I smiled. "I have the perfect plan."

"Oh no." She nibbled on her lower lip and looked up at me through her lashes. It was the first time I'd ever gotten a hard dick from a simple look. "Can you be trusted, cowboy?"

"Almost certainly not," I said, leaning down to put my lips next to her ear. "But I can guarantee we'll have fun."

14

LILY

The next morning I didn't hide when Evan knocked on my door. I greeted him with a cautious smile. "Are you sure about this?" I asked.

"Of course." He handed me a metal thermos this time. "We're taking our coffee with us. No time for flirty banter this morning, sweetheart."

"You have to at least talk to me and distract me from my nerves." I pulled the blue door shut behind me and turned around just in time to catch Evan openly gawking at me. "What's wrong? Am I dressed alright?"

"Those fucking jeans should be illegal on a body like yours," he said in a gruff voice.

"You like?" I jutted out a hip and turned in a circle. "I think I was born to be a cowgirl."

Evan grunted and rubbed the back of his neck. "I'll reserve judgment on that until I see you in a pair of chaps." He winked at me. "And nothing else."

"In your dreams, cowboy."

"Every night," he replied with no hint that he was teasing.

"What else am I doing in your dreams?" I asked, enjoying watching the flush creep up his neck.

"Let's just say that in my dreams, you don't need riding lessons." He gave me a sexy, crooked smile and then headed to the stables.

This was his grand plan for getting me to trust him. He was going to teach me how to ride a horse. According to Evan, there was a lot of trust involved in riding. Trust in the instructor, trust in the horse, and trust in yourself. All of those were going to be a challenge for me.

Evan insisted that I learn all the basics, including grooming the horses, mucking out their stalls, and putting on the tack. We worked all morning and I still hadn't even learned how to mount a horse, let alone ride one. But I enjoyed the work. The horse I would be riding was named Blaze because he had been rescued from a burning stable before coming to the ranch. His original owner thought he would be too skittish to ride again, but Evan said that Blaze was one of the best horses he'd ever ridden.

"What would've happened to him if you hadn't taken him in?" I asked as I stroked Blaze's nose. He really was a sweet horse.

"Nothing good," was all Evan said.

"Do you rescue a lot of horses?"

"No, not really. Working with rescues takes a lot of time and focus and it's not profitable. That makes it hard to justify taking time and resources away from the ranch."

Evan came over to check that I'd followed his instructions. After tugging on the saddle, he nodded. "That's good. Are you ready to try mounting?"

"We're talking about Blaze, right?"

"That's your choice." Evan winked. "Either way, I guarantee you an enjoyable ride."

I pretended to consider it. "I'll stick with Blaze. He has already proven himself to be an excellent kisser."

"He stuck his wet nose on your face. You really think I can't do better than that?" Evan asked indignantly.

I ignored him. "What do you say, Blaze? You want to take me for a ride?"

"Fuck my life," Evan muttered. "My horse has more game than me."

Evan helped me with the strap on my helmet and then walked me through the proper mounting technique. I pretended to find it confusing just to get him to demonstrate it for me. Watching that man mount a horse was quickly becoming foreplay for me.

When it was my turn, Evan stayed close. He used a guiding hand to make sure I didn't fall backward and then I was upright in the saddle.

"I did it!" I stared at him with wide eyes.

"You did." Evan was eyeing me with complete joy. For someone like him, a simple horse mount couldn't be very impressive but he looked proud. "Let's do a lap to get you used to the feeling."

He guided us around a slow lap of the circle and instructed me on how to correct my posture as I swayed in place. Blaze was a consummate professional and he didn't care at all that his rider clearly had no idea what she was doing. He also waited patiently while Evan walked me through the steps for a proper dismount. Once my feet were back on the ground, I wrapped my arm around the horse's neck and kissed his nose. "We did it, Blaze." He grunted and fluttered his long eyelashes at me.

"You're a natural, Lil."

I was in such a good mood that I decided Evan deserved a hug, too. He rocked back on his heels from the force of my body colliding into his, but he quickly recovered with a laugh and a strong arm wrapped around my back. "You did good, city girl."

"*We* did good," I said, wondering if he could feel my heart pounding. "Thank you for teaching me, Evan."

"You're welcome." He pressed a kiss to my temple and gave me a gentle squeeze. "Let's get Blaze put away. Dad is expecting us up at the house for lunch."

That was new. Sunday family dinners were a tradition, but I'd never had a Saturday lunch with Tom. "Is it a special occasion?" I asked nervously.

"You could say that." He pulled back. "My little brother is in town."

"Which one?"

"Noah. His team already clinched for the playoffs and he's got a few days off while they wait for the wild card to play out." Evan brushed my hair over my shoulder. "It will be fun introducing you to him."

"Why?"

Evan chuckled and started to walk toward the stable,

Blaze following close behind. "Because I get off on showing my brothers what they can't have, sweetheart."

And that was the first time I'd ever thought about jumping a man over a single sentence. I could push him up against the wall and let him have me, in any way that he wanted me. Our only witnesses would be the horses and I knew that Blaze would never rat me out. He was the loyal type.

"I think you got too much sun, Lil. Your face is mighty red." Evan raised a challenging eyebrow. "Or has something else got you hot?"

The cowboy was a damn mind reader. "I was just picturing Noah in his tight baseball pants," I lied.

Evan's gaze turned molten. "Is that really what you like, city girl? Were you faking it all the times I caught you staring at my ass?"

"I don't fake anything when it comes to you," I said. "And definitely not my attraction to you."

He chose to let that confession hang in the air and quickly removed Blaze's tack. He went through the motions so quickly since it was something he had done thousands of times and I found the certainty of his movements insanely hot.

When it was time to go, Evan was back to acting shy around me. He kept a foot of distance between us as we walked up to the main house. The ranch was always quieter on the weekends and the silence between us was extra pronounced.

"Did I say something wrong?" I finally stammered out when I couldn't take the quiet any longer.

"Don't be ridiculous." Evan's hands were in his pockets.

"Then why does your body language read like you want to hit something?"

He inhaled sharply and let out a hard breath. "Because I'm fighting the urge to throw you on the ground and fuck you until you can't see straight," he said harshly. "Normally, I wouldn't fight that urge, but I did promise my father that we wouldn't be late and sweetheart, when I do fuck you, I'm going to need a few hours. Possibly days."

"Oh." It was the only thing I could say as I stared at him. His look was the definition of smoldering and desire raced through my body, heating my core.

He lifted a hand to my face, tipping up my chin to close my dropped jaw. "If you keep that mouth open, I'll be forced to put something in it." Then he pressed a kiss just to the side of my mouth. "You'd look so fucking hot with those lips wrapped around my cock."

My brain started functioning again and I narrowed my eyes at him. "Be careful what you wish for, Sullivan. If that ever happens, you will never want anyone else's lips around your cock. You'll be mine."

When I walked away, I swore I heard him mutter quietly, "I'm already yours."

Noah Sullivan was nothing like his older brothers. He was quiet and polite but easy with a smile. He was every bit an athlete and looked nothing like a man who had spent eighteen years on a ranch.

Tom always looked happy when he was around his family, but he was downright bubbly to have his youngest sitting at the dining table. He peppered Noah with questions about the upcoming post-season.

"How's the arm? You looked a little tight in your last outing," Tom said.

"Tight?" Chase barked a laugh. "He pitched like shit."

"Thanks, bro." Noah didn't even look insulted. He was used to Chase's blunt comments. "My arm has been a little sore, but it's nothing serious. The trainers say I need to bulk up a little this winter. The added muscle should take away some of the strain."

"There are plenty of hay bales around here for you to throw around," Evan said. "If you decide to come back to the ranch, that is."

Despite Evan's big talk earlier, he had resorted to long glances across the table rather than any outward signs of affection. He was still keeping our blossoming relationship a secret and that was alright with me. We hadn't even kissed yet, so there was really no need to get his family involved in our relationship.

"So, Lily. What do you think of the ranch? Is it everything you hoped it would be when you agreed to take the job?" Noah asked in his calm, friendly voice. Whenever Tom and his brothers weren't asking him about baseball, he had been asking me about myself.

"The ranch is amazing. I really do love it here. Evan is

even teaching me how to ride." I smiled at him, doing my best to keep it friendly and not flirty.

Harper snorted out a laugh. "I'll bet he is," she muttered.

I aimed a kick at her leg under the table and flinched when Nate jerked back. "What the hell, Lil? What did I ever do to you to deserve a kick to the shin?"

"Sorry. Spasm." I grabbed my drink and took a big gulp of ice water, hoping it would cool the flush in my cheeks.

"What else has our brother been teaching you, city girl?" Chase asked, not bothering to hide his smirk.

"Did I say that I love it here?" I asked, turning to Noah. "I meant to say that I find the people who live here to be very annoying."

Noah laughed in his quiet way. "Me too, Lily. But I think I like you, so don't let these idiots scare you away." Then he looked right at Evan and said, "Don't fuck this up."

15

EVAN

Lily and I hadn't told my family that we were dating, or whatever we were doing, but somehow they all seemed to know. Even Noah, the guy who had spent one meal with us and already pegged me for being a goner for Lily.

When Dad had thrown together lunch plans, we all knew that it would turn into a much longer affair. We didn't get to see Noah very much outside of winter and we all wanted to spend as much time with him as we could. After lunch, we jumped on the ATVs and raced around the ranch. Noah had agreed to clauses in his contract that forbid him from doing certain things on the ranch, but we all looked the other way.

Chase and Nate rode together while Noah was with me. Harper had insisted that the girls stick together, so Lily was with her.

"Your girl is pretty cool," Noah said as we whipped past the stables. "She's pretty, too."

"She's not my girl," I said, slowing as we approached the main road. The guest ranch had better land for riding where we wouldn't have to worry about frightening the cattle with our shenanigans.

"Bullshit." He gripped the metal frame as we bounced over the uneven ground. "You didn't take your eyes off her once during lunch. How long have you been hooking up?"

"We haven't." It was the truth.

Noah let out a disbelieving laugh. "Man, you are a fucking monk these days. A smart, beautiful woman was dropped on your doorstep and you aren't going to do anything about it. Why do you keep refusing to let yourself be happy?"

"I am happy, Noah. I've got the kids and the ranch."

"Your kids are going to be grown up in no time and then what? You'll just spend all your time working until you can't, just like Dad? Don't you want more than that?" Noah swore when I took a turn too fast. "Look, I'm not trying to give you shit for how you live your life. I just want you to be happy, whatever that looks like for you."

"This speech is pretty ironic coming from you," I said, shooting him a glance. "You talk to Ava lately?"

"Fuck off." Noah scowled and looked away.

I felt bad for digging a knife into an open wound. "You should call her," I said. "We all like Ava."

"Yeah." His normally friendly face had gone dark. I should've known better than to bring up Ava.

"Lily has a list of things we can do this winter to get the guest ranch prepped for its expansion in the spring," I said, quickly changing the subject to something less upsetting. "If you're going to be here, can I put you down to help out?"

"Sure. Of course." Noah had never wanted to be a rancher in the regular sense. He didn't love dealing with the cattle, handling horses, or most of the other things we did every day. But he was always willing to help with projects. Building things, tearing down things, and creating something new. He had helped when I built my house and a had worked on the newer stable and barns we built a few years ago.

"I might be around more next year," Noah said. "I think I'm going to get traded in the off-season."

"No shit?" That was hard to believe. Noah had been having a record-breaking season and his team was favored in the playoffs. It seemed ridiculous that they would trade their star pitcher.

"Management knows about my arm. They know that I've been struggling and they want to get rid of me before I become a liability." Noah rotated his pitching arm. "Colorado is the team expressing the most interest."

"You might be coming home?" I felt bad that he was struggling, but I loved the idea of having him closer. "It would be nice to be able to come to your games. I know the twins would love that."

Noah nodded. "It could be good. I wouldn't mind being able to see the family more often."

"And we could put you to work more often," I joked.

"I expect nothing less from you, Ev." He was back to

his usual, smiling self. "Do me a favor and don't mention this to the others. Nothing is definite yet and I don't want to get their hopes up."

"I won't say a word." I was more than happy to keep his secret. That was kind of a tradition with us. With the ten years between us, I had always felt protective of Noah. He had still been young when we lost our mom and he had lost a lot of his childhood growing up with a dad who was overcome with grief. But he had gone on to be insanely successful and was a great guy. I was proud of him.

"I won't say a word about you banging Lily either," Noah said with a grin.

I regretted every nice thing I'd ever thought about him.

WE SPENT the afternoon wasting time on the guest ranch. No one was in a rush to get back to their normal Saturday plans and we carried the fun right back to the main house where Dad had fired up the outdoor pizza oven. In the last few months, he had become obsessed with making the perfect pizza and he had plenty of people willing to indulge in his obsession.

"I think this is your best one yet," Harper said, teeth sinking into his most recent creation.

Everyone was scattered around the backyard. Dad was near the house where the pizza oven was located while Chase had talked Noah into playing catch out in the yard.

Nate and Harper had taken over slicing the pizzas as they came out of the oven.

"The kids are going to be bummed they missed this," I said, grabbing a plate and adding what had to be my fifth piece of pizza.

"We can do this again next weekend," Dad promised.

"Is that for me?" Lily asked, snatching the plate from my hand. "Thanks, Boss."

"That'll come out of your paycheck." I faked a glare that no one believed.

Lily grabbed the slice and took a big bite. There was nothing sexy about watching her chow down on pizza, but there was no way for me to look at that mouth and not be turned on. She finished chewing and smiled. "Delicious," she said, flicking her tongue out to lick her lips.

I was about to pop a boner right in front of my whole family. She knew exactly what she was doing to me because she winked before handing me the plate and walking away. I dropped the plate on the table and headed after her.

"You can't just walk away from me like that, sweetheart." I caught up to her and brushed my hand against hers.

"I need a beer. You want one?" She hooked her pinky finger around mine while looking into my eyes. "You can come inside with me."

Oh fuck. That innuendo had definitely been intentional. I didn't bother to check if my family was watching us go into the house together because I no longer cared if the whole damn world knew about us. I wanted Lily. All of her.

She was already in the kitchen and she turned just as I came up behind her. Her mouth parted as if she knew what I was about to do.

"Evan..." She leaned in as I reached for her, sliding an arm around her waist. "Your family is right outside."

"I don't care." My nose brushed against hers. "Unless you stop me, I'm going to kiss the fuck out of you, city girl."

"I'm not going to stop you." Her lips started to tip up, but I devoured her smile. I'd been wanting to feel her lips on mine for so long that I gave myself over to her magnetic pull. She offered no resistance when I prodded her lips with my tongue and then I was inside, sweeping against her equally hungry tongue. A low moan caught in her throat and I nearly lost what little control I had maintained.

"Fuck," I said, moving her back against the counter. I lifted her onto the countertop and she parted her legs to let me step between them and then I was kissing her again as she wrapped her legs around me, pulling my hard length against her core with just layers of denim between us.

Her fingers tangled in my hair and she tugged gently as I kissed down the column of her throat. Her skin tasted like vanilla and she quickly became my favorite treat. She tugged on my hair again, dragging my face back to hers. Her lips were swollen and her skin was red from the drag of my stubble over it. She looked so damn fuckable.

I didn't resist when she kissed me again, this time slow and searching. My hands skimmed up her sides and I stroked the sides of her breasts with my thumbs. She wasn't wearing a bra underneath her shirt and my cock strained against my jeans.

"Ahem."

We froze, lips still touching. Lily's eyes stayed closed as she released my hair while I let my hands fall away from her body.

"You already had a meal, son," Dad said. "No need to devour Lily in my kitchen."

"Your timing is impeccable, Dad." I tried to pull away from Lily, but she had buried her face in my chest and her legs were still tight around me. It was for the best since I had no desire to turn around and have my dad see my painfully obvious erection. "Any chance you'll go away?"

"None." Dad went over to the fridge. "Lily, can I get you a beer?"

She lifted her head and smiled sheepishly. "Sure, Tom. Thanks."

"I'll take one, too," I said.

"Actually, you and I need to talk." Dad shut the fridge door and opened the beer bottle before handing it to Lily. "If you can still use your mouth after Lily is done with it." He had the nerve to wink at us before walking away. "I'll be in my office, Evan."

Lily reached up a hand and smoothed down the mess she had made with my hair. She didn't say anything, but I knew we wouldn't be doing more kissing in that kitchen.

"That man certainly knows how to ruin a moment," I said, kissing Lily's forehead before stepping back.

"It was probably for the best." Lily put the beer bottle to her lips and took a sip. I was irrationally jealous of that bottle. "The things I want to do to you are way too unhygienic for a kitchen."

"Fuck, Lil. The things that come out of your mouth…" I sucked in a deep breath through my nose.

"And yet not nearly as naughty as the things I put in my mouth." She wagged her eyebrows suggestively. "You should go. Don't keep Tom waiting."

I nodded absently, still visualizing siding my cock into her mouth. "Can we pick this up later?" I asked hopefully.

She hopped off the counter and put a hand on my chest, pushing up to kiss my cheek. "Come to the cottage. You can keep your promise about fucking me for hours. Or days."

"Definitely days," I said, sinking my fingers into her ass as I gave one cheek a firm squeeze. "I'll be there as soon as I can get away."

Lily smirked as I stepped back. "Look at me, riding a horse and a cowboy on the same day. I guess I'm no longer a city girl."

"No," I agreed. "You're *my* girl now, sweetheart."

16

LILY

I had to mingle outside for a little while before I was able to leave without drawing any suspicion. Harper looked a little skeptical when I said that I had work to do, but the guys just waved me away.

I was on my way to the cottage when my phone rang. I was going to ignore it since the people I cared about were here on the ranch, but something made me pull it from my pocket to see who was calling.

"Aunt Vi?" I braced myself for bad news.

It was rare for my aunt to call out of the blue. We had a standing phone call every Sunday night. For her to be calling on a Saturday meant that something had happened.

"Hey, kiddo." Violet sounded exhausted. "Did I catch you at a bad time?"

Almost, I thought. "No. What's up?"

"I... well, there's no good way to say this. Your mom is

Ready to Ride

dead. She overdosed last night. I was notified a couple of hours ago." Violet sounded annoyed that she'd been pulled into anything involving my mom. "You'll need to come home and handle her affairs."

"Me? Why the fuck would I do that?" I hadn't spoken to my mother since I was twelve.

"Because you're her next of kin. I'll help you get everything squared away, but you need to be here to sign off on the cremation and closing her bank accounts." Violet let out a low breath. "I'm so sorry, flower. I know that woman doesn't deserve a second of your time, but I can't do this without you."

If my mother had called and asked for help, I would never have gone. But this was Violet. The one person who loved me. The person who took me in when I had nowhere else to go. I couldn't tell her no.

"It's going to take me a while to get there. I could leave in about an hour."

"You can wait until morning," Violet said.

"No, I'd rather leave now." I wanted to get this done as quickly as possible. "I think it will be about a four-hour drive. I'll get there before midnight."

"I'll leave the porch light on," Violet said. "You drive safe, kiddo."

I promised that I would and hung up. When I reached the cottage, I pulled my suitcase over to the wardrobe and started throwing things inside. Since I hadn't brought much with me to begin with, it ended up only taking me about fifteen minutes to pack. Evan still hadn't arrived by then and I didn't want to sit around waiting not knowing if it was going to be just a few more minutes or possibly hours.

I wrote him a note explaining that I had a family emergency and had to leave town for a few days. I taped it to the front of the blue door and then loaded my car. If I hadn't been numb from shock, I probably would've felt more guilty about sneaking away without talking to Evan in person. But I couldn't face him right now. I didn't want to talk through feelings that I didn't have.

When your mother died, you were supposed to be sad. You were supposed to grieve. Instead, I just felt burdened by her death. Like she had found a way to pull me back into her shit from beyond the grave.

I pulled my car around and headed up the dirt road to reach the main road. The main house was a shining beacon ahead of me, a sign that happy families did exist and that I now had a home that wasn't full of trauma and sadness. I hadn't even left the ranch yet and I couldn't wait to get back.

It took two days to get the arrangements finalized for Mom's cremation. After signing the paperwork, I was informed that I could pick up her ashes the following day. Violet was by my side through everything, always good for a snarky comment that would make me laugh.

It had been a long time since I'd spent a few days with Violet. When I had been busy with my old job, I'd barely had time to visit, and even when I had, I'd never stayed for more than a day. When I saw how happy my aunt was to have me there, I felt guilty for staying away for so long.

"I'm going to hire someone to empty out the trailer," I told Violet over lunch. "I have no desire to go back to that place."

"Are you sure? There might be something sentimental that you want."

"Like what? One of mom's pill bottles?" I couldn't think of a single thing I would want from that trailer.

Violet shrugged. "You never know. I think we should do one quick visit. Just to make sure. Maybe she'll surprise us."

"Fine. If you want to go, we can go." I didn't have the energy to fight her.

"I don't want you to do this for me. Do it for yourself. For closure." Violet had an annoying way of convincing me to do the right thing, even when I was determined to do the opposite. "Is your employer okay with you taking this time off?"

"Yeah. It's not a problem." I hadn't actually spoken with Evan yet, but he had texted me a few times asking what he could do to support me. I told him that I just needed a few days to take care of some stuff and that I would be back as soon as possible.

"I have to admit that I was surprised when you agreed to take that job. I thought you were happy in Denver." Violet wasn't good at hiding her feelings. Right now, she looked confused. "Did something happen to drive you away?"

I hadn't told her about Drew or how I'd been forced

out of my job. I had been too embarrassed to admit it to anyone but Harper at the time. "It wasn't the right fit for me anymore," I said, truly meaning those words. The ranch was the right fit for me. So was Evan.

"You could've come home," Violet said.

"I know, Aunt Vi." I reached across the table and squeezed her hand. "I appreciate how you've always been there for me."

"Of course, I'm here for you. I love you." Violet had never shied away from telling me that she loved me. She was the only person who had ever told me that when I was a kid.

"You should make a trip out to the ranch. It's really beautiful there. I think you would love it."

"Any older attractive cowboys on that ranch?" she asked with a playful smile.

I thought of Tom and Marv and laughed. "Actually, yes. You would have your pick."

"Then I may have to take you up on that offer." She glanced at my phone. "Are you going to tell me who Evan is and why you're ignoring his texts?"

"Nope." I waved to the waitress to bring our check.

"Oh, come on. You never tell me about the guys in your life. I worry about you." Violet was good at laying on a guilt trip.

"Fine. Evan is my boss." I was hoping that would satisfy her curiosity.

"Is he texting you about work? Don't you need to reply to him?"

Of course, she wasn't going to let me off easy. "He's not

messaging me about work. He's just checking in to make sure I'm okay."

"Sounds like a nice boss." She clearly didn't believe my bullshit excuse. "Is he single?"

I nodded and threw some cash onto the table. "He has two kids. Twelve-year-old twins. But he's not with their mother."

"Is he a deadbeat dad?" Violet knew about my own absentee father better than anyone.

"No, the exact opposite, actually. He has joint custody and he's an amazing father. He is friends with the kids' mother and they co-parent really well."

"If you aren't dating that man, I'm going to give up on you completely."

"We're...something. I don't know what. More than friends." I had no idea how to label our relationship. We'd had one date, one kiss, and a month of sexual tension. "We're figuring it out. Or, at least we were before I had to abruptly leave town."

"Do you want to work something out with him?"

I didn't have to think. "Yes, I do. Evan is a great guy."

"Then figure it out. Stop pulling your usual bullshit and give yourself a chance to be happy, flower." Violet made it sound so simple. She hadn't even acknowledged the fact that Evan was my boss.

We left the diner and headed across town to where I'd lived with my mother. Her trailer was still on the same lot and looked exactly the same as it had when I lived there. Neither of us had a key and I was worried we would have to break a window to get in, but when Violet tried the door, it was unlocked.

"Wait. Did they find her in here?" I was worried about what we might find. If her body had been sitting in there for a while, it was likely also going to smell horrible.

"No, she was found out here." Violet gestured to the lawn chairs scattered in front of the trailer. "She never made it inside after she overdosed."

I didn't know what to do with that information, so I chose to file it away in the back of my brain and forced myself across the doorway. I had expected to be hit by a wave of emotion at finally returning to the place that had haunted my nightmares, but I felt nothing. The trailer hadn't changed, but I had. I wasn't that scared little girl anymore, shaking my mom after she passed out on the floor, worrying that she was dead and I would be alone.

"Let's make this quick," Violet said, kicking aside an empty beer can.

The trailer was small and aside from the piles of trash, Mom didn't have a lot of stuff. She always spent her money on alcohol and drugs. Violet found a pair of earrings that she said belonged to their mother and I found one of my old report cards shoved in the back of a dresser drawer.

"This is just depressing," Violet said after she uncovered an entire cabinet filled with empty alcohol bottles. "Was it this bad when you lived here?"

"Most of the time, yes. I tried to clean up after Mom but it would never last long. She would invite her drug buddies over and they would trash the place." I felt tears prickling my eyes for that young girl who had so desperately wanted a normal mom in a normal house. She had deserved so much better. A few blinks cleared the tears that I refused to let fall. "I've seen what I need to see. I'll wait for you outside."

Violet put down the stack of mail she'd been inspecting. "I'm coming with you. I'm done here."

It was an anti-climactic ending to our adventure. Neither of us had gotten closure and it only further solidified my anger toward my mother. Violet must've felt the same way because she stopped me at the car.

"I'm so damn sorry, Lily. I had no idea it was this bad. The fact that my sister would raise a child in that trailer..." Violet didn't bother fighting the tears that streamed down her cheeks. She threw her arms around me in a fierce embrace. "I should've saved you from this place. You shouldn't have had to save yourself."

I wanted to tell her that it wasn't her fault. That I didn't blame her for my childhood. I wanted to tell her that she was the only adult who had ever cared about me. That she had taught me I was capable of loving and worthy of being loved. But those words lodged in a knot in my throat and all I could do was hug her back.

17

LILY

I headed back to Crestwood the next day, right after picking up my mom's ashes. They were strapped into my backseat and I eyed them repeatedly during the drive as I tried to decide what to do with them. I had no intention of keeping them.

Violet had suggested flushing them down the toilet, but that would only make me feel like a terrible daughter. I was hoping I could find someplace on the ranch where I could dump them. Maybe near one of the ponds.

I still hadn't talked to Evan since I left, but I had texted him to let him know that I was headed back. He responded to let me know that he was headed out of town to deliver a couple of horses to a ranch in Wyoming. We were two ships passing in the night.

He was only supposed to be gone one night, but he had the kids this week. We wouldn't have any chance to be alone until after dinner on Sunday. I was anxious to see him again. We had a lot of unfinished business, plus a few unfinished orgasms.

Pulling under the horseshoe arch felt like coming home. I smiled as I passed the main house and drove down to my cottage. As I walked toward the familiar blue door, my breath caught in my throat. A vase full of beautiful lilies was waiting on my welcome mat. I momentarily forgot about my luggage and picked up the flowers and the folded piece of paper that was beneath them.

Welcome home, city girl. I missed you.

Simple. To the point. So very Evan. It made me miss him even more. This wasn't something I was used to feeling. I wasn't someone who got easily attached to guys. Even with Drew, I had never found myself pining for him. Evan was bringing out a side of me that I hadn't thought existed.

I took the flowers and my suitcase inside. It was almost lunch time and I was in desperate need of sustenance after skipping breakfast. My grocery supply was running low, so I headed over to the guest ranch to grab something to eat there. They had an amazing chef who made three meals a day for our paying customers. Chase usually ate lunch there, too, to spend time chatting with everyone. He was the social butterfly of the Sullivan clan.

"The prodigal city girl returns!" he called out when I entered the dining room.

"It's good to be back." I skirted around the tables until I reached the one where he was seated with a notebook in front of him. It was the notebook where he was always jotting down information or ideas relevant to the guest ranch business. "What's on the menu today?"

"Fajitas. You want? I'll put in your order." I nodded and he bounced up from his seat to head over to the counter. He circled something on the notepad and then ripped off the top page and slid it through the kitchen window. "Marla makes a mean steak fajita."

"I have no doubt." I'd eaten more than a few of Marla's meals and they had all been fantastic. "How has your week been? Anything exciting that I missed?"

"Besides my brother moping around all pathetic?" Chase leaned forward, resting his elbows on the table. "You know, there's a kitchen right over there if you are craving some kisses from a Sullivan male."

"Fuck my life. Did Tom tell you?" I hadn't expected him to tell the others what he had interrupted in his kitchen.

Chase chuckled. "No. You just missed the giant window behind you that Noah and I could clearly see from the backyard."

I groaned. "Does everyone know?"

"Afraid so. Noah and I saw for ourselves, but Dad spilled the details to Harper and Nate after you left. He gossips more than the church ladies in town." Chase fidgeted with the edge of the notebook. "We all suspected it anyway. Neither of you are good at keeping secrets. Nate has the bruised shin to prove it."

"Do other ranch employees know?"

"Why do you care?" Chase looked at me like I was insane. "You're a grown adult, Lil. You were hired because of your impressive resume. No one is going to think you're sleeping with the boss to get ahead. That's not how shit works on a ranch anyway."

I couldn't tell him why it bothered me without telling him about Drew and my past experience of getting caught in bed with a boss. "I just don't like the thought of everyone knowing my personal business. The guys might act weird around me."

"They already do. Most of them spend all their time acting like damn fools when you are around. Gippy nearly broke his thumb the other day when he smashed it with a hammer when you walked by while he was patching the barn roof."

Two plates slid through the window and Chase jumped up to grab them. He placed them on our table with a flourish.

"Stop worrying about what other people think of you and dig in," he said.

I couldn't argue with that. The food smelled delicious and I was sure it would taste even better. I was so hungry that I didn't let it properly cool before shoveling it into my mouth and promptly burning my tongue. It was worth it, though.

Chase decided to stop giving me a hard time about Evan and we spent the next hour going over the corporate event we were hosting next week. A group of executives were coming to Lucky Charm for what Chase called a cowboy cosplay outing. They would ride horses and go into the woods to hunt. Rich men were willing to spend big money to shoot helpless animals.

"I'll ask Evan and Nate to help out. With the kind of money they are paying, we'll want to make sure they have the best possible experience." My brain was running through all the logistics we needed to prepare. "I'll work with the cleaning staff to get the Airstreams ready. We should stock them with booze and cigars. We'll need to test the internet speeds, too. Executives never really disconnect from work."

"I guess you would know." Chase made another note in his notebook. "It's supposed to be pretty cold next week. You should have them switch the sheets to our flannels and make sure firewood is stocked by the communal fire pits. We can pull the boot dryers out of storage too. Wouldn't want the fancy boys to have wet feet and I highly doubt they'll have the right footwear."

"We should consider offering that as part of the package in the future. We could add on boots, clothing, and cold-weather accessories. We could even put our branding on it."

Chase nodded and made another note. "That's good. We should start stocking more of that in the gift shop, too. We only have a few basic T-shirts and sweatshirts now. Harper has been pushing me to add more stuff, but I haven't had the time to deal with it. Maybe you could work with her on some ideas?"

"Sure. I've got some good connections on the manufacturing side, too, and I can get us a good deal."

"I get why Dad hired you," Chase said. "We were doing fine before, but we weren't pushing ourselves. We were complacent. You've sparked something in all of us. We can

Ready to Ride

see the potential now for what we could do to set this place up for future generations."

"Most of these ideas are yours, Chase. You could've done all of this without me." Tom and his sons had done a great job running the ranch. They were profitable every year and still had a ton of room for growth. They had made my job easy.

"We could've done it, but we wouldn't have," he said with certainty. "We needed you to light a fire under us, city girl."

"Let's just hope I don't burn everything down," I joked.

"Eh. If one of us boys hasn't done that yet, I think you'll be fine." He pushed back his chair. "Come on. Let's visit the village."

Past the welcome lodge, the rustic cabins, and the stables, a large area held ten vintage Airstreams. They had all been converted into permanent lodging. Each one held a queen-size bed and a tiny kitchenette area with a mini-fridge and microwave. It was the epitome of glamping and perfect for a group of executives looking for a cowboy experience without the hardships of actually working the land. There was a shared bathing quarters with toilets and showers. In the center of the Airstream circle, two large fire pits were surrounded by rustic chairs.

"We should put more solar-powered lighting along the path," I said. "Just to make sure no one gets wasted and accidentally wanders into the woods."

"Good call. You updated our legal waivers, right?" Chase asked.

"Yep." The last thing we needed was some CEO shooting his buddy and then suing the ranch.

We made detailed notes of everything that needed to be done within the next few days and then I headed back across the road. It had been a long day and I felt a familiar, dull ache between my eyes. I was hoping that I was just tired and dehydrated.

I decided to take it easy and eat a quick dinner and do some work before going to bed early. I had barely slept at my aunt's house and wasn't sure if that would continue, but something about the cottage relaxed me to my core. The only explanation for that feeling was that the cottage was my home.

I woke in a daze many hours later after possibly the deepest sleep of my life. It took me a moment to realize that someone was knocking softly on my door. I pushed back my hair and stumbled to my feet. I already knew who would be on the other side of the door before I opened it, but I still felt a rush of excitement when I saw Evan standing there.

"You're back," I said, my voice heavy with sleep.

"Got back late last night. I'm sorry I woke you up, but I couldn't wait to see you." He grinned as his eyes scanned me. "I didn't expect to be seeing quite so much of you."

"Shit." I forgot that I was wearing my pajamas, which in this case was just an oversize t-shirt that barely covered my ass. "Let me throw something on."

"Don't do that on my account," Evan said with a chuckle.

I laughed. "Just wait here."

It only took a few seconds to pull on sweatpants and join Evan on the porch. He handed me my usual mug full of coffee and leaned against the porch railing. "You still look ridiculously hot, Lily." He hooked a thumb into the waistband of my sweats and tugged me toward him. It was a chilly morning and I was happy to lean into his warmth. "I missed you, sweetheart."

"I missed you, too." I cupped the mug between my hands to absorb the heat. "Did you have a good trip?"

"It was fine." His hand covered my hip. "Are you ready to talk about yours?"

"I don't really want to start my morning talking about that." I was desperately trying to ignore the fact that my mother's ashes were sitting on my kitchen counter next to the vase of lilies. "Thank you for the flowers. That was a very sweet surprise when I got home."

"You're welcome." He smiled big enough that his dimple appeared. "I'll bring you flowers every damn day if you promise to open your door like you did this morning."

I looked down at my shirt and winced. "You probably won't think that once I tell you that I stole this shirt from my ex."

Evan groaned. "You didn't have to tell me that, Lil."

"Maybe I can replace it with one of yours in the morning." I put a hand lightly on his stomach. "Do you have the kids tonight?"

"No, I was supposed to get back late tonight so they are staying with their mom until tomorrow." Evan's hand slid under my shirt and softly stroked my side. "Come over for dinner again. This time we'll have dessert, too."

"Okay." I leaned in when he slid his hand to the back of my head and pressed his lips to my forehead. It was such a gentle, comforting gesture that I nearly gasped. No one had ever treated me so sweetly. Without knowing that I was going to say anything, words sprang out of my mouth. "My mother died. That's why I left."

"Fuck." Evan tilted my chin up to look me in the eye. "I'm so sorry, Lily."

"It's fine. Really. I haven't talked to her in over eighteen years. My aunt just needed some help handling logistics. I'm the next of kin, so I had to sign off on the cremation and some financial stuff."

Evan studied me for a long moment and then put both arms around me without saying a word. He just pulled me into his warm embrace and dropped his chin on top of my head. It was that gesture that finally pulled tears from my eyes. He somehow knew exactly what I needed.

"If you need some time, you don't have to come over tonight." He stroked a hand down the length of my hair. "Or you can come over and we can just talk. Or not talk. Whatever you need, Lily."

"You," I said. "I need you. I want to be with you tonight."

His chest rose sharply with his sudden breath. He let it out slowly and said, "I'm all yours, sweetheart."

18

EVAN

It was almost impossible for me to leave Lily at her cottage. It would've been hard under any circumstance, but knowing she was quietly processing her mother's death alone broke my heart. I knew she had a troubled relationship with her mother and that almost made it worse. She couldn't grieve in a normal way.

If I didn't have a million things to do around the ranch to make up for being gone yesterday, I would've stayed with her or made her take a walk around the ranch. Since I couldn't be there for her, I did what I hoped was the next best thing. I called Harper. She quickly agreed to check on Lily while I was busy working.

Nate was the one to break the news that we needed to haul some hay bales over to Rick's ranch. It was technically on the same land as Lucky Charm Ranch, but it was at the far edge of the property. Dad had given him that part of the land to grow his business, but we still handled most of the maintenance.

"You can't do this on your own?" I grumbled after we'd loaded the trailer.

"I could, but it will go a whole lot faster if you're there to help me unload." Nate tugged on the brim of his hat. "It's your call, Boss."

It was strange to hear someone other than Lily call me that. It didn't sound nearly as enticing in Nate's gruff timber. "Alright, let's get this over with."

It shouldn't take long to make the delivery and I knew Nate would appreciate the help. Just because he *could* do it by himself didn't mean I should let him. We headed down the road and got to work piling the hay bales at the back of the thoroughbreds' barn. Two of the trainers were in the outdoor arena with the horses and they never looked in our direction. Even though Rick's elite horse training facility was still part of our family business, it never felt that way.

For one thing, the style was incredibly different. He had built state-of-the-art facilities for both the trainers and the horses, including a climate-controlled barn with a white and black exterior, and large windows at the front and smaller windows for each stall. The horses here had nicer accommodations than some people.

We had just finished unloading when our uncle made an appearance. He had an office on site, but he didn't visit often. Usually only when a new horse or trainer was brought in, or if he was trying to woo an elite jockey to join his team.

"Must be my lucky day to have two nephews visiting my facility," Rick said, leaning against one of the wood beams. "I figured you would send your lackeys."

"We don't have those on the ranch. Everyone does their share," I said flatly.

"Everyone, huh? Including that bitch your dad hired?"

I took a step toward him, fists clenched. "You're going to want to shut the fuck up right now, Rick."

"Oh, I see. You really are fucking that girl." He laughed harshly and blood filled my ears in a loud whooshing noise. Before I even knew what was happening, I had him pinned to the side of the barn, my forearm pushed against his throat. His eyes bulged as I applied enough pressure to block his airway.

"Don't talk about Lily like that." My voice came out low and rumbling. I had never heard myself speak that way.

"Evan." Nate's hand tugged on my shoulder. "We need to get back to the ranch."

I hadn't realized just how much rage I was holding in when it came to my uncle. He had always been a surly prick. I could even remember him making rude comments about my mother when I was a kid. He had thought that she'd only married Dad because of his money. Dad had kicked Rick off the ranch on more than one occasion, but he always took him back.

When I asked my dad why Rick was so angry, he told me that it was because their father had been a weak man who made terrible decisions. I didn't understand what that meant at the time, but I had figured it out when I got older and Marv told me about my grandfather.

John Sullivan had been married to a woman named Celia. They had been high school sweethearts and were married a week after graduation. They had one child together, Rick. Celia had always wanted more children, but they had trouble conceiving again. A few years later, a beautiful woman moved to town and John left his wife and kid. That woman had been my grandmother, Louise.

Needless to say, Celia had not been pleased by the turn of events. She was even more frustrated when John and Louise had a baby boy– my dad. John had stayed with his second wife and son. He had doted on them while only seeing his older child every other weekend. This had pitted Rick and my dad against each other.

When John died, he left the ranch to Dad. Rick was left out of the will completely. Dad had felt bad about that, so he brought Rick in to run part of the business. Dad had always wanted to repair their relationship, but Rick couldn't let go of his hurt and his jealousy.

Nate tugged on my arm again and I finally removed my forearm and stepped back. "You are a sad, pathetic man. I generally don't give a fuck how you live your life, but you leave Lily's name out of your fucking mouth or I will make you regret it."

"She's only after your money," Rick continued as if testing to see whether I would follow through on my threat.

Nate just laughed. "You're a fucking idiot, old man. That woman has plenty of money and none of it is tied up in this place. The only freeloading money seeker on this ranch is you."

"Then why has she been spending so much time digging into our financials? She hasn't just been reviewing our balance sheets and cash flow records. She is digging into *everything*. Including shit she has no business seeing, like insurance policies." Rick glared at me beneath the brim of his hat. "Haven't you wondered why she is so interested in every aspect of our business? Do you even care, or have you been too busy staring at her ass and trying to get between her legs?"

"She is doing what Dad hired her to do," Nate said.

I was too angry to consider whether there was any validity to his concerns. Lily had done nothing to make me question her integrity.

"Dad may cut you slack because of some weird family loyalty, but that doesn't extend to me. If you fuck with Lily or even look at her wrong, I will destroy you." I stormed away before he could say something else that would piss me off.

We were back on the road before Nate said anything. "Did you?" he asked.

"Did I what?"

"Get between her legs?" Nate grinned and wagged his eyebrows.

My answer was a hard punch to his arm.

19

LILY

When Harper showed up at my door, I knew it was Evan's doing. He had looked so skeptical about leaving me for the day, even after I told him several times that I was fine.

Harper didn't believe me either and she spent most of the morning with me. When she finally had to leave to open the bookstore, I headed up to the main house to meet with Tom.

Maybe I'd been spending most of my time on the ranch with the Sullivan sons, but the Sullivan patriarch was still my favorite cowboy. Tom greeted me with a big hug and a cup of coffee before escorting me into his office.

"Evan told me that you had to leave for a couple of days for a family emergency. I hope everything is okay," Tom said, gesturing for me to take a seat on one of the leather chairs. He sank into the one next to it.

"My mother died," I said bluntly. There was no point

in keeping it to myself now that Evan and Harper knew. "We were estranged and had a terrible relationship even before that. I only went because my aunt needed some help squaring away some logistics."

"I see." Tom leaned forward with his elbows on his knees. "If you need more time off, you should take it."

"I actually prefer to keep busy." I appreciated his concern, but I didn't want to talk about this anymore.

"Okay then," Tom said, nodding. "I can keep you busy. But you have to promise you'll let me know if you need anything. Deal?"

I let out a relieved breath. "Deal."

"Have you had a chance to look through those additional files I gave you?" Tom leaned back, smoothly transitioning into business talk.

"I spent some time looking them over last night. There is definitely money missing."

I hadn't wanted that to be the case. When Tom first reached out about hiring me, this had actually been his primary reason. He suspected that someone in the business was syphoning off money. His records for the last couple of years just weren't balancing.

Tom suspected it started when he had stepped back after his stroke. He hadn't been able to be as involved and the transition to having Evan take over a lot of the work hadn't been smooth. It wouldn't be surprising if someone had been able to take advantage of that situation. Because Tom wasn't sure who was taking the money, he hadn't told anyone about his suspicions. Except for me.

"I have a speculation where some of the money might

be," I said, tapping my nails against the coffee mug. "I want to check on some stuff at Rick's place. Do you think that will be a problem? It might draw suspicion."

"I'm going with Rick next week to check out a racehorse at another ranch. You'll have the whole morning to do whatever you need to do." Tom hesitated. "Have you mentioned any of this to the boys? To Evan?"

"No. You asked me not to." I felt terrible for not being forthcoming with Evan about why I'd been brought to the ranch, but Tom was adamant that no one else should know. He didn't suspect his sons, but he also didn't want them casting blame on innocent parties.

"Once we have some definitive proof, we'll loop him in," Tom promised. "I know it can't be easy for you to keep this secret, especially from him."

"I was hired to do the job, Tom. That's what I'm doing." I wasn't about to start talking to Tom about my feelings for his son. He'd already seen enough of that.

Tom ran a hand over his chin, stroking his graying beard thoughtfully. "I know my opinion doesn't matter, but I like you with my boy. You make him smile. He's different when you are around. It's like he's finally allowing himself to want something more than just being a great father and a good employer.

"He's a good man and he carries a lot on his shoulders. He's done a great job with the ranch and with raising his kids. But I worry about him. About him ending up alone because he spends too much time worrying about everyone else. And I think you could use someone to worry about you."

"He's not going to be happy when he finds out we've been keeping this investigation from him." I hadn't known Evan long, but I knew him well enough to know that he would feel betrayed.

"You let me handle that. None of this was your idea and I won't let you take the blame." Tom turned toward the large window that looked over the ranch below. "I have to do what I think is right when it comes to this place. This will be my legacy that I leave to my children and I want it to be the best one possible."

The love that Tom had for his kids had never been more clear. He wore it right on his face, like a badge of honor.

"I think you're wrong about that, Tom," I said. "Your legacy isn't the ranch. It's those six human beings who have never once had to question whether their father loves them. It's the people they have become and the way they carry your example everywhere they go." Tom didn't give himself enough credit for how he'd managed to keep his family so happy and united after the death of his wife. "You know, Harper was my first real friend. She knew me for about five minutes and decided that I was going to be her special project. I didn't know how badly I needed someone like her in my life and I'll be forever grateful to her for showing me what real love looks like. She learned that from you, Tom. I see that same instinct in all of your kids.

"They were raised to love and care for others. To care about their family, friends, and the ranch employees. Nate has lunch delivered every Friday for his team. Chase knows the birthdays of everyone who works at Lucky Charm and he has Marla make them a special birthday dessert. And Evan knows the home situation of every one of his employees. He makes them leave early if their kids have a special event or lets them come in late if they have a doctor's appointment. He will work late on Friday night so they can all be with their families a little longer on the weekends."

I was continually impressed by how thoughtful all of the Sullivans could be. Harper and her siblings had all grown up under an umbrella of impressive wealth. They could've easily been raised to be spoiled and ungrateful.

"Face it, Tom. You raised good humans. And I'm just grateful that you have allowed me the chance to get to know them." I reached over and patted his arm. "Your legacy is safe."

He looked at me with watery eyes. "You are part of that legacy now, Lily. I didn't just bring you into my business, I brought you into my family. My daughter thinks of you like a sister." Tom smirked. "Which makes what I discovered you doing with my son in my kitchen a little unsettling."

"Oh god." I put a hand over my eyes. "Can we not talk about that?"

"Didn't I just tell you that you are family now? I am obligated to give you shit. I did the same thing with Evan and he took it like a champ." Tom's smirk transformed into a genuine smile. "He cares a lot about you, Lily. That might not seem like a big deal, but I don't think Evan has ever cared for a woman the way he cares for you."

"Evan is right," I said with a sigh. "You are a bigger busybody than the church ladies."

Tom let me leave a few minutes later after just a couple more teasing comments about Evan. He was clearly delighted about the situation, but that didn't mean he was going to make it easy on us. And even though I rolled my eyes more than once, I kind of loved how invested he was in our relationship. If Tom supported it, then it had to be a good idea.

It was good to have that confirmation since I no longer trusted my own instincts with men. Even if Evan was easily the least problematic man I had ever met. He was also the hottest man I'd ever met, too. I had no idea how I'd scammed him into wanting me.

Since Evan was once again making dinner, I sent him a text letting him know I was making dessert, not just providing it in bed. Then I grabbed some apples from the large apple tree by his house and got busy baking a pie. I wasn't much of a cook, but I enjoyed baking. This was the pie recipe that Aunt Violet had always used and I thought the results were impressive. Hopefully.

This time, I was waiting when Evan knocked on the door. Even though I had told him I was fully capable of finding his house on my own, I knew he wouldn't listen.

"Damn, cowboy. You clean up good." If I hadn't been holding the pie, I might've thrown myself at him right there on my porch. In his dark jeans, light gray sweater, and neatly combed hair, he looked positively gorgeous.

He surprised me by leaning in and pressing a light kiss

on my lips. "I can't decide what I want to eat first. That pie or you."

"Hm. I didn't realize I was going to have competition tonight." I pretended to consider my options. "Maybe I'll just leave the pie here."

"Bring it. There's no competition. I would choose you every time." Then he kissed me again and plucked the pie from my hands. "You look beautiful, Lily." His dimple appeared and my heart fell into my stomach. That man had no business looking so damn good.

"I may have told Harper about our dinner plans and she may have insisted on doing all this." I gestured to my hair and makeup. It still looked good even though I'd been sporting it for a few hours. "It's a little creepy how determined she is for us to hook up tonight."

"She's a surprisingly good wingwoman." Evan shifted the pie to his other hand and put his free arm around me. "I hope you know that I don't have any expectations for tonight. I just wanted to make you dinner and spend time with you."

I groaned. "I really hope that's not all you want because I'm incredibly horny."

Evan let out a harsh, surprised laugh. "You and me both, city girl. But we've got plenty of time to satisfy those urges. We don't need to rush into anything."

"If you didn't already have two kids, I'd suspect that you are a virgin with that kind of talk." It was sweet that Evan was trying not to pressure me, but I was making it clear that I wanted to get naked with him.

"You've had a rough few days, Lil. I'm here for whatever you need. Or want. And if that happens to be my face between your thighs, I'm here for that, too." He brushed his lips over my ear. "And I am very eager to satisfy that need."

I ducked my head as my cheeks flushed. He somehow knew exactly what I'd been dreaming about for the past month. I allowed myself to glance at him and the unguarded desire on his face made my entire body flush with warmth.

"Should we just skip dinner?" I said, a little breathlessly.

"You're going to need something to fuel your body for what I have in mind." Evan stepped away to open his front door and then held it open until I was inside. His manners were impeccable. "Everything is in the oven, but we've still got a little time until it will be done. Can I get you a drink?"

I nodded. "Whatever you're having."

"I was going to have a beer. Are you sure you don't want something else?" He set the pie on the counter and opened the fridge. "I've got wine and Harper left some of her fruity drinks in here."

"Beer is good." I didn't bother adding that wine always gave me a headache and as someone who was prone to migraines and had been feeling one coming on for a couple of days, I had no interest in doing anything to exacerbate the problem.

"Let's sit outside for a bit. We won't be able to do that

much longer without freezing." He handed me a beer and took my other hand. It felt so natural to slide my fingers between his. He led us onto his back deck where he had two chairs facing the open field. The sun was mostly set now and the view was beautiful.

"I missed this view while I was gone," I said after settling in one of the chairs.

Evan pulled the other chair closer to mine before sitting. "Careful, Lil. You're starting to sound like a country girl."

"Would that be such a bad thing?"

"Only if it gets my hopes up that you're going to stay and then you don't follow through." There was too much honesty in his words.

I wanted to tell him that he didn't need to worry about me leaving, but that wasn't true. Once I finished with Tom's investigation, my job on the ranch would be done. If I wasn't working there, I couldn't continue living in the cottage for free. Evan probably wouldn't want me staying anywhere close to him once he learned that I had been lying about why I was there.

"We can't start worrying about what is going to happen in the future," I said. "Let's just enjoy tonight."

Evan watched me quietly for a moment. "I don't want just tonight with you, Lily. I want a future with you."

"I can't promise you that." I knew that wasn't what he wanted to hear. I reached for his hand and was relieved when he didn't pull away. "I like you Evan. A lot. I like being here on the ranch and spending time with your family. I like having coffee with you every morning and a big part of me really likes the thought of still doing that with you twenty years from now. But in my experience, when I plan too far ahead, everything tends to explode on me."

"Well, your experience doesn't include me. I'm not going to explode on you." He squeezed my hand. "I do plan to explode inside of you, however."

"Ugh. That was terrible. That was something Chase would say." I couldn't even be too dismayed by his joke because I knew he only said it to make me stop doom spiraling.

"I've got a proposition for you, Lily. You give me a chance and I promise to prove to you that you are worthy of good things and of being loved exactly as you are."

"And what do you get out of the deal?"

He raised one eyebrow. "Besides the hot sex?"

"You'll be getting that no matter what," I said, stroking the back of his hand with my thumb.

"If I succeed, you have to stay here. You can go back to the city whenever you want or travel anywhere else you want, but this will be your home. This is where you'll return and I'll be here waiting for you." He brought my hand up and kissed the back of it, just like he had the first time we met.

"What if I decide to travel the world for two years? You'll keep the cottage ready for me and be sitting on the porch waiting when I get back?" I asked doubtfully.

"Sure. Why not? Well, except for that part about the

cottage. If things go the way I'm planning, you'll be living in my house."

"Yikes." I didn't bother hiding my discomfort. "Ev, we've known each other for just over a month. This is our second date. Don't you think you're moving a little fast?"

Evan brought the beer bottle to his lips but stopped before drinking. "I'm not sure about much in my life, but I am sure about the way I feel when I'm with you. When you were gone these last few days, I missed you. I'm a man who is used to being alone. I've never really missed anyone except my kids. But I missed you. My life is just better with you in it."

"You always say the right thing. How the hell are you still single?" I let myself get lost in his eyes until I felt like I was drowning in their blue depths. Even though I'd been denying it, I felt the same way about Evan. I had never felt so comfortable with another person, like I had found a missing piece of myself. "I think you might be my endgame, Evan Sullivan."

Evan smiled his dimple-flashing smile. "Us romantics call that a happy ending, city girl."

"Call it whatever you want. Just as long as you call me yours."

He got to his feet while still holding my hand, pulling me up too. "You can't say that to me and not get the shit kissed out of you, sweetheart."

His lips were hot and urgent against mine. I was ready for him, my tongue sliding between his lips and colliding hard against his tongue. He tasted like beer and a hint of mint. I appreciated that he'd most likely brushed his teeth right before coming to my cottage.

Both of his hands circled past my hips until he was cupping both ass cheeks. His teeth sank gently into my lower lip and he tugged slightly as he pulled away. "Mine," he said in a growl. "And you better not ever fucking forget it."

I had never in my life belonged to anyone. My own parents hadn't wanted to claim me as theirs. Drew had washed his hands of me as quickly as possible. I had long ago accepted that I wasn't someone that people wanted to keep around. In the strangest twist of fate, I now belonged to the most amazing man I'd ever met.

He pressed the gentlest kiss to the tip of my nose. "Let's get dinner over with so I can enjoy the real meal." He squeezed my ass hard before stepping back.

When the warmth of his touch left my body, I craved for it to return. I had quickly developed an addiction to Evan's electrifying presence. At first, I blamed the dull ache in my head on the withdrawal of his affection. But after we sat down to eat the delicious roast chicken and vegetables that Evan had made, my headache started to worsen. I told myself that it was a self-inflicted ache, my body's way of sabotaging the only thing in my life that I truly wanted.

Evan was telling a story about Nate getting stuck in a well when they were kids and I focused on getting lost in his eyes. When his phone rang, neither of us noticed it at first. He reluctantly checked who was calling and frowned. "Shit. It's Marv. I need to take this." He gave me an apologetic look that I waved away.

"Of course. It must be important for him to be calling you this late." I knew that Marv would've left the ranch a couple of hours ago, so he wouldn't be calling about normal work matters.

"What's up, Marv?" Evan asked, pushing back from the table.

I watched him closely as he listened. Evan was typically very guarded in showing his feelings, but he had dropped that shield around me. He grabbed the back of his neck and muttered several swear words. "I'll call my brothers and head out there. You don't need to come back. We'll handle it."

Before Evan had even hung up, I stood up and started clearing the table.

"Lil, I'm so sorry but I have to head out. Marv's buddy called him and said that he noticed part of our fence is down near the highway. We've got to get that fixed right away before we lose some cattle." He took the plates from my hand and put them in the sink. "I'm not sure how bad it is, but I hope it won't take too long."

"I can help," I said, ignoring the growing ache in my head. "Just let me run home and put on my boots."

"No, Lil. You should stay here. It can be dangerous moving around on the ranch when it's dark if you aren't familiar with the land." He squeezed my arm. "Just put your feet up and eat some pie. I'll be back before you can even miss me."

"I already miss you," I said, feeling my body lean toward him as if pulled by an invisible magnetic force.

Evan did his best to smile, but I could see the worry in his face. "I'll be back as soon as possible. Please don't go home. It's going to be so much easier for me to leave if I know you'll be here waiting for me when I get back."

"Then that's what I'll do." I gave him a gentle nudge. "Go."

He hesitated in the doorway, having some sort of internal debate before giving his head a slight shake. "It would be easier walking away from you if you weren't so damn beautiful."

Then he was heading down the hallway to put on his boots while calling his brothers. I turned my attention to putting the rest of the food away, washing dishes, and cleaning up the kitchen. When I was done, the pounding in my head was quickly becoming debilitating. I could hurry back to the cottage and try to find my prescription, but I was almost certain that I had forgotten to fill it after my last migraine. I also didn't want to break my promise to Evan and not be there if he returned.

Instead, I crept down the hallway and went into the first bathroom I found. After searching the top shelf of the medicine cabinet, I found some over-the-counter painkillers. I popped three of them into my mouth and swallowed them down with water from the faucet.

I stumbled back down the hallway and went past the kitchen until I was in the large, inviting living room. Harper had done an excellent job choosing the furniture. The plush suede couch that I sank onto felt like I was sitting on a cloud. I closed my eyes and curled into its warmth, wishing that the migraine would pass soon even though I knew it wouldn't. My migraines never ended until half a day had passed. Or longer.

The only thing that could save me from the pain and nausea was the blissful relief of sleep. So that was exactly what I did.

20

EVAN

The fence repair took a lot longer than I had hoped. Based on the damage, it looked like someone had veered off the highway and plowed directly into the fence. That wasn't a far-fetched theory because we'd had that happen a few times. The road was dark at night and people often drove way too fast and often times the drivers were in an inebriated state.

Chase was extra snarky after having his night ruined while Nate was his usual unflappable self. I would normally be inclined to encourage Chase's grumbling with some of my own anger, but it was impossible not to imagine how great my night was going to end when I got home.

"Why do you keep grinning like a damn fool?" Chase asked as we were packing up our tools. "This type of shit usually pisses you off."

"He's getting laid tonight," Nate said, removing his work gloves.

"You and Lily?" Chase grabbed his shovel. "It's about damn time."

"Both of you need to butt the fuck out of my personal life." I had no idea how Nate had reached such an accurate conclusion about my night. I hadn't told him that I was having Lily over for dinner.

"Don't forget that if you seal the deal tonight, you'll lose our bet," Chase said.

I just rolled my eyes. There was no way I was letting some stupid bet dictate my relationship with Lily. "You need to worry about your own sex life, brother." I headed toward the ATVs.

"There's no need to worry about that. It's doing just fine." He started to climb into his ride. "Enjoy it while you can, Ev. That woman is way out of your league."

"Of course she is. But I'm not planning to tell her." I had no business being with a woman like Lily. She was incredible. But if she didn't mind dating a guy like me, I wasn't going to stop her.

I got back to the house around midnight. It wasn't obscenely late, but I knew that Lily always went to bed much earlier. Part of me expected her to have gone back to the cottage for the night. I felt a sense of relief when I saw that her shoes were still by the door.

"Lil?" I called softly as I shucked off my boots. The house remained peacefully quiet.

I followed my instincts and went into the living room. Aside from the light filtering in from the kitchen, the room was dark. I could just barely make out Lily's still form on the couch. She was curled on her side and had one arm shielding her eyes. She almost looked like a sleeping cat.

My first instinct was to wake her. I really wanted to hear her voice and see her smile. A better part of me knew that would be selfish so instead, I grabbed a blanket and went to tuck it around her. Once I got closer to her, I realized that her body was trembling.

"Lily." I put a hand on her shoulder and flinched. She was really warm. When I touched her forehead, her skin was clammy. "Lil, honey. What's wrong?"

She mumbled something that was indecipherable.

"Okay, I'm really worried. Please look at me." I knelt next to the couch and stroked her hair. "I can't help you if I don't know what's wrong."

A small moan left her lips as she inched her head back from the couch cushion and whispered. "Migraine."

"Okay." I stroked her hair again and thought quickly. While I had spent many nights taking care of my kids' various sicknesses, I had no experience with migraines. "What can I do to help you?"

"I..." She moved suddenly, pressing one hand to her forehead and one over her mouth. "I think I'm going to be sick."

Now that was something I had experience dealing with. My kids had both gone through projectile vomiting stages. Unfortunately, that had ended a few years ago so I didn't have a puke bucket nearby. "Okay. We're moving locations." I stood and then bent over to scoop her into my arms, one arm tucked beneath her knees and the other around her back.

Lily let out another moan and kept her hand pressed over her mouth. The bathroom was only a few feet away and we were almost there when I felt Lily's body heave. I rushed forward and just made it onto the tile floor when she heaved again and I felt a warm dampness soaking my shirt.

"Oh my god," she muttered. "I'm so sorry."

"It's okay." This wasn't my first time being thrown up on. It never got any easier, but at least I knew how to handle it. "Do you need to do that again?"

"I'm not sure."

I put her on the floor in front of the toilet and lifted the lid. "Let's give it a little time and see what happens."

While Lily hunched over the toilet, I carefully peeled away my shirt. Then I grabbed a hair tie and worked on scraping Lily's hair away from her damp skin. While she moaned into the bowl, I crafted a quick braid and tied it off. She had somehow avoided throwing up on her hair and I wanted to keep it that way.

"Still feeling pukey?" I asked.

"And spinny," she said.

I stepped into the hall and grabbed a washcloth from the linen closet. After quickly running it under cold water, I placed it gently on the back of Lily's neck. This time her moan wasn't completely one of distress.

"That feels good."

"When you're up for it, we need to get you cleaned up." I tried not to think too hard about the logistics of cleaning Lily. "You need to drink some water, too. Puking can make you dehydrated."

"Just leave me here," Lily said softly. "You don't have to do this. I mean, I just threw up on you."

"One time, when they were toddlers, both of the twins had the stomach flu and they took turns throwing up on me for hours." I sank onto the floor next to Lily, leaning back against the shower glass. It felt like ice against my bare back. "This is nothing."

"You're never going to want to have sex with me now," she groaned.

I laughed. "Oh, sweetheart. That's not going to be a problem. Once I get that puke washed away, you'll be good as new and I'll still want to fuck your brains out."

"Honestly that sounds amazing. Then I wouldn't have a brain pounding inside my skull right now." She lifted her head and when she looked at me, her eyes were glassy and unfocused. "I think I'm done."

"Alright. Time to strip, city girl."

"I pictured this moment as being much sexier than this," she said as I reached for the hem of her sweater.

"I can't imagine ever not finding you sexy, Lil." I pressed a kiss to her forehead before gently pulling the sweater over her head. She helped me tug away the arms and then I wrapped an arm around her and lifted her to her feet. "We need to get rid of these pants, too. You wiped your pukey hands all over them."

"I'm disgusting," she said, letting her head rest on my shoulder. "You could do so much better than a pukey city girl who can barely ride a horse."

"Hush. I don't want anyone else. I want you." I stroked a hand lightly over her waist. "Now let's end this date right and let me take your pants off."

She laughed and stood still while I slowly peeled down her leggings. Then I lifted each foot and pulled them all the way off. "At least you're getting a chance to see the sexy lingerie I wore for you."

I was still on my knees in front of her and her lacy thong was right in front of me. Under any other circumstance, I wouldn't have hesitated to push aside the delicate fabric and run my tongue over her until she came on my mouth. But that was the last thing she needed right now.

"You look beautiful, sweetheart," I said, getting to my feet. "Let me just clean off your neck and then I'll help you lay down again."

She kept her eyes closed as I took the wet washcloth and carefully wiped down her neck and across her chest. I wasn't a damn saint, so I did let my fingers stroke a little lower than was necessary, gently caressing over the swell of her breasts.

"Alright. Good as new." I tossed the washcloth into the sink. "Can you walk?"

"I'm not sure."

"Let's not push our luck." I scooped her up again. This time, she put a hand on my shoulder and pressed her face into my chest. "I've never carried a nearly naked woman down my hallway. We may have to recreate this someday when you're feeling better."

She just murmured against my skin and her nails scratched lightly over my chest. The sensation it created was so startling that I froze in the doorway of my bedroom. I looked down at Lily curled so contently against my body that I couldn't believe this was only the first time I had held her like this. Despite the reason why we'd ended up like this, it felt so incredibly right.

"I'm going to get you one of my shirts to wear," I said as I set her on the bed.

I grabbed one of my flannels since that would be easier to get on her than pulling something over her head. She obligingly held out her arms and let me slip in on. I buttoned just a couple of the buttons. "Okay. You're all set for sleep. Let's lie you back."

She let out a soft breath when her head touched the pillow. "Thank you, Evan. For everything."

"Happy to help." I brushed her hair back. "I'm going to grab some stuff you might need, but I'll be right back. I'll keep the light off for you, okay?"

"Perfect," she whispered, already half asleep.

I hurried to grab a small trashcan, a bottle of water, several painkiller options, and an icepack. When I brought them into the room, Lily didn't acknowledge me. I thought about waking her to explain what I had brought, but sleep was bringing her relief from the pain and I didn't want to ruin that for her. Instead, I pulled a blanket over her and left her to sleep away the migraine.

I should've felt exhausted after a full day of work, preparing dinner, repairing the fence, and taking care of Lily, but my adrenaline and hormones were both racing. I had been able to keep myself in check by focusing on her clear physical suffering, but the sight of Lily in that lingerie wasn't something I could easily forget. I had never been as attracted to anyone as I was to that woman.

"Get ahold of yourself," I grumbled, making my way back to the bathroom to clean up. I threw our clothes in the washer and jumped in the shower, hoping the cold water would help settle me. Instead, I jerked myself off to the visual of me shoving aside Lily's thong and plunging myself deep inside her body until she was yelling my name.

After I spilled all over the tile, I felt like a total pervert. Here I was having sexual fantasies about a woman who was currently passed out from pain. And then I remembered that she was in my bed, wearing my shirt and I was hard again. I hadn't been this pathetically horny since I was a teenager.

The shower and two releases did have the benefit of settling some of my restlessness. I was officially tired, but I couldn't go to bed. Lily was in there and even though I knew she wouldn't be upset if I chose to sleep next to her, it didn't feel right to me. Not when she couldn't consent to me being that close to her in such a vulnerable position. Plus, I didn't want to risk waking her.

I settled on the couch instead and the cushions still faintly smelled like Lily, vanilla and lightly floral. It was the next best thing to having her in my arms. My eyelids grew heavy and before I could think about all the ways my plans for the night had been ruined, I drifted off to sleep to visions of Lily wrapped in my arms.

21

LILY

The morning after one of the most embarrassing nights of my life was anti-climactic. My brain was still hazy from the remnants of my migraine and it took me a long moment to realize I was in Evan's bed, wearing his shirt. I vaguely remembered him stripping me out of my puke-covered clothes and gently cleaning me with a washcloth before bringing me to his room. I was so mortified by the whole thing that I wanted to hide under the covers.

I didn't need to do that, though, because Evan had already left for work before I woke up. I discovered this when I noticed the note lying on the bedside table, next to a bottle of water and several varieties of over-the-counter pain relief.

Good morning, sweetheart. Hope you are feeling much better. Sorry I had to leave so early, but I left you fresh coffee in the kitchen. I've got the kids after work tonight until Sunday, but I'll try to check in with you later. I washed your clothes and left them on my dresser. I think you should keep the flannel, though. It looks good on you. Stay as long as you'd like. Just lock the door when you leave. ~Evan.

He washed my clothes. I had to read that part twice. When did he have time to do that? He was up until the early morning hours taking care of me and then got up before the sun to start work. I felt even worse seeing that the bedding next to me was still untouched. He hadn't even slept in his own bed for the couple of hours of sleep he got last night.

My migraine was thankfully almost gone. I popped a couple of pain pills just in case and then made the bed. I pulled on my leggings from last night, but I kept Evan's flannel like he had suggested. I liked that it smelled like him, woodsy and masculine. Before I left, I checked to see if anything else needed to be cleaned, but Evan had also taken care of the bathroom.

"You are too damn perfect," I muttered to myself, remembering the way Evan had carefully pulled back my hair while I heaved into the toilet. "I can never face you again, but I'll remember you fondly."

Talking to myself was the least of my concerns. I was supposed to be meeting Chase to go over our last-minute details for the corporate retreat starting Wednesday. We still had a lot to do and I was already behind schedule. I did steal some of Evan's coffee before heading back to the cottage and taking a quick shower.

Chase was already at work unloading wood near the fire pits. "Welcome, sleeping beauty."

"Sorry, sorry. I had a rough night." I knew I wasn't going to get off without taking some shit from Chase.

"I'm sure you did. Evan has a lot of stamina. He's used to riding for hours." Chase cocked an eyebrow at me as he dropped a stack of wood.

"It wasn't like that." I went to the ATV's trailer and grabbed a stack of logs. "I had a migraine and spent the night puking all over Evan."

Chase flinched. "Really?"

"More or less." I pushed my hair out of my face. "Evan had a pretty terrible night."

"Damn. I was really hoping that guy would finally get laid." Chase leaned forward with his hands on the trailer bed. "Are you feeling better?"

"Much." I frowned. "Also mortified."

Chase waved that away. "Eh, don't worry about it. Evan is used to taking care of people. He always took care of us when we were sick after Mom died. Dad doesn't have a great bedside manner, so Ev stepped up. And then he had the twins and was constantly changing diapers and wiping snotty noses. Last night was old habit for him."

"Doesn't that make you sad? That Evan has always had all the responsibility for taking care of everyone around him?" I had only ever had to take care of myself and most of the time that was exhausting. I couldn't imagine how tired Evan was. "Who takes care of him?"

He shrugged. "Feel free to apply for the job, city girl."

"He's a good man," I said, emotion catching in my throat.

"He is," Chase agreed. "And he wants you, Lil. Don't

question it, just be grateful. I've known him my whole life and he doesn't rush into anything. If he's pursuing this thing with you, he knows it is right."

I turned back to grabbing firewood and Chase turned back to giving me shit for being late. It was just good-natured teasing and I appreciated the return to normal order. I wasn't sure how I felt about the genuine Chase, the one saying nice things about Evan and giving me advice.

Distracting myself with work was my usual mechanism for avoiding my personal problems and there was plenty of work to be done. We only took a break to grab lunch and then we got right back to work.

"Hey, I need to take off a little early. I think we got everything done if you can handle taking these boxes back to storage on your own." I felt bad that I'd arrived late and now was leaving early, but Chase nodded.

"Yeah, of course. You did good work today. It would've taken me forever to get all this done on my own." Chase raked a hand through his hair. "I don't think manual labor was part of your job description."

"It was a flexible description," I said with a laugh. "I'm pretty sure dating my boss wasn't listed in those responsibilities either."

I left Chase at Lucky Charm and headed back across the road to get my car. While I was walking, I placed a call to Harper and then fired off a text to Evan. The drive downtown was quick and it didn't take long to run my errands and make it back to the ranch. When I knocked on Evan's door, he was still dressed in his work clothes.

"Hey." His smile was warm and familiar. I could hear the twins laughing at something on the television inside the house. "How are you feeling?"

"Much better. Thank you." I held up the paper bag I was holding. "Harper said this was your favorite restaurant in town. She told me what you and the kids usually order so if I got it wrong, it's all her fault."

"You didn't have to do this, Lil." He took the bag and then grabbed my hand. "But thank you. I don't know the last time anyone handled dinner for me."

"I figured you would be really tired tonight after staying up so late to take care of me." I squeezed his hand. "I know you aren't great at putting yourself first, so I decided to take over."

Evan leaned in and pressed a soft kiss to my lips. "Thank you. I'm glad you're feeling better."

"I had an excellent nurse."

"Why don't you come in and eat dinner with us? We still need to tackle that incredible pie you baked for last night." He tugged me gently toward him.

"No, it's your night with the kids. I know you want to spend time with them. Besides, I promised Harper and Tom I would head up to the main house for dinner tonight." I squeezed his hand again and stepped back. "Have a good night, Ev. Enjoy the pie."

"Good night, Lil." His smile was a little sad and I understood why. As much as I knew I was doing the right thing by not forcing myself into his family time, I hated leaving him. I was happier when I was with Evan Sullivan.

Dinner at the main house was nice and relaxing. Since

the whole family wasn't there, it was much quieter than usual. Without his sons egging him on, Tom was much gentler with his words. I didn't hear him say a single swear word the entire time which had to be some kind of record for him.

I went to bed as soon as I got back to the cottage. My migraine spells always left me tired for a couple of days afterward. A good night's sleep was the only cure.

I wasn't surprised to hear knocking on my door the next morning. In fact, I was already dressed and ready to greet Evan with a big smile.

"This is definitely the best part of waking up," I said when he leaned in for a long, hungry kiss. Two mugs of coffee sat waiting on our usual step, but I ignored them and clung tighter to Evan.

"I missed you last night," I said, sliding my hands through the soft waves at the back of his head. Evan looked damn fine in a hat, but I preferred when he wasn't wearing one because I could give in to the urge to run my fingers through his hair.

"I missed you in my bed," Evan said, his lips lightly grazing my ear. "My pillow smelled like you."

"Oh god. Like vomity me?" I asked in horror.

"No." Evan chuckled. "Like your normal, sexy smell. Like a delicious treat that I can't wait to taste."

I couldn't wait for that either. "I think it would be frowned upon to do that on the porch. Want to come inside?"

"Hell yes, I do." He smirked and grabbed my ass with

one hand. "But I have to take the kids to hockey practice in a bit, so I'm afraid we don't have time for that."

"You are such a tease," I said.

"Think of it as extended foreplay." He pulled me toward the steps. "I've got about twenty minutes for some coffee and chatting. Tell me about your day yesterday."

This was easily my favorite tradition on the ranch. There was something incredibly intoxicating about having time every morning to bask in Evan's undivided attention. I loved how interested he was in the mundane parts of my life and how easily he answered my own questions. I was enjoying learning more about what made Evan happy. Most of that was his kids. He told me every detail about their lives, from their school accomplishments to who won the board games they played last night. I found myself falling more and more for Evan with every story he told.

When it was time for him to go, he collected the coffee mugs in one hand and gave me a deep kiss that I never wanted to end. Evan seemed to agree because his free hand pressed hard into my back as he held me close. "I think I'm developing a pretty severe addiction to you, sweetheart."

"I know the feeling." My heart was racing wildly in my chest. It kept racing even after he had gone and I had a suspicion that it wasn't just a fleeting thing. Evan was the spark that brought me back to life and I had the startling feeling that it would be impossible for me to live without him.

22

EVAN

Aside from the morning coffees I had with Lily, I didn't get to see her until dinner at the main house on Sunday night. The twins had a lot of extracurricular activities on the weekends that always kept us busy. Plus, I wanted to spend that time with them since my week of custody had been cut short with my out-of-town trip falling right in the middle of it.

I was grateful that Lily understood how important that time was to me. She stopped and chatted with the kids when she saw them riding their bikes outside, but she didn't force herself into our time together. Even though I wouldn't have cared. I wanted her to have that time with us, too, but I didn't want to rush anything. It made more sense to ease her into my life and my family, starting with our Sunday dinners.

We were running a little late for dinner and the rest of the family had already gathered. Lily and Harper were laughing at something Dad said while they were setting the table. Emma immediately beelined in their direction. She was just as obsessed with Lily as her dad. Lily gave Emma a big hug and complimented her hair.

"Dad did it," Emma said proudly, stroking her braid.

"Huh." Lily grinned at me. "Evan Sullivan, a man of many talents."

"Don't give him too much credit," Harper protested. "I taught him everything he knows about hair care. He called me up in a panic the first time he had the twins overnight and had to handle Emma's hair in the morning."

I rolled my eyes and inched closer to Lily. "I'm sorry that I ever asked you for help, Harp."

"Mom says that Dad does my hair better than she does," Emma said, twisting the braid around her finger.

"I'm going to grab a beer. You ladies want anything?" I let my hand brush lightly against Lily's back on my way past and she smiled shyly at me.

"I'll take one," she said and Harper echoed her request.

It was hard to walk away from Lily without giving her a kiss. My dad and siblings all knew that Lily and I were dating, but the twins didn't know yet. I knew they both really liked Lily and I didn't want them to get too invested in our relationship until things felt more solid with her. I was also enjoying this early stage where expectations were low and every small interaction was still exciting.

No one was in the kitchen, but I wasn't alone for long. A soft hand ran up my back and warm lips pressed to the side of my neck. "Thought I could help you with the beers, Sullivan," Lily said.

I turned and snaked an arm around her waist. "I'd rather have you help me with something else."

"The twins are going to their mom's tonight, right?" She gave me a hopeful look.

"Right after dinner." I kissed her quickly. "How's your head?"

"Migraine-free." She smiled suggestively while stroking a hand over my stomach. "Your place or mine tonight?"

"I'll come to you once I drop the kids off." I put my lips to her ear. "I want to be able to enjoy undressing you this time."

"Ev! Where's my beer?" Harper continued her tradition of ruining a perfect moment.

Lily kissed my cheek and stepped back. "To be continued, cowboy."

It was the longest family dinner of my life. I ended up sitting directly across from Lily and watching her smile and laugh throughout the meal only made me wish that I could get her alone and capture those lips with my mouth.

Nate was keeping her attention with some story about a drunken streaking incident while he was stationed overseas and I appreciated the opportunity to look at her without getting caught. Her complexion had taken on a nice tan after all the time she'd been spending outdoors and her hair had soft honey highlights framing her face. They accentuated the golden flakes in her eyes. I had thought she was beautiful the second I laid eyes on her, but damn if she wasn't even more gorgeous now.

"It's rude to stare," Emma said, hitting me with a look that was too knowing for someone who was barely twelve.

Her comment brought Lily's eyes back to me and we both hurried to look away. "I just zoned out for a second," I said, clearing my throat. "It's been a long day."

"Sure, Dad." Emma rolled her eyes. "I'm young, but I'm not stupid."

"But you *are* annoying," I said, flicking her braid. "Maybe you'd like to tell your uncles about your new little boyfriend on the hockey team."

"Dad!"

"Wait, what?" Nate exchanged a look with Chase. "Did you hear that?"

Chase nodded. "I did. What's his name, Em?"

"I'm not telling you." She stuck out her chin.

"You are too young for a boyfriend," Dad added.

"He's not my boyfriend!" Emma's cheeks were a rosy red. "We're just friends and Dad only called him my boyfriend to distract everyone from his obvious crush on Lily."

Dad let out a barking laugh and Lily's cheeks burned scarlet red. Nate reached over and tugged a strand of Lily's hair. "We've all got a bit of a crush on Lily," he said. "Look at this pretty hair."

"Country boys always fall for city girls," Chase added.

Ronan had been sitting very quietly at the far end of the table, but even he chimed in. "I'm still waiting for her to accept my date request," he said, sliding me a conspiratorial wink.

I was grateful that they had all picked up on my desire not to involve my kids in my relationship yet. Lily nudged my foot under the table. "I don't know, Ronan. If I've got my pick of cowboys, I think I might like one that knows how to braid my pretty hair."

That made Emma giggle happily and turn back to her meal. With the attention off of me, I was momentarily distracted by a visual of wrapping Lily's braided hair in my hand and tugging hard on it while I plunged into her from behind while breathy moans escaped her parted lips.

"Do you need some ice water?" Chase said, nudging my arm. The longer I sat at the table, the harder it was getting to keep my raging hormones in check. I was done holding back when it came to Lily.

"Kids, take your plates to the kitchen. We need to get going. Your mom is expecting you soon." We had about an hour before I was supposed to drop them off, but I couldn't take much more of looking at Lily without being able to touch her. All over.

It took another fifteen minutes to help clean up plus another fifteen minutes to drive to Naomi's house. The drive back to the ranch was the most excruciating fifteen minutes of my life. I parked in front of the cottage and took a deep breath before exiting my truck. I had a moment of panic where I convinced myself that Lily was going to fake another migraine just to avoid me. But then the blue door opened and Lily stood there wearing her sexy lingerie, cowboy boots, and a big smile.

"I'm ready for my ride, cowboy," she said, beckoning me forward with one finger.

My cock was already hard before I even stepped inside the cottage. I reached for her, slipping a thumb into the lacy fabric on her hip. "Sweetheart, tonight is going to be the best ride of your whole damn life."

23

LILY

Evan kicked the door shut behind him and I was already clinging to his strong, enticing body. Arms around his shoulders, one leg wrapped around his thigh as I pulled him close. Our lips collided in a pulse of heat and hunger. His tongue swept between my lips as his hard cock pressed directly against my throbbing core.

I had been wet since dinner and even though I'd only just put on this thong, it was already soaked by my desire. Evan turned us around until my back was pressed against the door. He slid a hand over my thigh and between my legs.

"Fuck, Lil." He swallowed hard and pushed aside the lacy fabric to run his fingers through my wetness. "You are so wet." His lips moved down my neck and I moaned as he continued to stroke me. "Just so we're clear, I'm about to make you my dessert, city girl."

I looked down at him as he kissed his way over my breasts and stomach. "Eat up, cowboy," I said, my chest heaving with each shaky breath I managed to take.

Evan pressed his lips to my hip and slowly guided down my thong. His eyes never left mine until he had removed it completely and tossed it aside. Then he lifted my right leg and hooked it over his shoulder. "You might want to hold onto something," he said in a low growl before kissing the inside of my thigh.

I groaned when he gently sucked the tender skin and rubbed his fingers over my swollen clit. When I squirmed and tried to force myself closer to him, he stopped and shook his head at me. "I'm in charge now, sweetheart. You'll come when I want you to and only then."

"Fuck," I breathed, desperate to feel his lips on me.

He slowly licked his lips as he eyed my arousal. "I'm betting you're going to taste even sweeter than I imagined. And believe me, Lil, I've been imagining this moment a lot."

"Me too," I said. "But there was less talking."

His laugh was warm against my skin as he brought his lips closer. "I guess I'll have to find something else to do with my lips," he said and then he closed them around my clit in an urgent suck that sent a surge of pleasure through my entire body that was so strong I banged my head against the door.

"Fuck, Ev. That feels incredible." I slid one hand into his hair, pulling him closer.

He stopped sucking and used his tongue to lick me

from my entrance to my clit, letting out a murmur of pleasure. "So damn sweet," he said before taking another languid lick. "This is now my favorite meal."

His hand clutched tighter to the thigh resting on his shoulder while his other hand parted my folds to give his tongue even more access. When he slid a finger inside me, I gasped and clenched around him. "More," I panted.

"Easy girl," he said. His finger hitched until it found the right spot and softly caressed while his tongue circled my clit. As his mouth closed over me again, he shoved a second finger inside and began pumping them slowly, always stroking in just the right way before pulling them out. The heat and throbbing grew so intense that I was having a hard time keeping my balance on one leg as I rode Evan's mouth and fingers.

"I'm almost..." I couldn't finish the sentence. My eyes fluttered shut as a familiar tingle grew stronger than it ever had before. "Evan..."

"Now, sweetheart. Come for me." He latched on hard and sucked hungrily on my clit while he pounded his fingers inside me all the way, flicking and twisting them masterfully until I was contracting hard around him as my orgasm crescendoed. "Fuck, Evan."

I was delirious from the high of release and had almost no awareness that Evan had stood and picked me up until I felt my legs latch around his hips. His cock was threatening to replace his fingers inside me.

"Don't quit on me yet, city girl. I still need to take you for a ride." Then he tossed me onto the bed and yanked off his shirt.

I pushed up on my elbows to watch the show. "Your body is incredible," I said, taking in every taught muscle. He had earned them through hard work and not a gym membership. I wanted to trace every one of those muscles with my tongue, including the ones leading straight down to the giant cock that sprung free as he pushed off his pants. "I think I'm going to have fun riding that stallion."

Evan laughed as he finished removing his clothes and then flicked a hand at me. "Take that bra off. I want to suck on those perfect tits."

"As you wish, Boss." The bra landed on the floor next to his boots.

I shook one of my feet at him. "What about these?" I was still wearing my own boots.

"Keep them on. You'll need them for the ride." His eyes flicked down as he opened the condom wrapper and rolled it over his length. "Part those pretty legs, sweetheart."

I happily complied and watched as he knelt on the bed and crawled between my legs. He quickly kept his promise and sucked each breast, pulling the nipples into his mouth and twirling his tongue around them. He buried his nose in the valley between them and took a deep breath. "I really want this to last as long as possible, but I'm already on the edge, Lil."

"That's okay." I slid my fingers into his hair and tugged. "I am, too."

He was breathing just as hard as me and I could feel his heart pounding in rhythm with mine as he leaned down to kiss me. I could taste my own desire on his lips, but the urgency of his kiss was all his.

"Lil, are you okay with this?" he asked as his cock pushed hard against my entrance.

"More than okay," I said, brushing back his hair. "I want to feel you move inside me, Evan. I want to come apart with you."

His hand lifted my butt at an angle as he eased just the head of his cock into me. I had seen for myself that he was large, but I hadn't given enough appreciation to his girth. My body had to stretch to accommodate his size.

"Keep going, Ev," I said when he hesitated. That was all the encouragement he needed. He pushed in the rest of the way, aided by my eager wetness and I gasped in pleasure at the fullness I felt as he filled every inch of me.

"Fuck, Lil. You feel so incredible. I didn't expect you to be this tight." He spoke through gritted teeth. "If I'm going to make this last, I need to start slowly, okay?"

I nodded and resisted the urge to clench around him knowing that would only make things harder for him. His first withdrawal was achingly slow. His next couple of thrusts were tentative as he adjusted to the feeling of being inside me. When he picked up his pace, I was already about to explode again.

"Evan, I'm not going to make it," I said.

He stopped moving and kissed me hard. "I promised you a ride," he said before grinning wickedly and rolling onto his back, taking me with him until I was straddling him with his cock still inside me. His palm made a satisfying noise when he smacked my ass. "Giddy up, sweetheart."

I laughed and pushed myself up, hands resting on his hard pecs. This new angle allowed me to sink down and push him further inside me. "Oh fuck," he breathed. "I didn't think this through."

I grabbed both of his hands and put them on my breasts as I started to move. His fingers dug into my flesh and his thumbs stroked my hard nipples. When I started moving harder and rocked my hips with each descent, he slid his hands down my body and grabbed my ass, pulling me hard against him and meeting me with eager thrusts.

"Are you close?" he grunted.

"Yes." It came out as a breath.

Evan moved one hand to my center, pushing hard against my clit in time with another thrust and then I was lost to the orgasm that ripped through me. I screamed his name as my body convulsed and then I felt his release jerk inside me as he pulled me down and swallowed the last of my moans with his kiss.

I collapsed on top of him as I struggled to steady my breathing. Evan carefully pulled out of me, making sure not to lose the condom. "That was..." I couldn't find the right word for what I'd just experienced.

Evan had no such problem. "Perfect," he said, stroking a hand down my back. "That was perfect and so are you."

I lifted my head and looked into his beautiful blue eyes. "I have the answer now."

"What answer?"

"Forget riding horses. I only ever want to ride a cowboy from now on."

Evan laughed and pulled me down for another kiss, this one slow and sweet. He tucked my hair behind my ear and said, "Not just any cowboy. From now on, you'll only ride me, city girl."

24

EVAN

From the second that Lily opened her door, I was hers. She owned me, body and soul. Nothing that I'd been imagining was anywhere close to being as good as the real thing. Her body was incredible, her taste was intoxicating, and being inside her was the only place I ever wanted to be. From that first push inside, I felt myself claiming her as mine. Each thrust was a plea for her to claim me, too. And then she did.

Afterward, when I told her that she would only ride me from now on, she laughed, traced my lips with her fingers, and promised, "Only you."

Just like that, she was mine and I was hers.

To seal the deal, we had sex two more times that night and twice again in the morning. Lily insisted that she was more sore than she ever would be riding a horse and I was a little worried that I'd gone too far with her. Once we got started, it was hard for me to quit.

"Lil, you know that you can tell me no, right? I won't be offended if you're tired or sore and need a break." We were drinking our coffee at the tiny table tucked against the wall in her kitchen area. The table was so small that our knees touched beneath it.

"Of course I know that," she said. "But I'm fine, Evan. I mean, yeah I'm a little sore, but in a very good way. My body has never withstood that many consecutive orgasms."

"Your body is a masterpiece, Lil. Getting to touch it... taste it... and be inside it... well, I'm a lucky man."

Lily's cheeks flushed and she looked down at her coffee. "Ev, how long had it been for you? Since the last time you were with a woman, I mean."

"Was it that obvious?" I asked with a nervous laugh.

"No!" She grabbed my hand and squeezed. "You were incredible, Evan. By far, the best I've ever had. But you mentioned to me that it had been a long time. I'm just curious."

"About three years." I laughed at her dramatic eye-widening. "Not my favorite fact about myself, but it's the truth."

"But how? Why?" She gestured to me with her other hand. "Have you seen you? Have you had sex with you?"

"Well, technically... yes." Especially since meeting Lily. My hand and I had spent a lot of time together over the last few weeks. "Look, there were a lot of women when I was younger. High school, college, and right after I moved back to the ranch. But then the twins happened and I stopped being so damn reckless. I decided to only sleep with a woman if I thought I might have a future with her. That didn't happen often. The older I got, the less interested I was in any kind of meaningless fling."

"Who was she? The woman before me?"

I grimaced. "Do you really want to know that?"

"Yeah, kind of. I want to know everything about you, Evan."

"Her name is Tara. We went to high school together, but we ran in different groups. She got divorced a few years ago and moved back to town. We went on a few dates and got along well. But we disagreed about some pretty big things."

"Like what?"

"She was only here temporarily. Just trying to get her feet under her and then she planned to leave. That was never going to be an option for me while the kids are still young. It didn't make sense pursuing something with her that was never going to work long-term." There had been other reasons, too, but that had been the deal breaker for me.

Lily contemplated that answer. "But otherwise you got along with her? You would've stayed with her?"

"No. I may have stayed with her a little longer because I've been so damn lonely, but we were never going to last. She didn't like the ranch." I didn't have a lot of requirements when choosing a partner, but I did require them to not despise my home.

"Don't you need to get to work?" Lily looked at the time on her phone. "You are running so late, Ev."

"It's fine. I texted Marv and told him I would be late.

I've got a little more time to enjoy being with you." I could count on my hands the number of times I'd been late to work.

"Are we... telling people about us?" She gave me a hesitant look. "Are you ready to do that?"

"Sweetheart, you can tell anyone you want about what we did last night." I laughed when she kicked my foot under the table. "Look, my whole family already knows exactly what we are up to. I'm not interested in pretending you're not the best thing in my life right now. But I also don't want to get the kids too invested yet. Not until we know what this is going to look like in six months or a year."

"You mean if I'm going to stay?" Lily looked hurt.

I tapped my fingers on the table. "Lil, it's not about whether you are going to stay or not. I meant it when I said that I would support you if you needed to go back to the city. We could work something out. You could split your time between there and the ranch or I could try to come out and visit you when I don't have the kids. But this is my home. It's always going to be my home. If we're going to be together, I need it to be your home, too. The place where you return." I didn't want her to go, even if it was just for a week. But I could do long distance as long as I knew she would return to me.

"You seem so certain that I'm going back there," she said, looking bewildered. "Why? What have I done in the last six weeks that has led you to believe I want to be anywhere but here?"

"It's only been six weeks. You used Crestwood and the

ranch as a way to escape your past. But once you heal from that, you might decide you don't need or want to stay away any longer. The city was your home for a long time."

"It was where I lived," she said, shaking her head. "But it was never my home. I spent so much time working, constantly traveling, because I had nothing keeping me there. Nothing that I was eager to return to. Even in the short time that I've been here, I have people that I would miss if I left. I have a place to live where I wake up every day and I'm glad to be here. I felt that way even before I had you." Lily traced her thumb over my knuckles and even that slight touch set my body on fire. "Crestwood Valley is my home. This ranch is my home. *You* are my home, Evan."

"Does that mean you're staying?" I needed to hear her say it in order to believe it.

"I'm not going anywhere unless you tell me to." She smiled slightly. "This is your house, after all."

"Technically, it belongs to the whole family. And Harper would never let me kick you out." I grinned. "Well, except for maybe if I was moving you into my place."

Lily's eyes widened again. "Um..."

"Relax. We're not there yet." I looked around the cottage. "Honestly, I like the idea of having this place even if you eventually move in with me one day. We're going to need someplace for riding practice where the kids won't interrupt us."

"Riding practice? Is that what we're calling it?" Laughter danced in her eyes. "I think we both know that I don't need any practice in that area."

"Speaking of riding, I do need to take off soon. We've got a bunch of cattle that need to be moved today." I was sure the team was already well underway, but we'd need every rider available to help out. I stood and took my coffee mug to the sink. "Do you want more coffee?"

"No, I'm good. Thanks." She stood and leaned against the counter behind me, watching while I cleaned my mug. "I can do that, Ev."

"I'm sure you can." I was just so used to washing dishes that it never would've occurred to me to leave this one for someone else to clean. When I finished, I dried my hands on the towel and turned. "Do you have plans after work?"

"More orgasms if you're up for it." She looked so damn beautiful with her teasing smile, sparkling eyes, and sex-mussed hair.

"With you? Always." I stepped forward and kissed the top of her head. "Have a great day. I'll be here after work, ready to deliver."

"Be careful out there," she said.

It was a request that made me hesitate at the door. My safety wasn't something I thought about often on the ranch. Not directly anyway. We had plenty of safety procedures in place that were required to be followed by every ranch employee, but it was just part of my daily life. It was habit. I never thought too closely about it because no one had ever told me that I should. I didn't have someone worrying about me coming home every night.

Not until now. Not until Lily.

As I had expected, everyone was already saddled up

and ready to ride. Marv had gotten Blaze ready, too, and all I had to do was mount him. We worked hard all day to move the cattle to the lush pasture closer to the mountains. The grass there was still thick and would be for several more weeks.

"You've been weirdly smiley today, kid. Good night?" Marv said as his horse trotted next to mine.

We both knew what he was implying. "Let's just say I took your advice. Decided not to fuck up what the universe gave me."

"About time you stopped being stupid." Marv nodded to himself. "I like that girl. She's been good for the ranch and she'll be good for you. Reminds me of my wife."

"How is Nellie? Has she been feeling better?" We didn't often talk about his wife's health because I knew Marv worried about her all the time. I'd often catch him frowning and staring across the fields.

"She's been on some new drugs for the last three months and they have really helped. Cost a pretty penny, but she's worth it." He smiled like a man in love. I would know. It was exactly how he'd caught me smiling today.

"That's great, Marv. Maybe you could bring her out sometime and we could have dinner together with our girls." I loved Marv's wife. Nellie was a kind woman with a quick sense of humor.

"That would be nice." He tugged on the brim of his Stetson. "I have to admit that I was a little nervous when Tom told me he was bringing in an outsider. You've done a great job with this place since your daddy got sick and I was worried someone was going to come in and ruin everything."

"You and me both," I said with a dry laugh.

"I'm happy to admit that I was wrong."

I pictured Lily as I'd seen her this morning. Those damn eyes and that intoxicating smile. I couldn't believe that there had been a time when I hadn't wanted her to be a part of my life.

"Me too, Marv. Me too." I had never been so happy to be wrong about something in my life.

25

LILY

The beginning of the week was a blur of busy days working on the ranch and slow nights in the cottage with Evan. We made the most of our time together, first falling into a heated frenzy the moment he walked through my door before settling down to eat a quick dinner and then spending the next several hours satiating our desires.

I never got sick of his mouth on mine, his hard body pressing down on me as our bodies came together. His low groans became my favorite sound in the world. He always showered before coming to my place, washing away the sweat and grime from a hard day of work. The smell of his pine-scented soap was like a drug to me. It lingered in my sheets long after he had left every morning.

On Wednesday morning, we woke a little earlier than

usual to squeeze in a few extra minutes of time together. I was going to be busy working the executive retreat for the next three days and nights. Evan was also going to be putting in some time to help with the guided hunts, and both of our schedules weren't going to allow much time for us to be together.

I headed across the highway on my own. Evan still had work to do on his ranch this morning, so it would just be me and Chase getting everyone settled. I really wanted this event to go well. Booking more corporate retreats was a big part of our financial strategy for next year and impressing a group of executives from various companies would go a long way toward helping us achieve our goals.

"Hope my brother managed to let you get some rest last night," Chase said.

We stood on the large porch at the welcome lodge, sipping coffees as we waited for our guests to arrive. Chase had hired chauffeurs to drive them from the airport and so far, everything was going to plan. Even the weather was perfect. I was able to stand outside comfortably in my Lucky Charm Ranch t-shirt. It was one of our new merchandise items. Chase was wearing an identical t-shirt after I had convinced him that the "Get Lucky on the Ranch" t-shirt would not be appropriate for this moment.

"The first van should be here any minute," I said, ignoring his innuendo. "I'll take them inside for coffee and tea while you wait for the second van."

"Are you excited to finally be around your people again?" he asked with a wry grin. When Chase looked at me like that, he reminded me a lot of Evan.

"These aren't my people." I had never felt a kinship with the CEOs I had encountered, even if we'd all been working toward similar goals of running successful companies and making a lot of money. "I like my men in Stetsons and chaps, not Armani and Rolexes."

"Don't discount a man in a nice suit yet," Chase said as the first black luxury van barreled down the main road. "You haven't seen us Sullivan boys when we dress fancy."

He had a point. I knew that Evan would look damn fine in a suit, but I really loved him in worn jeans and flannels. I set my coffee mug on the porch railing and waved to the staff members who had been patiently waiting inside the open doorway.

"This is it, everyone. Let's show these city boys what they've been missing." I plastered on my best smile as the van pulled to a stop. We had hired two vans to accommodate the guests' different arrival times.

The doors slid open and Chase and I stepped forward to make introductions. The rest of the staff scrambled to unload suitcases from the back and pile them onto our ATV trailers to transport out to the Airstreams. We had decided that asking these men to carry their own bags wouldn't go over well.

The five men who now stood before us were all dressed in their interpretation of casual. Five-hundred-dollar jeans and cashmere sweaters. Italian leather boots that would be a mess in just a few hours. They reminded me of myself on my first day on the ranch.

"Let's go inside and I'll tell you more about Lucky

Charm Ranch and what you can expect during your visit." I gestured for them to follow me.

"This is beautiful land," the man who had introduced himself as Brian said. "How long have you worked here?"

"Not long, actually. I was in Denver up until a couple of months ago." I couldn't believe that it had only been that long. "But I fell in love with this place right away and I intend to stay as long as the Sullivan family lets me."

"You were in Denver? Where did you work?" Brian had a nice smile. He reminded me a lot of the men I had been attracted to when I lived in Denver.

"I worked for a tech company," I said vaguely. There was a good chance that these men would immediately recognize my old company's name and they may also remember the stories that had circulated when I'd been forced out. At least one of the men probably also knew Drew. "But I think I was always meant to be a country girl. I really love it here."

I veered into our largest community room where the staff had set up a coffee bar and breakfast buffet. "I highly recommend the coffee. It's a special blend from a local shop. Once the rest of the guests have arrived, we'll take a tour around the property and show you to your sleeping quarters."

"Do you also sleep on the ranch?" I thought this second man had said his name was Steve. He looked like a Steve.

"I live across the highway, actually. On the working ranch. Both properties are owned by the Sullivans." I could see Steve running the dollar signs through his head as he tried to figure out how much wealth Evan's family had.

"How much land do they have?" he asked.

I shrugged. "A few thousand acres." I knew the exact number, but it was none of his business. Evan and his family never felt the need to brag about the impressive size of their land. They didn't care about impressing anyone, and definitely not these men from the city.

"Please, grab something to eat and drink." I gestured to the buffet and started to back away. These men all reminded me too much of Drew and my old life.

"I know exactly what I'd like to grab," Steve muttered, his eyes trailing down to my chest.

"Unless you want to end up in the hay baler, I'd advise against that." Chase's threatening tone traveled easily from the doorway. He was staring hard at Steve. "My brother wouldn't take kindly to you touching his girlfriend. Neither would I."

That was the first time anyone had referred to me as Evan's girlfriend. The feminist in me wanted to be annoyed that Chase had felt the need not only to defend me but to also use his brother as the reason why I shouldn't be harassed. But the professional in me was grateful to have support from a coworker. And the woman in me... well, she liked being called Evan's girlfriend.

"Ah. You're one of those." Steve smirked and shook his head. "I should've known."

I knew exactly what he was implying. He assumed I'd

gotten my job because I slept with the boss. A lot of men had made that same insinuation about me at my old job, too. And part of me had wondered if they were right. I *had* been sleeping with my boss then. I was sleeping with my boss now.

Steve walked away and Chase strolled over to me. "Want me to take care of that?" he asked, a hopeful gleam in his eyes.

"No. We can't start off this event with a fight." I punched his arm. "Thanks for having my back, Sullivan."

"Always." He hooked a thumb toward the doorway. "The next van is pulling up and Evan and Nate are here to schmooze with everyone."

"Let's go." I was happy that I would get to see Evan, but I was nervous about how he would react if Steve was dumb enough to repeat his harassment in front of Evan.

The second van had just been parked when we walked onto the porch. Evan and Nate were already at the bottom of the steps, wearing their standard ranch gear. But they were both dressed in clean clothes, likely attempting to impress our guests. I had to admit that their cowboy look was way hotter than the preppy outfits coming out of the van.

I was so busy looking at Evan as I descended the porch steps that it took me a moment to realize that I knew one of the new arrivals. Knew him quite well, in fact.

"Lily?"

I was frozen in disbelief at the man who had so confidently greeted me by name. A man whose voice had once moaned my name in bed. A man who I had never wanted to see again.

All three Sullivan brothers were staring at me in confusion, but I avoided their questioning looks as the reality of my situation came into sudden focus.

Then I let out one word in an exhale of breath. A name. "Drew."

26

EVAN

Lily recovered from her unexpected visitor faster than I did. She forced a smile that everyone else would've mistaken as genuine, but I saw the way it didn't reach her eyes. Chase easily detected that something awkward was playing out in front of us and he stepped in to welcome everyone and make introductions.

Nate and I had decided on a whim that we would come over and meet everyone when they arrived rather than waiting until tomorrow morning when we were taking the men hunting. We had never done a guided hunt like this and were still working out the kinks. Just getting the legal and licensing aspects squared away had taken Chase a long time to figure out. I wanted this first outing to go well for him. And maybe I wanted to mark my territory a little bit with so many rich guys invading my ranch.

But now I was forced to watch as Drew approached

Lily, his mouth forming a cocky smile that made me want to punch out his perfect fucking teeth.

"It's been a long time, babe. You look good." His eyes scanned her with a sense of familiarity that made my stomach clench along with my fists. "I have to admit that I never in my wildest dreams would've expected to see you in a place like this."

"I have to admit that you haven't been in my dreams at all." She managed to keep her tone neutral, but I could see the tenseness in her shoulders and jaw.

"Hey, Lil. I need you to look over some paperwork," I said, touching her lightly on the elbow. "Chase and Nate can handle getting our guests situated."

Lily nodded without looking at me. Drew looked at me for the first time and quickly made an assessment that had him taking a step back. "We'll catch up later, Lil."

I wrapped my hand around her elbow and started leading her away, a little unsettled that she wasn't saying anything or even looking at me. I took her to the welcome center's office so we could have privacy.

When the door shut behind us, she finally looked at me. "I'm so sorry."

"What? Why?" The last thing I had been expecting was an apology.

"I didn't know he was one of the guests. I swear. I never looked up the names. Chase handled the booking and the contract stuff. I didn't invite him or–"

"Lily, stop. I believe you." I had never seen her this frazzled. "I know you didn't invite that asshole to our ranch. If you want me to tell him to fuck off, I'll do it."

"You can't." She shook her head quickly. "We need this retreat to go well. Neither of us can piss off Drew or any of those other men."

I scoffed. "If you don't want me to make him leave, I won't. But I can't promise you that I won't do something to piss him off if he keeps getting you upset like this."

"I'm not upset. I'm fine." She lifted her chin defiantly. "I was just surprised to see him and I didn't want you to feel like I had somehow planned this."

"It would be a poor decision to invite your ex to a hunting outing where it would be very easy for me to shoot him and dispose of the body." I smiled so she would know I was kidding. "Hey, come here." I slipped a finger through her belt loop and tugged her forward until she leaned into my chest. It felt so natural to wrap both arms around her like I'd been doing that for years instead of just days. "If you want me to take over for you, I will. I can leave Marv in charge for the next couple of days and I'll pick up your responsibilities over here so you don't have to deal with Drew."

"I appreciate the offer, Evan, but I'm not going to let Drew run me away from another job that I love. He doesn't get to win this time," she said firmly, looking up at me through her long lashes. She had looked at me that same way last night while kneeling in front of me.

"That's right, sweetheart. This time, *I've* won." I pressed my lips to her forehead. "Because you're mine now. That fucker never deserved you, Lily. He has to be the dumbest man alive to have let you go."

"He's no Evan Sullivan, that's for damn sure." Lily raised onto her toes to kiss me. "Will you do me a favor?"

"Anything."

"Fuck the memory of him right out of me." The heat of her gaze was scorching. "Now."

I didn't have to be asked twice. Apparently, a mutual hatred of her ex-boyfriend was the only foreplay we needed because by the time I had yanked down her jeans and bent her over the desk, she was wet and I was hard. A few forceful thrusts were all it took for both of us to find our release. I leaned over her and pressed a kiss to her cheek. "You good?"

"Much better. Thank you." She sighed contentedly as I pulled her up. "I think your dick might be able to solve all my problems."

"I'm willing to test that theory." I took a moment to dispose of the condom in the trashcan and tucked my favorite appendage back into my pants while Lily fixed her clothes. She frowned as she touched her hair. I had thoroughly messed it up by tangling my hand through the waves while sliding into her. "Sorry about that."

"I'm not." She snatched a rubber band from the desk.

"Hang on." I caught her hand as she was about to pull her hair back. "Let me fix it."

"Oh, that's right. I forgot those hands of yours are capable of more than eliciting orgasms."

I turned her around and lowered her onto the edge of the desk to get a better position to start gently combing out the tangles with my fingers. "This is a little easier than trying to keep you from puking on your hair in my toilet."

"I thought we both agreed to never speak of that night." She moaned softly as I kept combing through her hair. "You are way too good at this."

"Emma has given me lots of practice. What style do you want? Regular braid? French braid? Low bun? Pigtails?"

"Pigtails?" she gasped through a laugh.

"That was Emma's most frequent request from ages four through seven."

"I think maybe we should just stick with something that doesn't infantilize me." Her head dipped back and her eyes closed. "Your pick."

I decided to go with a regular braid. Lily had thick hair and I thought that would look best on her. But then again, I'd never styled anyone's hair beyond the age of twelve so I really had no idea what I was doing.

"We're going to be doing this every day from now on, cowboy," Lily said when I plucked the rubber band from her hand. "I've always wanted a personal hair stylist."

I finished tying off the braid and then pressed a kiss to her neck. "We haven't really talked about how you want this to work around the ranch."

"This?" She craned her neck to look at me. "Us?"

"Yeah." I shrugged. "I mean, my siblings obviously know we're involved. I'm sure some of the workers suspect it, too. But what about when we're with other people?"

"Like the asshole in the next room?"

"Among others. I can keep things professional for the most part, but my body reacts to you, Lil. My face gives away that I'm infatuated with you. Sometimes so does my dick. I'll do my best to hide what I can, but I can't guarantee that people won't figure out I'm obsessed with you."

"Then don't try to hide it. Evan, I don't care if people know about us. I don't care if Drew knows you just fucked me on that desk." She leaned into me as my arms circled her from behind. "But I do think it would be best for us to maintain some decorum over the next few days. We both need to stay focused and..."

"And?" I could feel the tension already returning to her body.

"I know those men out there. Not specifically those men, but men like them. If they think I'm only here because I'm sleeping with you, I'm going to lose my credibility. Especially if Drew decides to open his big mouth about our past."

"Then I promise to keep my hands to myself once we leave this room." I gave her breast a firm squeeze and smiled as she squirmed in my arms. "And if Drew opens his big mouth, I'll shove my fist into it and rip out his tongue."

I was not a violent man, typically. I'd only ever been in two real fights in my life. One was when I caught some stranger grabbing my sister's ass in a bar and the other was when Ronan got jumped by some older kids in junior high. But for Lily, I'd fight anyone who even thought about hurting her.

"You can't rip out his tongue," Lily protested with a laugh.

"I absolutely can." Another squeeze and then I

stepped back. "Let's finish getting them settled so I can get back to the ranch and take over from Marv."

"You don't have to stay over here if you've got things to do."

"I've still got some time. I'd rather spend it with you." That part was true. The part I wasn't telling her was that I didn't like the thought of leaving her alone with a group of rich men who weren't used to hearing the word no. I knew men like these men, too, and I knew exactly what they were capable of saying and doing to a woman like Lily.

"Okay." Lily didn't exactly sound thrilled about that. I tried not to take her response personally. She had been clear about wanting to focus only on her job today and I was going to do my best not to get in the way of that. "Can you make sure all the luggage is getting taken to the Airstreams? I'm going to walk the group over there soon and I don't want them to have to stand around and wait."

"I can do that." I moved to open the office door, but she caught my hand and pulled me back. Her lips were on mine, branding me with a firm and searing thank you.

Lily hadn't asked me about my feelings around having her ex-boyfriend on the ranch and I was glad she hadn't. I wouldn't have been able to lie to her and she didn't need to hear about my jealousy. It would only make her apologize again for Drew being here even though it wasn't her fault.

Nate tagged along with me and the staff members who were carting over the luggage. Chase stayed behind with Lily and was going to keep an eye on Drew on my behalf. I didn't even have to ask. He sent a text letting me know that he was going to make sure the asshole didn't make a move on my girl. His words, not mine, but I agreed with them completely. Especially the part about Lily being my girl.

"So... what do we know about the guy who was checking out Lily?" Nate asked as we rode toward the Airstreams.

"Which one?" I figured he was talking about Drew, but I'd caught nearly every man checking out Lily.

"The one who actually seems to know her." Nate gave me a pointed look. "The one you looked like you wanted to knock out."

I sighed. "His name is Drew. He was the CEO of the company where Lily worked before coming here." I hadn't asked her if she wanted anyone else to know about her relationship with Drew. I felt like I might betray her trust by telling Nate too much.

"Did they fuck?" he asked bluntly. It was the kind of question that I would expect from Chase, not Nate. Except I knew he was only asking because he was looking out for me. He wanted to know if he was supposed to hate Drew on my behalf.

"They have a complicated history," I said vaguely. "He's the reason she left that job."

Nate hummed. "In that case, I think we owe him a thank you. If he hadn't done whatever he did, Lily wouldn't have ended up here. I like having her here."

"Me too." I wasn't willing to give Drew any credit for that, though. "Let's give our thanks to Harper and Dad for bringing her to Crestwood. Drew doesn't deserve anything good when it comes to Lily."

"So, you two are... together? Like really together?" he asked.

"Yeah. We are together." It felt good to finally be able to say that. "We're not telling the kids yet until we're sure it's going to work out, but I know it will."

Nate was quiet for a moment as he looked at me. "You love her." It was a statement and not a question.

"I do."

"Have you told her that?" The nosy asshole knew me too well.

"Not yet."

He groaned. "You need to tell her, man. A woman like that should hear it every day."

"It's too soon. I don't want to freak her out. She hasn't had the best experience with men in the past." I was making excuses and we both knew it. I was the one who had never told any woman that I loved her. I was the one who had doggedly avoided commitment or vulnerability with anyone outside of my family. "We're in a good place right now. I don't want to fuck it up."

"You think that not being honest with her about how you feel is the way to go?" He shook his head and laughed. "No wonder you're still single at 38."

"Like you're doing any better? At least I've got Lily."

Nate slammed on the brakes harder than was necessary and my head snapped with an abrupt jerk. "I'm happy for you, Ev."

"Thanks." I didn't know what to do with a sincere comment like that from Nate, so I just got out of the ATV and walked toward the nearest Airstream.

The entire space looked different than the last time I was there. More chairs had been added to the fire pit areas and someone had strung up lights from each Airstream to the center of the space, creating a canopy of lighting that I was sure would look amazing at night. The outside of the Airstreams had been thoroughly cleaned and they were shinier than when Chase had first bought them.

He had salvaged them from across the state over the last couple of years and methodically rebuilt them into trendy little homes. This was our first event where we had rented them out and I hoped it went well. I was proud of what my brother was trying to do with the guest ranch and I wanted him to be successful.

"It looks great out here," Nate said, sounding as impressed as I felt. "I take it some of this was Lily's touch." He gestured to the decorative welcome mats in front of each shiny door and the flowers that had been planted all around.

"She probably did the finishing touches," I admitted with a proud smile. "But the rest of this was Chase. He had this all figured out before he even bought the first rusty trailer."

"Lily has this plan to get a group of influencers to come out here. She knows someone with, like, 50 million followers or something. She thinks we could make some tweaks to make the ranch more appealing to women. She said the horseback riding, sunrise hikes, hot cowboy instructors, glamping motif would be a big hit with women in their twenties and thirties. Girls' trips, bachelorette parties, stuff like that." Nate gestured to the lights above us. "I think she's right. I always thought this place would be better suited for families. But the corporate retreat stuff was right on point and I think the focus on women is a good call, too."

I'd had this same conversation with her a couple of days ago as she excitedly told me her ideas. Her face had lit up when she talked about expanding Lucky Charm Ranch to include more lodging for larger groups, making one of our ponds into a swimming hole, clearing a field to put in tennis courts, and adding in hot tubs and outdoor showers. In the winter, she thought we could target couples with romantic horse carriage rides through the snow and secluded A-frame cabins in the woods.

I thought all of her ideas were great and it sounded like Nate agreed. I was sure she'd already told my dad, too, and I knew he would be on board. Lucky Charm Ranch had been my mother's pride and joy. She had poured her heart into making it something that people loved and Lily had that same spark for it. She loved it the way that Chase loved it.

I could hear voices coming down the path from the main part of the ranch. Our guests were quickly approaching and I knew we'd be too busy for me to pull Lily aside and tell her how I proud I was of everything she'd been doing. But I hoped she could see some of that pride when she came into view and I smiled happily at her. She wore an identical smile, her eyes locked on mine.

The only thing more impressive than what she'd helped Chase create over the last few weeks was the fact that I had gotten a woman like Lily Jameson to fall for me.

27

LILY

The retreat was going well. We'd gotten everyone settled into the trailers with their luggage and then offered a tour to anyone who wanted one. The entire group decided to come along. Even Drew. He'd mostly been avoiding me so far and that was just fine with me. As Chase pointed out all that Lucky Charm Ranch had to offer, I stayed off to the side with Nate and Evan to take in the reactions of our guests.

For the most part, they looked impressed. Some even looked excited. Only Drew and Steve looked bored, like they hadn't come here voluntarily. But I wasn't deterred by that. The real draw for these men had been the guided elk hunting that we were offering the next morning. Most of these men just wanted to take a picture with their kill so they could brag to their friends.

I wasn't someone who understood the point of hunting simply for bragging rights. It seemed like a strange way to prove the size of your dick, but whatever. They were paying us big money for the opportunity and we planned to donate any meat from the animals that wasn't used to feed the group over the next couple of nights.

Evan kept his promise to keep his hands to himself, but he stayed close to me as we walked everyone around the ranch. So did Nate. Having a large, strong cowboy on either side of me might have been why Drew kept as much distance between us as possible.

When the tour was over, I turned to them. "We're going to take the guests to the dining room for lunch now. You don't need to stick around for that."

"But what if I want to?" Evan asked with a playful smile. "What if I've got a crush on one of the tour guides and I want to stick around and flirt with her?"

"Sorry, Mr. Sullivan. She's taken." I let myself get lost in those blue eyes staring at me from under the brim of his hat. "And she's completely obsessed with her sexy cowboy."

"She better be." His fingers grazed the back of my hand. "We'll be back over tonight to help with dinner."

Chase and I had arranged for dinners to be made over the campfires every night. We wanted to create a luxury camping experience that just wouldn't be possible inside the dining room. Chase had volunteered Evan to cook up a large batch of his Sullivan-famous cowboy stew and I couldn't wait to try it. I knew it would be delicious.

"Thank you, Ev. I appreciate everything you and Nate are doing to help out."

"I'd do anything for you," he said easily, quickly squeezing my hand and then stepping back. He tipped his hat at me. "See you soon, sweetheart."

This man... he knew exactly how to turn me on. I wanted him inside me again so desperately that I had to clench my thighs together. Evan didn't miss that or the flash of desire in my eyes and he winked before walking away.

Lunch went very well. Marla had outdone herself with her culinary masterpieces, having her staff create customized meals for each guest. Chase and I sat at different tables to mingle and make sure everyone was having a good time. The men at my table were all friendly and polite. They asked a lot of questions about both Lucky Charm and the working ranch. It was nice to be able to brag about both Chase and Evan.

After lunch, everyone was given the option to go hiking or take a trail ride with our guides. The group split pretty evenly, with only Drew and another man choosing to stay back and work. We had a business center next to the dining room and I hoped Drew would stay in there while I was busy helping the staff clean the dining room.

"Lil."

My wish was not delivered. Drew had stayed behind to talk to me.

"What do you need?" I asked, trying to sound friendly and failing miserably.

"I was hoping we could talk." He rested his hands on the back of the chair across from where I was stacking plates.

"Unless it's about this trip, there's no need for us to talk to each other."

"Don't be like this, Lil."

"I'm busy." That wasn't a lie. I had a lot of work to do.

"Doing what? Bussing tables? Cleaning? Babe, what are you doing here?" Drew looked at me like I was doing something truly crazy.

I didn't miss how casually he'd dropped that term of endearment. He had hardly ever called me that when I was sleeping in his bed every night. "I'm working, Drew. Not that I owe you an explanation."

"I could've helped you find a new job in Denver. I *told* you I would set you up."

"I didn't want your help. I'm doing just fine on my own."

"Are you?" He gave me an exasperated look. "You are working on a ranch in the middle of nowhere. You are wearing jeans and cowboy boots." He said that the same way someone would tell you that you were wearing cow shit and mud.

"And she looks damn good in them." Chase must've noticed that Drew had decided to linger. He was supposed to be taking one of the groups out to the tour guide for their hike. "Did you need me to escort you somewhere, Drew?"

"Are you fucking this guy?" Drew asked, wrinkling his nose as he looked at Chase. "I guess you really did decide to slum it, Lil."

"Speak to her like that again and I'll throw your ass off

my ranch." Chase sounded exactly like Evan when he was pissed.

"Ah. I see." Drew straightened and laughed coldly. "Fucking the boss again, are we, babe?"

Chase made a move like he was going to hit Drew, but I grabbed his arm and yanked him back. "Leave it," I muttered. "Drew, go away. If you can't keep your shitty comments to yourself, I'll be happy to call you a ride back to the airport."

"Did you tell him everything about us?" Drew asked, eyes flashing with anger.

"Chase and I are coworkers. I never told him anything about you." I knew exactly why Drew was acting out. He was worried. Not about me, but about himself. He was worried that I had told people the full truth about what had happened between us.

"I don't believe you. You've always been a vengeful bitch."

I was still holding onto Chase's arm, but he wasn't the one I needed to be restraining. None of us had noticed that Evan had returned and he had Drew pinned to the wall before we could stop him.

"There are at least a dozen ways I could kill you and dispose of your body." Evan sounded lethally calm. "I think you probably have so many drugs in your system that no one would be surprised if you wandered off a trail and fell down a cliff."

"Fuck you." Drew didn't sound as confident as he had before Evan had arrived.

"Chase, call for his ride. Have the staff collect his

things. An emergency has come up that requires our guest to leave early." Evan gave him a hard push into the wall and then stepped back. Chase was quick to pull out his phone and follow Evan's instructions. "You'll wait right here until it's time to leave."

Drew rolled his shoulders and glared at me. "You told him, didn't you? I was wrong about the other guy. This is the one you're fucking."

"Don't talk to her." Evan was just barely holding onto his control.

"You shouldn't believe anything she tells you. Lily likes to play the victim. She set me up to lose my company, told lies about me to the board. She'll do the same thing to you." Drew looked right at Evan. "I hope you have a good legal team."

"Lil, why don't you go to the office? I'll join you once this prick is off the property." Evan spoke to me without turning away from Drew.

I didn't want to stay, but I was scared to leave Evan alone with Drew. He still looked like he was thinking about following through on that threat to kill Drew.

"I'll stay with them," Chase said quietly as he hung up his phone. "You should go."

I knew the guys weren't trying to make me feel bad by suggesting that I be the one to leave, but it felt like I had done something wrong. Like I was the one who couldn't be trusted.

They were in charge and if they wanted me to leave, I had to respect that. "I'll be in the office," I said, willing myself not to let emotion creep into my voice. I didn't want Drew to know just how much he had gotten to me.

The welcome lodge had cleared out except for a couple of remaining staff members who were mopping the floors. I walked past them with my head up and only let my first tears fall when I was safely behind the closed office door.

The wall that I had carefully constructed around me to keep out my old life was about to come crashing down.

28

EVAN

I wasn't sure how I hadn't killed Drew yet. I wasn't even supposed to be here for a few more hours, but my gut had told me that I should stop by and check on Lily. I'd arrived just in time to hear her asshole ex accuse her of fucking my brother before calling her a bitch. My vision had gone red and by the time he'd made another shitty comment about Lily, my anger had boiled over.

I wanted to do so much more than slam him into the wall. I wanted to drive my fist into his smug fucking face. I wanted to snap every one of his delicate fingers. If Chase hadn't been there, ready to stop me, I was sure that I would have inflicted the maximum amount of pain that I could short of killing him.

"You knew that Lily was here, didn't you?" I said after she'd left the room. When I had watched them that morning, Lily had been stunned to see Drew. He hadn't looked surprised at all. "You came all the way here just to fuck with her."

"No, I came to talk to her. She's been avoiding my calls and text messages. We have unresolved business." He scoffed as he looked at me. "Do you think she actually wanted to take a job on your ranch? A woman like that wants more than cow shit on her shoes and a roll in the hay. She's not here because she wants to be here. She's here because she is hiding." Drew laughed and smoothed the wrinkles from his shirt. "She's using you, cowboy. Just like how she used me."

"How did you find her?" I ignored his attempt to rile me up, focusing on the fact that this man had traveled hours to reach my home just to harass Lily.

"I run a successful tech company. Do you think it would be hard for me to track down someone?" Drew rolled his eyes. "Then again, a guy like you probably doesn't even know how to use your smartphone."

"Look, I don't give a fuck why you are here. I just want it to be clear that you are not welcome here. Not at the guest ranch and not at the main ranch. You are not welcome on any of my property." I widened my stance and crossed my arms, hoping that a more relaxed stance would keep me from pummeling him. "In fact, you need to lose Lily's number. Stop calling her, stop texting her. She's done with you, Drew. You lost the best thing that was ever going to happen to you. Lily is mine now."

"We'll see about that." Drew pulled his phone from his pocket. "If you'll excuse me, I need to arrange for my plane to be ready."

I walked to the other side of the room and Chase joined me. We kept our eyes on Drew while we talked.

"So that's Lily's ex, huh?" Chase said. "What the hell did she see in him?"

"She knew him before he became an entitled dick." Just like with Nate, I didn't feel right telling Chase the details that Lily had shared with me. "They went to college together before he started his company."

"How long did they date?" He kept his voice low even though Drew was busy yelling into his phone about making sure his plane had a fully stocked liquor bar.

"A few years I think." I didn't want to talk about Lily being with a man who wasn't me.

"You should go check on your girl. I can handle the loudmouth and escort him to his ride when it gets here."

"I don't know..." I did want to check on Lily, but I also felt the need to see Drew leave with my own two eyes.

"I'm not going to fuck this up," Chase promised. "Go."

I nodded and headed toward the office. Now that I was about to see Lily, I no longer gave a shit about not being the one to escort Drew off the property. I just wanted to give Lily a big hug and maybe finally admit to her that I loved her. That I had loved her for a while now.

I pushed open the door and felt like I had been punched in the stomach when I saw the tears streaking down Lily's face.

"Oh, sweetheart. Come here." I barely got my arms open before she'd buried herself against me. I wrapped one arm tight around her back and held my other hand to the back of her head. "Don't let that asshole upset you, Lil."

"I lied to you, Evan." She exhaled hard enough that I felt her warm breath through my shirt.

"Okay... About what?" The muscle in my jaw tightened.

Her fingers dug into my back. "It wasn't a lie, really. I just...didn't tell you everything."

"Spit it out then, city girl." I tugged lightly on her hair to lift her head from my chest.

"I'm not as done with Drew as I may have implied." She winced at my obvious flinch. "Not like that. There's an investigation. A couple of months after I was forced out of the company, I got a call from an FBI agent. They are investigating Drew for a laundry list of offenses. Apparently, he made a lot of false statements in the financial reports. At first, I thought the FBI was investigating me, too, but they quickly made it clear that the reports in question had never touched my desk. But the FBI is going to need me to work with the DOJ and potentially testify in court."

"Fuck." I didn't know what else to say, but I was more glad than ever that I'd gotten Lily away from that asshole.

"The FBI knew that I'd been involved with Drew and they thought I might know some details that could help their case. I didn't want to tell them what I knew because it would mean telling them about something that happened between us that I had never told anyone. That I never wanted anyone to know." She took in a shuddering breath.

"Rip off the Band-Aid, Lil." I was already running through a million scenarios in my head.

"I had broken things off with him about a month before the board forced me to resign. He didn't handle it well. He showed up at my house and he still had a key, so he let himself inside. He had been out at a club and was completely strung out on some drugs. But it wasn't the drugs he usually took that always made him sloppy. He was angry and he was violent." Her eyebrows pinched together and she stared at something over my shoulder. "He forced himself on me."

"Mother fucker." I turned away from her to storm right out of that office, intent on following through on my threat to kill Drew.

"Evan." The sound of Lily's voice cracking stopped me cold.

I clenched and unclenched my fists as I attempted to release some of the rage that had flooded my body. "Lily, I can't just let him walk away."

"You have to." She put a hand on my back. "Evan, I just told you something that I have never told anyone. I don't need you to go out there and punish Drew. I need you to be here with me."

My shoulders dropped and I turned back to her. "Of course. I'm here. I'm not going anywhere."

Lily stepped back and took a seat on the edge of the desk. "I know it's going to sound like I'm making excuses for him, but he had never been like that before. I truly believe the drugs exacerbated his anger, but I also know that he made the decision to take those drugs and come to my house when he knew he wasn't welcome there. I don't forgive him for what happened, but I also couldn't bring myself to report him. At the time, I just wanted to forget about it. I was still working for him and we were so close to the IPO. I was just trying to get to the finish line.

"He pulled me aside at work the next day and apologized. Said that he didn't remember most of what happened, but he knew that he'd gone too far. I asked him what drugs he took and he couldn't really remember that either. And then I asked him if he remembered the conversation we had after he..." She couldn't admit that Drew had raped her. For some reason, she couldn't say it out loud even though we both knew it was true.

"In his drug-fueled haze, Drew had gone on this rant about how he'd gone out of his way to protect me at work. That he kept me out of meetings so that I would have deniability. I had no idea what he was talking about at the time. I sort of thought he was talking about protecting me from having our relationship become public. But after the FBI agent called me, it all made sense."

"So he committed fraud to enhance the value of the company for the IPO? And the DOJ knows about it and is going to call you as a witness against him?" I was struggling to piece together everything she was telling me because I was still fighting the urge to hunt him down and kill him.

"And somehow Drew found out. He knows that he told me stuff that night when he came to my house, but he doesn't remember how much he told me. He doesn't know if he gave me enough rope to hang him."

A lot of things were suddenly making more sense. "That's why he calls and texts you. That's why he was so invested in tracking you down and showing up here."

"Yep." She nodded sadly. "Drew doesn't do anything unless it benefits himself. He probably hired a whole team of private investigators to hunt me down. When he found out I was helping host this retreat, it gave him a guaranteed opportunity to speak with me."

"Shouldn't we be calling the police? He can't intimidate you like this."

"He hasn't been charged with anything yet. The investigation isn't public and Drew isn't even supposed to know that I spoke with the FBI. He will easily deny that he showed up here to threaten me."

This was so much worse than if he'd just shown up trying to win her back. "Lily, that man is dangerous and now he knows how to find you."

"I'm going to call my contact at the DOJ. I know they are close to moving forward with charges and this might incentivize them to move faster. Or maybe there is something else they can do to legally prevent Drew from coming around me."

"I think you should move in with me. I don't want you in that cottage alone."

"I'm not moving in with you, Evan."

"Just for the next few days. Until we figure this out."

"He called for his plane. That means he's headed back to New York. We can pull up one of those flight trackers and make sure his plane leaves. No one else uses his plane, so if it's in the air, we'll know he left."

"He doesn't live in Denver?"

Lily shook her head. "Not anymore. He moved right before the IPO. He always had a place in New York because we had a second office out there. But with the way the business was shifting, he was spending most of his time out there so he finally decided to make the move."

"That makes me feel a little better, but you're not staying alone tonight. We can stay at your place if you prefer that, but I'm bringing over one of my guns."

"Whatever makes you sleep better, cowboy." Her playful demeanor was slowly returning.

"I really want to kill him for what he did to you, Lil." If I had known those details when Drew first stepped out of the van, no one would've been able to stop me from attacking him. Nothing made me more furious than men hurting women.

"I'm sorry that I didn't tell you everything before. It's hard for me to talk about." Her hands wrapped around the edge of the desk. "Drew used to be someone I trusted. One of my closest friends. I saw that man every single day for years and he had never done anything that made me fear him. That's why I have a hard time trusting people now."

"I get it." I would never fully understand what Drew's betrayal had done to her, but I understood why she had been reluctant to share the full story with me. "Are you sure you don't want to take the day off? We could go back to the cottage together. Or go riding again."

"I need to stay. For myself. I'm not letting Drew control me any longer."

I appreciated her determination, but I was uncomfortable with the thought of her wandering around the ranch on her own. "I want to stay with you," I said quietly, holding up a hand to cut off her protest. "I know you can take care of yourself and I know you don't want your boyfriend following you around while you work. I promise not to get in your way or make you feel smothered. I just... need to keep you close for today. Please."

I wasn't a man who begged to get what he wanted, but I would gladly prostrate myself before Lily to get her to agree with me. This whole thing with Drew had me on edge.

"Okay. You can stick around, but I'm putting you to work, Sullivan."

"Like you did earlier in this room?" I was impressed by how I almost made myself sound like I wasn't still inwardly panicking.

"Nice try." She pushed away from the desk and stepped in front of me. "I'm sorry you got pulled into my drama, Ev."

"I'm not." I hooked an arm around her shoulders and pulled her close enough that I could kiss her forehead. "You shouldn't have to deal with this alone, Lil. Nothing that happened was your fault. You trusted someone who didn't deserve your trust, but that's not on you."

She nodded and lightly touched my stomach. "We need to get back to work. Thanks for being here for me."

"There's nowhere else I'd rather be."

29

LILY

The rest of the retreat passed uneventfully. Everything went according to our plans and none of my ex-boyfriends showed up. The men seemed to really relax into ranch life when they returned from their hunt. Most of them had lost their fancy clothes for jeans and flannels and a group of them even asked Evan and Chase for shooting lessons the next day.

When it was time for them to leave Saturday morning, all of them had a lot of nice things to say and several mentioned wanting to come back with friends. They may not follow through, but I did think they would at least be complimentary about their time on the ranch.

The last van left just before noon and I could finally breathe a sigh of relief. We stood on the porch again, watching as the van turned onto the highway and accelerated away from the ranch. Chase gave me a firm side hug. "We did it, city girl."

"We did," I agreed, squeezing him around the waist.

"How should we celebrate?"

"I'm going to bed." I sighed at the thought of my comfy mattress waiting for me. We had all only gotten a few hours of sleep the last three nights.

Chase chuckled. "Alright then. Let's go."

"Try it and die," Evan growled.

"Come on. Someone has got to keep your girl satisfied while you're doing your fatherly duties." Chase apparently had a death wish.

Evan shoved him away and took his place at my side. His arm slipped around my waist so naturally that I couldn't believe we hadn't been doing this for years. "I don't have the twins until tomorrow afternoon."

"Nice. We're going drinking tonight." Chase pointed a finger at me. "Don't you dare try to get out of this. You have plenty of time to nap this afternoon."

"Why are you targeting me? I'm not the old man in this trio." I smiled teasingly at Evan. "This guy will want to be in bed by nine o'clock."

"Damn straight." Evan's pinky finger slid into the waistband of my jeans, softly caressing the skin over my hipbone. "Going to the Nest with you guys to get drunk is not nearly as appealing as a guaranteed good night with my girl."

I leaned into Evan, practically melting at how smoothly those two words rolled off his tongue. "Hate to break it to you, Ev, but your girl already promised Harper that she would go out with everyone tonight."

"Damn it." Evan held out his other hand. "Give me your phone."

"Why?"

"So I can block the numbers of every Sullivan who might try to steal you away from me on our last night together for the next week."

"You never did learn how to share." Chase clapped his hands once. "Time to get back to our regularly scheduled business. I have a guest ranch to run and the two of you need to get your orgasms out of your system so you'll be ready to party tonight."

I flinched slightly and avoided looking at Evan. We hadn't had sex at all for the last three nights. Both of us had worked long hours and we'd been exhausted when we finally went to bed, but I knew that wasn't why Evan had been cuddling me instead of fucking me. He kept a gun on my nightstand and insisted on sleeping on the side of the bed that was between me and the cottage door. His instinct to dive into protective mode was one of the reasons I hadn't wanted to tell him the full truth about Drew.

We ended up going back to Evan's place for lunch where he threw some burgers on the grill and we had a relaxing couple of hours just sitting and talking on his porch. I really had thought that I would be too exhausted to do anything other than sleep, but spending time with Evan was rejuvenating. I loved that we already had the kind of relationship where just sitting and talking with him was the highlight of my day.

"Can I ask you something, Ev?" I was unsure of the best way to broach this topic.

"Of course."

"Is there a reason why you haven't had sex with me since I told you about Drew?" I already suspected the reason, but I wanted to hear him say it.

"We've been busy, Lil. Late nights and early mornings. We both needed sleep."

I laughed. "Bullshit. You wouldn't turn down sex with me for a little more sleep. Tell me the truth, Evan."

"You weren't with anyone else between me and him, were you?" he asked abruptly.

"No."

"So the first time we... that was your first time since Drew assaulted you, wasn't it?"

I nodded. "It was. Does that bother you?"

"No. But if I had known, I would have done things differently. I wouldn't have been so demanding or aggressive."

"Stop. I wouldn't have wanted you to do things differently. Our first night together was perfect. I loved every minute of it." I put my hand on his forearm and squeezed. "What happened with Drew was terrible, but I'm not damaged because of it. I don't need you to treat me like I'm broken."

"I don't think you are broken, Lily. I think you are incredible. I think you've lived your whole life without anyone ever loving you the way you deserve to be loved." Those damn blue eyes of his saw right through me.

"That doesn't mean you can't manhandle me and talk

dirty to me. Especially when I'm begging you to do it."

"Good to know." He reached over and pushed back my hair. "I should've just talked to you about this three nights ago. I didn't want to upset you, but I was in my head worrying that you might be dealing with some trauma after seeing Drew. I thought maybe I would make that worse."

"Never." What had happened with Drew had never once crossed my mind when I was having sex with Evan. "Ev, when you and I are together, all I can think about is you. How much I want you. How good you make me feel. Honestly, that's pretty much all I can think about when we aren't together, too."

"Same, sweetheart." He leaned across the few inches between our chairs and cupped my cheek. "There's one other thing I can't stop thinking about."

"What's that?"

His lips formed an incandescent smile. "How much I love you, Lily."

"Oh." My initial instinct was to run away. No one had ever told me that they loved me besides my aunt. I had never said those three words to a man. But as the last couple of months flashed through my head, there was no denying that I had gradually fallen for the man in front of me. "I love you, too."

I had barely got the words out before he'd scooped me and was carrying me inside the house. We had been keeping our sexy times to the cottage and it was my first time in Evan's bedroom since the night I'd thrown up on him.

"Ah, lots of fond memories of this room," I joked when he put me on the bed.

"I detect sarcasm." Evan leaned down to kiss me. "But I'll never forget the sight of you in my shirt, in my bed. That was the night you became mine, Lily, even if you didn't know it yet."

"Enough of the sweet-talking, Ev. Get busy fucking me."

He let out a delighted laugh as he tugged my shirt over my head. "You always say the sweetest things to me, Lil."

"I had to watch you walking around in your sexy cowboy clothes for the last three days, doing all kinds of manly things, and then sleep next to you without a single orgasm every night. You've been torturing me and I can't take it anymore." I lifted my hips as he yanked down my pants and underwear together. I removed my bra and was then completely naked while he hadn't removed a single article of clothing.

"My apologies, miss." He yanked me by the hips until my ass was on the edge of the mattress. "I'm going to relieve you from that torture now. When you come, do you want my fingers inside you or my cock?"

"Your cock," I said instantly. I had been craving the feeling of him inside me for days. "And I want you bare this time, Ev. I'm clean and on the pill."

Evan paused, hands on my thighs. "I, uh, have honestly never done that. With anyone."

It made sense. After accidentally knocking up Naomi with twins even while wearing a condom, he had every reason to be extra cautious.

"Only if you want to. No pressure." I hoped I hadn't completely ruined the moment.

"Sweetheart, I'm not sure there's anything I could want more." Then he buried himself between my thighs in a flurry of lips, teeth, and tongue. He pulled my legs over his shoulders and latched hard over my clit, sending my back arching off the bed.

"Oh, god!" I slid a hand through his hair to pull his head even closer to my core.

Evan responded by slipping his tongue inside me. "Fuck, Lil. I can't get enough of you. I could eat your pussy for hours and never get sick of it."

"I won't stop you," I said through breathy panting.

"Except you already did, remember? You demanded my cock. Bare." He disentangled my legs from around his neck and stood. One hand ripped his shirt away while the other undid the button on his jeans. His hard length was begging to be set free. "Get on your knees and bend over, sweetheart."

I didn't have to be told twice. I knew that being penetrated from behind would allow Evan to drive as deep as possible into me, hitting me at just the right angle to send my orgasm into another world. I whimpered as I waited for him.

"Look at the fucking ass." He pressed a kiss to my right ass cheek while squeezing the other one. Then he grabbed both cheeks and spread them, baring me completely. His dick was already dripping his arousal when he slid it over my throbbing pussy. Without warning, he slammed into me and I let out a loud cry of pleasure. He felt so incredible moving inside me, nothing between our bodies except our own arousal.

"You feel so damn good, Lil." He slammed even harder into me, our thighs slapping in a steady, obscene rhythm.

One of his hands left my hips to reach in front of me, finding my clit with ease. The pressure he applied was timed perfectly to accelerate my orgasm and my whole body trembled as I clenched and pulsed around Evan's cock, his name leaving my lips in a breathless shout. He followed with his own release after one more thrust and I felt our combined arousals leaking out from where we were still joined.

I was a melted mess as Evan let me fall forward. "Look at you," he said hoarsely. One finger slowly traced where my body was still stretched taught around him. "Look at us. A perfect fit." His touch coaxed a few more aftershocks from my body and he groaned as I clenched around him. "Now who is the one doing the torture?"

"I just let you come inside me, cowboy. And I'll let you do it again as soon as you are ready. I'm not into torture, I'm into orgasms."

Evan bent forward, his warm chest resting on my back as he gathered my hair in his hand and I felt him hardening inside me. "Whatever my girl wants, my girl gets." He yanked my hair at the same time that he thrust deep into me and damn if my body wasn't ready for him. I would always be ready for him. Always want him. This was all I wanted. Me and Evan, together, giving ourselves to each other heart, body, and soul.

30

EVAN

I could've spent a week buried inside Lily and not grown bored. I loved discovering every tiny detail about her body and what turned her on. I loved hearing her moans and when she gasped my name. I loved everything about sex with Lily, except for the part where it had to end because my stupid siblings had insisted on meeting up at the Nest.

At least that gave us an excuse to shower together and afterward Lily sweetly asked if I would braid her hair. It was quickly becoming my second favorite way to make her happy.

"There is literally nothing you can't do with those hands," she said when I was done.

"You were going to look beautiful no matter what I did with your hair." I couldn't take any credit for the exquisite beauty standing before me. "We should cancel on my siblings."

"We can't." Lily laughed and patted my chest. "We had sex three times, Ev. We need to try doing something else for a couple of hours."

"Four times," I corrected.

"What, are you adding notches to your bedpost or something?" She fidgeted with one of the buttons on my shirt. "So... we didn't use condoms. You feel okay about that?"

I knew why she was asking. "Both of us are clean. You said you're on the pill. I trust you, Lily."

"I trust you, too." She tilted her head and smiled. "I love you."

Fuck if that wasn't the hottest thing she had ever said to me. I cursed out loud when her phone rang.

"Easy, cowboy." Lily's giggle was such a sweet sound. She checked the caller on the phone screen. "It's Harp."

I stepped away when she answered and perched against the wall. I liked finding moments like this where I could watch Lily doing mundane things, like talking to my sister on the phone while she poured coffee into a mug.

Seeing her move around in my kitchen so casually tugged at a desire I'd never thought I would have. A desire to make this a regular occurrence. To make my home *her* home.

"Yeah, we'll be there. Evan is so excited to get out of the house and see everyone." Lily flashed me a teasing smirk.

Challenge accepted, Lily Jameson. I pushed away from the wall and quickly invaded her personal space, backing her into the cabinets. Her eyes widened as I deftly yanked down her pants just enough to give my hand access to her already-wet pussy.

"Evan." She pressed the phone to her shoulder as I slid my hand through her wetness. "We can't..."

I just grinned and slid two fingers into her slick entrance. "It would be rude to ignore your phone," I said quietly, stroking her in an internal massage.

"Fuck," she breathed, bringing the phone back to her ear. "No, sorry. I'm here. Uh huh."

Her breathing was rapid and hard. I put my lips to her neck and sucked gently as she ground against my hand, chasing her pleasure. I sucked harder and she poked a finger between my ribs.

"No marks," she hissed at me.

I chose to ignore her, but I pulled the collar of her shirt down so that any marks I left wouldn't immediately be visible.

"Mhmm," she said into the phone. "Well, that's how... Harp, I need to let you go."

She was barely able to get words out without moaning as I continued pumping my fingers into her while using my thumb to circle her clit. "Yes. Yes." I couldn't tell any longer if she was talking to me or Harper.

"I promise. I'm coming!" She hung up just as her walls clenched around my fingers and she called out my name, head thrown back. "Oh fuck, Evan."

I trailed my lips up her neck and over her jaw, stopping at her ear. "You can come on *my* hand, *my* mouth, or *my* cock. Those are your options from now on, sweetheart."

"What about my own hand?" she teased, purposefully clenching around the fingers that were still inside her.

"Only if you're thinking about me while you touch yourself." I very slowly removed my fingers, trailing them up to her swollen clit and giving it a circling stroke. "I will be the last man to ever touch you like this. Understood?"

"Understood, cowboy."

"You're getting really good at riding me, city girl." I gave her pussy a gentle pat and then pulled her pants up. "Rode hard and put away wet." I winked at her and reached for the full cup of coffee she'd left on the counter. "Now, what did my sister have to say?"

Lily licked her lips and blinked a few times, chasing off the hazy afterglow of her orgasm. "Um, I honestly don't know. She was complaining about something that Ronan did and then everything went a little..."

"Yeah, sorry about that. I'll start working on my self-control." I wasn't really sorry. Getting Lily off was more enjoyable to me than just about anything else.

"We've got some time before we need to meet everyone." Lily hooked a finger through my belt loop. "Plenty of time for me to return the favor."

"Actually, let's leave now. I want to take you to dinner."

"Like a date? A date that's not in this house or my bed?" She grinned. "Evan Sullivan, you *like* me."

I rolled my eyes. "Duh."

"Duh?" She laughed and took the mug from me. "Do grown-ass cowboys say duh?"

"I just did." I pressed a soft kiss to her lips. "Finish your coffee. We need to leave soon if we're going to finish dinner before we're due at the Nest and my siblings send out a search party looking for us."

I turned away, but she called me back. "Hey, Ev?"

"Hm?" I smiled at her.

"You left a mark," she said, gesturing to the spot forming on her chest.

I shrugged. "It was only fair considering the mark you've left on my heart."

WE HAD a nice dinner at one of the fancier restaurants in town. It was nice to do something with Lily that didn't end with us getting dirty on the ranch or sweaty in bed. Lily told me some stories about different restaurants she'd visited while traveling for work and I liked hearing about her old life. She had led a much different life than me.

Aside from my four years away at college, I'd lived in Crestwood my whole life. I had rarely traveled outside of a few hundred miles from home. If things had been different and I hadn't had the kids, I might've been more interested in seeing the rest of the world. I was certainly interested in seeing the world through Lily's eyes.

"I always told myself that I would finally get my passport once the twins turn eighteen," I said as we shared a dessert after dinner. Lily had just finished telling me about an ill-fated trip to Italy where it rained for five days straight.

"You should get it now. Get the twins set up with one,

too, and plan a trip. They are old enough to travel without much trouble."

"Fine, but only if you come with us." I pushed the last bite of cake toward her. "That's all yours."

"You spoil me." She put the fork in her mouth and damn if I wasn't jealous of a fucking eating utensil. "Evan, I hope you know that I don't want to leave. Not Crestwood and not you. I'm happy here."

"Good. I'd do anything to make you happy, Lil."

Her eyes narrowed. "You don't need to do anything to make me happy. Just being with you makes me happy. I know you have spent most of your life feeling responsible for everyone around you, but that's not how I want our relationship to work. It's not going to be you just taking care of me all the time."

"I don't mind taking care of you." I shifted in my seat.

"I know you don't. I love how caring you are and I would never ask you to stop being that way. I'm just saying that sometimes I'm going to take care of you, too."

"You already do, Lil." I leaned back in my chair and smirked. "Who knows, maybe I'll get really drunk tonight and you can hold my hair back while I throw up in your toilet."

"I'll even braid your hair," she said, sporting one of her adorable smiles. "But I probably won't be carrying you to bed."

The waitress arrived with our check and I dodged Lily's attempts to snatch it from me. "We *just* talked about this. Let me take care of you by paying for your meal."

"Fine." She pouted slightly. "I will put away my independent woman card."

"Keep it handy. I have a thing for independent women." I took care of the bill and then we headed down the street to the Nest. One of the advantages of living in a smaller town was that a lot of things were in close proximity and it was only a quick walk to any place downtown. We had only made it a few feet down the sidewalk when Lily's phone rang.

"It's probably Harper making sure that we're not bailing." She checked the screen and frowned, her steps faltering. "I need to take this."

"Okay." Based on her reaction, I was worried that it was Drew calling. But I didn't think she would answer a call from him.

"This is Lily," she said as her greeting. Her brow furrowed as she listened, but the rest of her reaction was unreadable. "I understand. Is there anything else you'll need from me?" She listened again, nodding slightly. "Okay. Thank you for letting me know. Bye."

She ended the call and looked at the phone for a moment before drawing her gaze to me. "That was my contact at the FBI. Drew is dead."

31

LILY

Evan reacted to the news exactly the way I expected him to react. He first offered me a hug, but I declined. Then he suggested we go home, but I told him there was no need. I was fine. In fact, I could use a drink or five. I could use a night out with friends to take my mind off things.

The FBI agent had told me that Drew's death looked like a suicide. They had been planning to arrest him the next day and he'd somehow found out. I guess he had decided that death was a better option than twenty-plus years in prison. Whatever the case, I almost couldn't help but feel relieved. My nightmare of dealing with the mess he had made was over. I no longer had to worry that he was going to pop up when I least expected him.

And yet some part of me still grieved. Drew and I had started as friends. Good friends. We had stayed up late studying in college and attended football tailgate parties together. We had built a business as colleagues and helped people grow their careers. Some part of us had once loved one another, even if we'd never admitted it.

Evan could tell that I was processing a lot of emotions at once and I knew he didn't think that going out was the best idea. He didn't try to convince me to go home, though. Instead, he bought the first round of drinks at the bar and when we had finished those, he bought the second. Then, he grabbed my hand and took me to the dance floor.

We two-stepped and slow-danced song after song. Chase and Nate each cut in and took me for a spin, but Evan was always quick to hurry them away after one song.

"Can't have anyone getting the idea that you aren't my girl," he said when I asked why he was being so attentive.

It was sweet, if not a little annoying. But I knew that he was only looking out for me because he knew I was trying to distract myself from the news about Drew. I had begged Evan not to tell his siblings yet. I didn't want anyone acting weird around me when we were supposed to be cutting loose and having fun.

"I need to pee. Are you planning to follow me into the bathroom, too?"

"If that's what you're into," he joked.

I pressed a kiss to his cheek. "I'll be right back. Could you grab me a water from the bar?"

"Of course." He was a little reluctant to remove his arms from around my waist. I understood because I was also a little reluctant to leave his arms.

There was a line to use the bathroom and I bounced

impatiently in my boots while I waited. A few women were at the sinks, fixing their hair and checking their makeup. I caught them studying me in the reflection of the mirror before exchanging wordless glances with each other.

Even in my newly acquired Levi's and boots, I didn't fit in with those women. I still stood out as an outsider and I probably always would. They had all gone to school together and been friends for years. When they looked at me, they saw the city girl who was dating one of the locals. Probably one they had all hoped to date.

I did my business as quickly as possible while avoiding eye contact with anyone. When I returned to the main room, I couldn't find Evan. The Nest was busier than usual and the crowd was oppressive. I finally made my way to the bar and tried to flag down the bartender.

"Want some help?" A large hand pressed against my lower back. I didn't have to turn around to know that the hand didn't belong to Evan.

"No thanks," I said, gritting my teeth. I hated it when strangers felt the need to touch me.

"Come on, sweetheart. Let me buy you a drink." The hand slipped down my back until it grazed my ass. I jerked away and whirled, fully prepared to tell him off.

"Touch her again, Sawyer, and I'll break every finger on that hand." Evan stepped smoothly in front of me.

"Fuck. Relax, Sullivan." Sawyer took a step back. "I was just offering to buy the girl a drink."

Evan's glare was menacing. "And then slip something

into it and try to take advantage of her like you did with my sister?"

"That never happened." Sawyer was a terrible liar.

"If you don't walk away right now, I'll drag you out of this bar myself." Evan was eyeing Sawyer with almost as much hostility as he had directed at Drew on the ranch.

"You're being as dramatic as your sister." The man had zero self-preservation skills. He did at least have enough sense to turn and walk away.

"Friend of yours?" I joked, running a hand down his arm to pull his attention back to me. The muscles beneath my hand were tense.

"He's been staring at you all night." Evan was frowning when he turned to me. "He saw you with me and still thought he could grab your ass."

I smiled a little at his obvious jealousy. "Ev, he was doing all that just to fuck with you. That guy didn't care about me or my ass. He wanted to piss you off."

"Sweetheart, every man in this bar has been looking at your ass. You are not just a pawn in some stupid game, Lily. You're the whole damn prize."

Ugh. This man. He really was perfect. "You are so getting lucky tonight, Sullivan."

"I got lucky the minute you stepped foot on my ranch, Lil." He squeezed my shoulder and pressed a kiss to my temple. "Now, let me get you that water."

When he turned toward the bar, my gaze landed on a stunning woman sitting at the opposite end of the bar. She was facing out into the crowd and wore an impressive scowl. The cocktail she was holding stood out in a place that was known for its beer and hard liquor. I followed her hostile glare through the crowd and landed on a familiar broad back. Chase.

"Huh."

Evan turned to hand me a glass of water, a beer in his other hand. "What?"

"Your brother has an admirer." I nodded toward the woman.

"Admirer?" Evan chuckled dryly. "Hardly. That's Riley Parker and she absolutely hates my brother. I didn't know she was back in town."

"What's their story?"

He shook his head. "It's a long one and it's not my story to tell."

"Should we be warning Chase that this woman is here?"

"Nah. I'm hoping she might throw that pink monstrosity of a drink in his face."

I thought he was joking, but then Chase turned around as if he felt the imaginary daggers being thrown at his back. He stared right at Riley, the pain in his eyes overwhelming. In a crowded bar, it felt like I was watching an intensely intimate exchange. When Chase didn't back down from the scorching glare, Riley downed her drink in a big gulp and slammed her empty glass on the bar hard enough that I worried it was going to shatter. It didn't, and Riley shot off her bar stool and headed straight for the door. It was swinging shut behind her when Chase said something to Nate and then headed after her.

"That's going to be interesting," Evan said. "Those two are like fire and ice."

"Did they date or something?"

"No. Chase used to date Riley's best friend." That was apparently all he was going to say because he took a long pull from his beer bottle. "Will you be ready to go home soon?"

I was smitten by the way he asked so casually, like we had left parties to go home together all the time. Like we shared a home. "I'm going to need another slow dance first, cowboy."

"You can have as many slow dances as you want." His fingers grazed my neck as he brushed my hair over my shoulder. "From now on, all my dances are yours."

We ended up staying for another hour because once I got my arms around Evan, I didn't want to let go. Evan was happy to give in to my dancing demands even though he had stopped drinking so he could be our sober driver. I should've followed his lead because the additional drinks I had were enough to have me stumbling as we walked to Evan's truck. Once we were on the highway, the steady thrum of the wheels on the asphalt and the heat blowing from the vents quickly lulled me to sleep.

Evan didn't even bother waking me when we got home. He carried me from the truck right inside his house and placed me on his bed.

"Do you want me to help you change out of these clothes?" he asked, already tugging off my boots.

"Strip me, Boss!" I demanded happily.

"Don't say it like that," he said with a groan. "I'm only

trying to help you get ready for bed. This is not a sexual strip, city girl."

It took three attempts, but I finally managed to strip off my shirt. "Are you telling me you aren't turned on right now?"

His eyes flitted over my chest and I was surprised not to see the usual flicker of desire in them. His jaw locked tight as he went over to his closet. I finished taking off my socks and pants and waited on the mattress dressed in just my underwear.

Evan came back holding one of his flannels. "Here." He held it out without any attempt to touch me. "I need to take care of a couple of things before coming to bed."

"Oh. Okay." I hugged the soft fabric to my chest. "Is everything alright?"

"Yeah." His smile wasn't believable. "Everything is great. Go ahead and lie down. I'll be back in a little bit."

I watched him walk away and tried to remember if I had said anything that had caused his abrupt emotional shift. I lifted his shirt and took a deep whiff of the pine scent that was so very Evan. As I put my arms through the sleeves and tugged it around my shoulders, I glanced down at my body and gasped. I was covered in small bruises. Bruises on my hips from where Evan's hands had gripped me. Bruises on my thighs from him attempting to restrain me as I had bucked wildly against his face. And the larger bruise on my chest from where he had intentionally marked me.

Only that one mark had been intentional and the others had just been an inevitable result of vigorous sexual activity. None of them hurt and I hadn't even know they were there until just now. I doubted that Evan had known he left them until he saw them. At least now I knew why Evan had shut down so abruptly once I took off my shirt.

I waited for him to return, tucking myself under the warmth of his bedding and further surrounding myself with his intoxicating scent. I wouldn't let myself lie down even though I was exhausted. Evan and I needed to talk.

He didn't come to bed until almost an hour later. When he stepped into the room and saw me still awake, sitting against the headboard, we exchanged a look that said exactly how we were both feeling.

"I'm sorry," Evan said.

"You don't need to be sorry." I put a hand on the space next to me. "Sit with me. We need to talk about this."

Evan nodded and quickly stripped off his clothes down to his boxer briefs, his usual sleep attire when he wasn't passing out naked after sex. The mattress shifted as he settled his sturdy frame into the space next to me.

"You're okay?" he asked softly.

"I was until you took one look at my naked body and ran away."

"Lil." He put a warm hand on my thigh. "That's not what happened. I just saw that mark I left on you and it surprised me. And then I saw what I did to your hips and thighs. It looks like I..." His voice broke off.

"You didn't hurt me," I said. "I know what it looks like, but it was just good sex. I enjoyed everything you did to me, Evan."

"You'd tell me if I ever did anything that hurt you, right?"

I nodded. "Of course. But you didn't hurt me."

"I got too carried away. I always do with you. It's like I have no self-control." His thumb stroked a slow circle over my skin. "But if you ever tell me to stop, I will. No matter what."

"I know that." I looked at him in confusion. "Where is this coming from? Have I done anything to make you think that I don't trust you? Or that I'm scared of you?"

"No. I'm just...in my own head."

He was holding something back. I thought about how he had reacted when I'd told him about what Drew had done to me. That pure rage at the thought of another man hurting me. Afterward, he had been so hesitant with me, worried that I was still processing the trauma of that night.

I moved quickly, throwing a leg over Evan until I was straddling him. I locked my arms around his neck. "You are not him, Evan. You didn't hurt me and I know that you never will. You are a good man and I love you."

"You could do better than me, Lil." An inexplicable sadness filled his eyes. "You deserve the world and all I can give you is this ranch."

"I've seen a lot of the world and I will take you and this ranch any day." I leaned close enough that our noses brushed. "You are the most impressive thing in my life, Evan Sullivan."

32

EVAN

"Explain to me again why we are here." I followed Lily down the ridiculously clean aisle between the stalls in Rick's stable. It was rare for me to visit this place and it was even rarer for me to be here when my uncle wasn't present.

"I've been checking through some records and I need to verify something," Lily said vaguely. She had been stopping in front of each stall and checking the horses' names against the list in her hand. "Rick buys a lot of thoroughbreds. He sells some, but I would expect more growth than what we've actually seen."

"You've lost me, sweetheart." I couldn't even pretend that my brain could keep up with Lily's insane genius.

"This stable was built about ten years ago. Rick paid for some upgrades last year, but that was mostly for a newer temperature-controlled system. The stable wasn't expanded in any way. No new square footage, no new stalls. But Rick has acquired a dozen new horses in just the last two years. He has sold seven horses. A couple died. Every stall holds one horse." She made her way to the next stall. "It was already at capacity two years ago. So where are those extra three horses?"

I shrugged. "We have lots of stables. Maybe he is boarding them offsite."

"No. I asked him about that during our first meeting. The only horses that are offsite are ones that are being transported for races, but they would still have an empty stall here." She tapped her chin with the pen. "I've never seen these horses mentioned anywhere except in the insurance paperwork."

"There would be more records. Veterinary records. Procedures have to be followed to get a racehorse insured." I had never dealt with those logistics myself, but I knew they existed.

"Rick cashed in two insurance policies last year. One horse was injured during a practice run. Another got sick." She studied the list in front of her. "One policy was for one million and the other was for two and a half million."

"Those aren't outrageous numbers. The most promising horses can be insured for five million."

"Rick has his own personal vet. It wouldn't be hard for him to forge documents and create a horse that never existed. Then he could wait a couple of years and fake a death. Cash in the policies and make a nice little profit."

I stared blankly at her. What she was saying sounded crazy. Rick's stable already produced a lot of successful thoroughbreds and he ran a profitable breeding business. It would be a dangerous risk to put his whole business in jeopardy to cash in a few million.

"He can make that much breeding one thoroughbred stud for a couple of years," I argued. "Why would he risk everything he has built?"

"Because Rick has a gambling problem. He approached Tom about a year ago and asked for a personal loan to cover his losses. Tom refused. He started to become suspicious about what his brother was doing to recoup the losses on his own and noticed that some of the numbers in the financials weren't adding up." The words were coming out fast, nearly tripping on one another as Lily began pacing. "Then Tom started looking at the rest of the financial records and he noticed more inconsistencies. Someone has been skimming money. Mostly small amounts at a time. A few hundred here and there. But on top of Tom's suspicions about Rick, he knew he had to look into it more seriously."

"That's when he decided to hire you," I said, shaking my head in disbelief. My father had been lying from the beginning. When I'd pressed him on why he thought we needed to bring an outsider into our family business, he had kept the truth from me. So had Lily. "You've been investigating all of us."

"No!" She stopped pacing and whirled. "Evan, no. It was never like that. Tom never thought that any of his sons were involved. He trusts you. I was never investigating you or Chase."

"Except you spent days following me around the

ranch. Learning every detail of my job." I pinched the bridge of my nose. "You've been lying to me this whole time."

"Tom asked me not to say anything. He was afraid that he was wrong and my presence here would upset everyone for no reason."

"That's why you lied when you got here. But you kept lying to me even after you knew that Dad was right. Did you disagree with him and think that I was the one stealing from the business?"

"Never. I never thought that." She stepped forward and tried to grab my hand but I jerked it away from her. "Evan, I know it wasn't you. I didn't tell you because..." Her eyes filled with tears. "Because telling you that I was hired for this investigation would mean that I would also have to tell you that I'd only been hired temporarily. That I would be leaving once all this was resolved. And I didn't want to admit that to you. Not when I had all these feelings for you and we were still figuring things out."

"So why are you telling me now? Now that you know I'm in love with you? Why did you think that now would be a good time to tell me that you aren't planning to stay?"

"I told you now *because* I'm in love with you. I didn't want to keep lying to you. I hated lying to you." One tear snaked down her cheek.

"You let me fall in love with you even though you knew you weren't going to stay. Even though I told you that I was looking for a real commitment and not a fling. Damn it, Lily." I shoved my hand through my hair and tugged. "How the hell am I supposed to give you up now?"

"You're not. I'm not leaving." This time when she reached for my hand, I let her take it. "When the investigation is over, I'm not going to leave. If I need to move out of the cottage, fine. I'll find someplace else to live. I'll find a different job that I can do from Crestwood or I'll take some time off. I'll do whatever I need to do to still be in your life, Evan."

"I can't ask you to do that."

"You're not asking me. I'm telling you what I'm going to do. Unless you ask me to leave, I'm not going anywhere."

"Why did you bring me here today?" I had thought it was strange when Lily told me she was visiting Rick's ranch and I had been even more confused when she asked me to come with her. But I had done it without question because it was Lily and I would do almost anything for her.

"Because I wanted to tell you everything. Tom invited Rick to a meeting this morning and then they are going to the main house for lunch. Tom is going to keep Rick there until I can get back. I wanted to do one last check to make sure I hadn't missed anything before we confronted Rick. But I didn't want to do that until I talked to you. Tom doesn't know I'm telling you."

"And what am I supposed to do with this information?"

"Help me." Lily had perfected the art of begging. "Tom and I are going to confront Rick. It would be good to have you there."

"In case he turns violent?"

"It's a possibility," she said with a shrug. "But that's not why I want you there. This is going to be hard for Tom. He didn't want to be right about this. He knows that once he tells Rick what we've been doing, he's going to lose his brother. Tom could use your support, Evan. So could I."

"You're expected there now?" I was still angry that I'd been lied to by two of the people I loved most.

"Yes."

"Then we should go."

Lily looked at where her hand was still wrapped around mine. "I'm sorry I lied to you. When I agreed to stick with Tom's story about why I was here, I didn't know I was going to fall in love with you."

"I know." It was obvious that she felt bad for lying, but that didn't make me feel better about the situation. "We can talk about this later."

She nodded and pulled her hand away. "I'm going to hold you to that, Evan. Because I'm not letting you give up on me."

"Good." I wanted to tell her that I forgave her, but I wasn't there yet. "I love you, Lily. We'll get through this."

Dad had taken Rick into his office after lunch and that's where we found them, sitting in awkward silence.

"Lily." Dad shot to his feet. "You brought Evan."

"I did." She offered no apology. "He's aware of why we are meeting."

Dad's jaw clenched and he looked at me as if he wanted to ask me to leave. "I know, Dad," I said softly.

"Know what?" Rick stood and I instinctively moved in front of Lily. My uncle already didn't like her and this meeting was only going to give him more reason to lash out at her.

"Rick, you asked me earlier why Lily was at your ranch. She was there because I sent her. She was looking for proof that you've been embezzling money from the business and committing insurance fraud to pay off your gambling debts."

Rick's broad shoulders pulled back and his nostrils flared. "That's a lie. Whatever that bitch told you is complete bullshit."

"It's not. I'm the one who suspected you first, Rick. I noticed the inconsistencies in the financials and brought in Lily to help me confirm my suspicions. She talked to your trainers. To your vet. Compared the horse insurance forms to the horses actually being boarded at the stable. The numbers don't add up, Rick."

I watched his eyes bounce around as he formulated his next move. He could keep lying, but Lily had the proof. He could get angry, but that wouldn't change the truth. Rick decided to resort to the only option that might actually work. Playing into my father's family loyalty.

"I tried to do things differently," he said. "I came to you for help a year ago and you turned me away. I had to do something or we would've lost our thoroughbred business. Our entire family business would've taken a hit."

"You started forging false documents years ago," Lily said. She was standing next to me now, uncowed by Rick's angry glare. "You put together this plan long before you spoke with Tom."

"Stay out of this, girl." Rick jabbed a meaty finger at

her. "This is family business and you are nothing more than a pretty bed warmer."

Before I could react, Dad was in front of Rick. "I will not stand by and listen to you attack that woman. She is here because I asked her to help me do the hardest thing I've ever had to do. Prove that you are exactly the piece of shit everyone has always said you were."

"You're going to believe that woman over me? I shouldn't be surprised. You let Penny convince you to push me off the ranch years ago. Then I finally started to build something of my own and now you're letting your son's girlfriend push me out of the business completely. You're just like our father, putting a piece of ass before your family."

It was clear now why Lily had wanted me here. Rick was going to do everything he could to retaliate against my dad. Decades of hurt and anger were boiling over for both of them. Rick was goading him to lose his temper. If Dad hit Rick, he would have leverage to hold over Dad and keep him from reporting the insurance fraud.

"Dad." I put a hand on his shoulder.

"Rick, I suggest you leave my house now and go call your lawyer. You're going to need the best one that money can buy." Dad took a step back, but he kept himself between Rick and Lily. "I've already reported your actions to the authorities."

"Fuck you, Tom. You always said that family comes first, but you never saw me as your family. You treated me like shit your whole life."

Dad sighed loudly. "I'm sorry you feel that way."

Rick wasn't done with his hateful comments. He directed his next words at me. "I tried to warn you. A woman like that would never be with a man like you unless she had an ulterior motive. She's a bitch just like your mother."

"Damn right I am," Lily said. "I called your bookie and gave him a heads up that you might be going to prison for a while and he won't be able to collect what you owe him. Who do you think will find you first– him or the police? Prison is going to be pretty miserable with a couple of broken kneecaps."

I just barely repressed a smile. Lily would never wilt after being called a bitch and I loved that she was proud to have been compared to my mother. Mom would've loved her tenacity and utter ruthlessness.

Rick failed to hide the panic that flashed in his eyes before he turned away and stormed out of the room. A moment later, the front door slammed shut.

"Damn, Lil. Remind me not to piss you off," I said.

"Rick was right about one thing. You're just like Penny. She never could stand Rick's bullshit." Dad was still staring at the doorway where Rick had exited.

"Did you really call his bookie?" I asked.

Lily nodded. "Yeah, but just to pay him off."

"I sold one of the thoroughbreds. It covered Rick's debt. We don't need to be worrying about any retaliation on top of the legal shitstorm we're going to face with the upcoming litigation against Rick." Dad went over to a bookshelf and grabbed a bottle of scotch. He started pouring it into a glass. "I'm sorry Rick spoke about you that way, Lily. You didn't deserve any of that."

"I'm sorry your brother betrayed you, Tom. You didn't deserve that." Lily was keeping her focus on Dad, avoiding looking at me. "I have some final loose ends to tie up on the investigation. And the two of you should talk."

"You don't have to go," I said.

"I think I do." She finally looked at me and smiled sadly. "If you want to talk later, you know where to find me."

And then there were two.

Dad reached for a second glass and poured in an inch before handing it to me. "You're mad that we lied to you," he said.

"Yes."

"Don't be mad at Lily. The lie was my idea. The fewer people we told, the better chance we had of Rick not figuring out that we were investigating him."

"Are you sure that's why? You never considered for a second that it might be me or Chase embezzling money?"

"No. I never thought that." Dad looked at me the same way he had when I was a kid and I'd asked him if he was disappointed in me because I had failed a test in school. "You are my son and I know you better than anyone. You're an honorable man and the heart of our family. We would've fallen apart when your mom died, but you kept us together, Evan. I can never thank you enough for everything that you have done for this family."

"You don't have to thank me, Dad." I took a swallow of scotch to wash down the emotion lodging in my throat.

"Not anymore. I think my debt is paid since I'm the one who brought Lily Jameson into your life." Dad winked at me. "Try not to be too upset that she went along with my lie. She obviously cares about you and would never intentionally hurt you."

"I know." Most of my anger was gone already. "She really does remind me of Mom sometimes."

Dad nodded with a wistful smile. "Your mom would've loved Lily. Just like the rest of us."

"She'll be out of a job now," I said, swirling the scotch. "There will be nothing keeping her in Crestwood."

Dad laughed hoarsely. "You're wrong about that, son. That woman isn't going anywhere."

33

LILY

Later that afternoon, I answered my door expecting to find Evan on my porch. Instead, Emma smiled nervously at me. "Are you busy?"

"No. You want to come in?" I glanced toward Evan's house but saw nothing except his truck. "Does your dad know you're here?"

"Yeah. I told him I needed some fashion advice." She rolled her eyes. "He's pathetic with that kind of stuff."

I wasn't sure I agreed given how much I liked what he wore every day, but I stepped back to let her in. "Fashion advice for what?"

"Oh. That was a lie." She grinned sheepishly. "I need some help and I didn't want to ask Dad. He would've been so embarrassing about it."

"Help with what?" I wasn't sure I was qualified to help a twelve-year-old with anything.

"I got my period about twenty minutes ago. It's my first

one. Mom keeps stuff ready at her house, but I doubt Dad is stocked up on pads and tampons. Can you hook me up?" Her cheeks turned pink.

"Of course. Come on. I'll show you where I keep everything." I took her into the bathroom and made sure she understood the logistics of how to use things before giving her some privacy. When she was done, I put together a little kit for her to take home with her.

"Did you tell your mom yet?" I asked.

"I texted her, but she's busy working. She's a nurse and she works long hours." Emma was curled up on the couch in a t-shirt sporting her favorite singer, drinking from a mug that I'd filled with hot tea.

"Did you have any questions about anything? I don't mean to brag, but I'm an eighteen-year veteran of the Menstrual Wars. I'm kind of an expert."

Emma laughed. "No, most of my friends have already had theirs so I knew what to expect."

"You really didn't think you could tell your dad?" If there was one thing I knew about Evan, he wasn't squeamish or easily embarrassed.

"If I had to, I know I could. But he's a guy. They don't understand what it's like." Her eyes narrowed. "Which is such bullshit, by the way. Men get off so easy in the reproductive area of life."

"Welcome to being a woman." I reached for one of the cookies I'd placed on the coffee table. "But at least we have a monthly excuse to eat chocolate."

"Excellent point."

"You should consider telling your dad. I think he

would want to know so he can support you. Make sure you have what you need at his house. I don't think he'll be embarrassing about it at all." I felt the need to advocate for Evan. He took so much pride in being a good father that he would probably be hurt if he knew that Emma hadn't felt comfortable talking to him about this.

"I'll consider it," Emma said quietly.

It was time to change the subject. Emma and I talked about school and her friends. I found out that her favorite singer, Madi Lee, was performing in Denver next month and I offered to get her tickets. One of my friends from law school worked as her agent. When I was just about to send Emma home for dinner, Evan showed up.

"Do I have to leave?" Emma asked with a bit of a whine. "We're having fun."

"I see that." Evan eyed the junk food we'd been eating and the way we were snuggled on the couch in front of a warm fire. "Hope you saved some room for dinner."

"Stop being lame and have a cookie," I said, holding the plate in front of him.

He narrowed his eyes at me. "Lame?"

"You're acting like a total dad," I added with a taunting smile.

Emma giggled and leaned her head on my shoulder. "She's not wrong."

"I see what's happening here." Evan snatched a cookie and gestured to us. "You're ganging up on me."

"Women have to stick together," I said unapologetically.

"In that case, do you want to join us for dinner?" Evan asked.

"Yes! Please?" Emma chimed in.

I blinked a few times, stunned by the invitation. Evan and I had been purposefully avoiding spending time together with just the kids. "I..."

"Please?" Evan added, lips tilting into the sweetest smile.

I was never going to be able to say no to that smile. "Okay."

"Yes!" Emma threw her arms around me. "Maybe now we won't have to talk about stupid boy stuff over dinner."

"Stupid boy stuff?" Evan put a hand over his heart. "You always like talking about that stuff."

"Because I don't have a choice." She rolled her eyes and threw back the blanket that we were sharing. She was walking toward the door when she stopped and turned back. "By the way, I got my period today. That's why I came to Lily's place."

"Oh." Evan stared at her for a moment, processing her words. "You should have told me. I've got supplies for you under the sink in the bathroom. Whatever you need."

"Oh." She looked back at him with the same bewildered expression. "I didn't think you'd be prepared."

"I'm your dad, kiddo. I've got your back. Always." He smiled at her in a way that made my whole uterus clench. The love he had for his daughter was so pure. "If I missed anything, just tell me and I'll pick it up next time I'm downtown."

"Okay. Thanks, Dad." Then she glanced at me. "You were right."

"I'm always right," I joked.

Emma left the cottage and Evan stayed back with me. He took his daughter's place on the couch. "Was she embarrassed to tell me?" he asked warily.

"Maybe a little bit. I think she mostly just didn't want to tell you because she knew you would feel bad that you weren't prepared to help her. But she was obviously wrong about that." I moved closer to kiss his cheek. "You are a good dad, Evan. She's a lucky girl to have you in her life."

"It's not a big deal. I also keep a ton of extra toilet paper on hand for my son who seems to use an entire roll every time he uses the toilet." Evan rolled his eyes. "People act like it's a big deal for dads to buy tampons for their daughters but no one talks about the utter humiliation of finding your teenage son's crusty socks under his bed."

"Oh god," I said, laughing. "Parenthood sounds amazing."

"I, um... we've never really talked about that. About whether that's something you want." He fidgeted with the frayed edge of the blanket. "It's not really negotiable for me. I have two kids and that's not going to change."

"Obviously. I love that you love your kids, Ev. They are important to you and that makes them important to me."

"But what about kids of your own? Is that something you want?" He draped his arm over the back of the couch and stroked my shoulder with two fingertips.

I was not expecting to have this conversation right now. It wasn't something I would normally discuss so early in a relationship, but I understood why Evan was asking. He was already a parent and had spent twelve years raising kids. He was in his late thirties.

"I've never wanted to have kids," I said, watching carefully for his reaction. "I like kids and I love being around the twins, but I've never wanted to have my own kids."

Evan just stared at me.

"Is that a problem?" I asked nervously. "Do you want more kids?"

"It's not a problem." He let out a hard breath. "It's a relief. I don't want more kids. I love the two I have and wouldn't trade them for anything in the world, but I'm twelve years into raising them and I'm not looking to start over. I know you're a lot younger than me, so I thought it might be something you wanted."

"It's not." I had only grown more certain of that fact over the years. "I wouldn't mind being a hot stepmom in the future, though."

Evan's laugh was so damn sexy. "I'm going to take you up on that offer, sweetheart."

WE HAD our first family dinner at Evan's house. The twins set the table and I helped Evan carry the food from the kitchen. Emma was grinning wildly as she watched me settle into the seat across from her dad.

"You knew where to find the silverware," she said.

"I did..." I suspected I was about to walk into a trap. "And?"

"And the glasses. And the serving spoons." She stabbed a carrot with her fork. "You've been in our kitchen before."

I looked to Evan for help but he just smiled and shrugged. "Your dad has invited me over for dinner when you are with your mom."

"Mhmm." Emma exchanged a look with Tommy.

"Dinner," he said, rolling his eyes. "Yeah right."

"Careful, kid," Evan cautioned him without much effort.

"Are you dating my dad?" Emma asked bluntly. "Do you sleep over when we aren't here?"

Evan choked on the sip of water he'd just taken and thumped a hand to his chest. "Em, that's not an appropriate question to ask."

"Why not?"

"Because you don't like it when your uncles interrogate you about boys, do you?" he asked pointedly and she nodded. "Same thing."

I kept my concentration on eating my food as fast as possible so I could make up an excuse and leave before Emma could ask more prying questions.

"She comes to Sunday dinners," Tommy said. "Only family comes to those."

I looked up and found Evan looking right back at me. "Lily and I are dating, yes. I like her a lot and she makes me happy. Is that going to be a problem for either of you?"

"Nope," Tommy said around a mouthful of food.

"Em?" Evan raised an eyebrow.

"No, Dad. We like her, too." She smirked. "And you

guys are terrible at keeping secrets. I saw your shirts in Lily's cottage."

Oh fuck. I hadn't even thought about hiding any traces of Evan when Emma had dropped by. *Sorry,* I mouthed to Evan. He shrugged.

"Maybe we didn't want to keep it a secret any longer," he said.

"I can't wait to tell Mom," Emma continued. "She saw Lily at our baseball game and said you were watching her like a lovesick puppy."

"Your mom should mind her own business," Evan joked.

"She was right. You are always staring at Lily like you are in love with her or something," Tommy said.

"That's because I am." He said it so naturally that the twins didn't seem to notice the importance of what he'd just admitted. It was one thing that he told me he loved me when we were alone together, but it was so much more serious that he'd admitted it to his kids.

I tried to subtly wipe away the tear forming in the corner of my eye, glad that the twins were now fighting over whose turn it was to do the dishes. Evan's foot tapped against mine under the table and when I looked up, he winked at me. My little emotional reaction hadn't slipped past his watchful eyes.

"Em, do you want to pick the movie we watch tonight?" Evan asked.

"Yes! Now that we have another girl in the family, I don't have to pick some lame action movie." Emma smiled happily at me. "I'll find something good for your first Sullivan family movie night."

"Ugh. She's going to pick some silly romance movie." Tommy stood and started to collect the empty plates while Emma bounced out of her chair and disappeared into the living room.

"I know I didn't exactly prepare you for tonight, but you'll stay for the movie, right?" Evan reached across the table and took my hand.

"I think I'd break Emma's heart if I went home now."

"Not just *her* heart." He brought my hand up and kissed the back of my fingers. "Thanks for being so nice to my daughter today. She really likes you."

"It's my pleasure. Emma is quickly becoming my favorite Sullivan." I took my hand back as Tommy returned to collect more of the empty dishes. "Here, Tommy. Let me help you with the dishes."

"You don't have to do that," he said quickly.

"I know. But if I help, we can start the movie sooner and I know you're dying to watch whatever Emma picks out."

Evan chuckled while Tommy grumbled something about stupid teenage girls and their terrible taste in movies. When I started grabbing plates, Evan stood and joined me. Between the three of us, it only took a couple of minutes to clean up.

Emma did indeed choose some silly romance movie and Tommy scrolled on his phone in a chair across the room instead of paying attention. Emma laid on the floor with her chin propped in her hands, legs swinging behind her. Evan had pulled me down next to him on the couch and after just a slight hesitation, he put his arm tightly around my shoulders.

It occurred to me that this was the first time the kids had ever seen their dad be affectionate with a woman. But if the three of them weren't going to make a big deal out of it, neither would I. Instead, I snuggled closer to Evan and settled my head on his shoulder. It was the first time in my life I'd been part of a family movie night and there was nowhere else I would rather have been.

34

EVAN

"You invited her to movie night?" Chase grimaced over his coffee mug. "When are you proposing?"

"Shut up." I'd already had coffee with Lily this morning, but I helped myself to more from Dad's coffee pot. We were having an emergency family meeting to update the rest of my siblings on what had gone down with Rick.

"I thought you weren't telling the kids yet?" Nate eyed me with a healthy dose of judgment.

"They figured it out. Em was spending time with Lily in her cottage and she saw a couple of my shirts there." I couldn't even be mad about it because I loved having my things casually tossed around the cottage. In a weird way, it was a lot like I was marking my territory, and Lily didn't seem to mind.

"You better not be using that girl," Dad said as he came into the room. "You don't have to propose right now, but I expect Lily to be my daughter-in-law someday in the not-too-distant future."

"We'll see. She might be sick of this family and how much they like to intrude into our personal business." I gave him a pointed glare.

"No way. Lily loves us." Chase looked past me. "Right, Harp?"

"Totally." She held up her phone so we could all see Noah's smiling face on the video chat. "Noah wants to know if you can make it a winter wedding so he'll be able to attend."

"December would be best for me," Noah said. "That still gives you a couple of months to plan everything."

"I'm not getting married in two months, dumbass." I forced extra annoyance into my voice because I actually wasn't that horrified by the idea of marrying Lily in a couple of months. I knew it was too soon, but I also knew that what we had was the real thing. Unless I completely fucked it up, Lily was going to be my wife someday.

"Which one of us gets to be the best man?" Nate asked.

"I'm leaning towards Brent," I grumbled.

"Fuck that guy." Chase reacted exactly how I knew I would. "He probably won't even leave his job long enough to come to the wedding."

"Whose wedding?" Ronan was the last to arrive. Though he technically wasn't a sibling, Dad always included him in our big family announcements. "And where's your girl? Isn't she pretty much family at this point."

"She's staying with the twins." It hadn't made sense for

her to be here since she already knew everything. Dad also wanted the opportunity to explain to all of us about his decision to hire Lily and keep her investigation a secret. He thought that would be easier to do if she wasn't there. More likely, he was worried one of my brothers would say something shitty in front of her before they had time to filter their feelings.

At the end of the day, Dad was the one who had wanted to keep the secret. Lily had only been following her boss's orders and she had done a great job. Not only had she achieved Dad's goal, but she'd also become an asset in her fake role of helping us improve the efficiencies of our business.

We settled in the living room for our meeting and Chase dialed in Brent to complete the invite list. Unlike Noah, he had insisted on a normal call rather than using video. He was probably sitting at his desk at work, multitasking as he listened to our family drama with a distant ear. Brent tried to stay as disconnected from the family business as possible.

Dad didn't mince his words as he explained what had happened with Rick. My brothers all sat stone-faced while Harper took on a smug look. Chase eventually pressed our dad on why he had lied to us. Dad explained his reasoning and also made it clear that Lily had only been following his directions.

"She's a good liar," Chase muttered. "Evan should probably be worried about that."

"Fuck off, Chase," Harper snapped before I could

jump to Lily's defense. "Lily did her job and she did it well. You don't get to be pissed at her."

"I'm not pissed at Lily. I'm pissed that I thought we hired someone who was actually really good at her job and could help us run this place only to find out that wasn't true. That Lily is going to be leaving us." Chase grunted and crossed his arms over his broad chest. "I was counting on her being here."

You and me both, I thought to myself. Lily and I hadn't really talked about what her plan was going to be now.

"Well, that's going to be part of this discussion." Dad leaned forward in his seat, elbows on his knees. "Now that she's done with the investigation, I'd like to extend a new job offer to her. She has been doing an incredible job finding ways to increase our profits and expand the ranch. Last week, she presented me with a five-year plan that would help set us up for decades of growth. If everyone agrees, I'd like to make her the operations manager for the business."

"But that's your job," Harper said with a gasp.

"And I've been ready to retire since the stroke. I didn't feel comfortable stepping back earlier when Evan and Chase were so busy running their respective portfolios. It's a lot of work to oversee the financials and logistics of the entire business, but Lily has an incredibly sharp mind. I have no doubt that she will succeed in the role."

"Agreed," Harper said with a big smile. "She has my vote."

"Same," Nate agreed quietly.

"I'm on board the Lily train," Noah added through the phone.

"I'll defer to the rest of you on this," Brent said, his standard response for anything to do with the family business.

Dad turned his attention to me and Chase. "Well, boys?"

"Yeah. Obviously yes." Chase let out a relieved laugh.

It somehow felt like this vote was about more than just the business. It was about my family accepting Lily as one of us. It was about us fighting to keep her.

"Yes," I said around a lump of emotion lodged in my throat.

"Good." Dad smiled and clapped his hands together. "Evan, you'll be the one to convince her to accept the offer. I have a feeling she won't say no to you."

"Given how she spends her nights, I'd say you're right about that." Chase grunted when Harper punched his arm.

Dad had already put together an offer letter and he presented it to me with a clap on the back. "We're keeping her," he said, giving me a pointed look. "She's a Sullivan now."

35

LILY

"She's beautiful, isn't she?" Marv leaned on the fencepost next to me.

"Yes. Is she new?" I spent a lot of days watching the ranch horses go about their daily business, but I only recognized a few of them. Like Evan's horse, Blaze, or Chase's horse, Zorro. This horse wasn't one that I recognized.

"She arrived a few days ago." Marv rested a dirty boot on one of the rungs. "Evan paid a pretty penny for her."

"I appreciate you taking a few minutes to chat with me," I said, my heart racing as I considered what I was going to say next. "I've been going over the budget for next year and checking some of the recent expenses. I noticed that in the last six months, we've had to buy a number of new machines. A couple of ATVs."

"Yeah, it's been a rough year on some of the equipment." Marv kept his eyes on the horse walking around the pasture.

I nodded and tried not to sound too accusatory when I said, "I checked the barn last week and I couldn't find those new ATVs. Same with the machinery. It all looks at least a few years old and the serial numbers verified that."

"I see." Marv's shoulders pulled back. "Have you told Tom?"

"No. I was talking to Evan a few nights ago and he mentioned that your wife has been sick. She has cancer?"

Marv nodded.

"Those treatments can be expensive." I hated what I was about to say. "Is that why you needed the money?"

"Yes." He barely got out the word.

"From what I could tell, it was only about $10,000 total. Does that sound right?"

"It does." Marv finally looked at me. There were unshed tears in his eyes. "I planned to pay it back. I've been working some jobs on the weekends to make the extra cash and I almost have enough to pay it back."

"Why didn't you just ask Tom? Or Evan? They would've given you the money." I knew that beyond a shadow of a doubt.

"I couldn't. Not after Tom told me about Rick asking him for money last year. He was so annoyed by the whole thing that my pride wouldn't let me do the same thing."

"It's not the same," I said firmly. "Your wife was sick and she needed expensive treatment. You didn't blow a million dollars gambling on races."

Marv looked away. "Tom knows what I did?"

"No. I haven't told him." I put my hand on his arm. "I'm going to tell Evan and let him decide what to do."

"That's fair." Marv offered a weak smile. "I really love this ranch, but I love that family more. I never meant to hurt them."

"I know. I think Evan will know that, too." I squeezed his arm. "I'm glad your wife is doing better. Evan says she's a sweetheart."

"She's the love of my life," he said simply.

I left the stables and headed toward where I had last seen Evan, fixing some loose boards on one of the barns. When he saw me headed toward him, he set down his hammer and removed his gloves.

"Hey, sweetheart." His smile warmed every inch of me. "My day just got a whole lot better."

I put my hand on his shoulder to balance as I pushed up to give him a kiss. "I'm afraid I might actually be about to ruin your day."

"That sounds ominous." He gestured to a bale of hay. "Let's sit."

Once I was seated close enough to him that I could steal his body warmth, I took a deep breath and told him about Marv. I explained that while I was investigating Rick, I'd noticed some expenses that didn't make sense. I couldn't tie them back to Rick and eventually discovered that they had come from Marv. Then I told him about my conversation with Marv and how he had confessed to needing the money for his wife's cancer treatments.

"Why didn't he just tell me?" Evan asked, sounding so

hurt that I wanted to hug him. "I would've given him the money."

"I know. Marv knows that, too. But he didn't want to be like Rick, using your family for handouts. He's been working side jobs to make the money to pay you back." I put my hand on Evan's back and stroked a slow circle. "I haven't told your dad and I won't unless you want me to. Right now, we can just pretend I never noticed it. Unless you want to handle it differently."

"No, I'm not going to punish Marv over this. It's my own fault for not noticing that he was struggling. Marv and his wife are practically family. I never should've put him in a position where he felt like he had to do this." Evan yanked off his baseball hat and hung it from his knee before running a hand through his hair. "I don't want Dad to find out about this. He'll feel terrible that Marv felt like he couldn't ask us for help."

"Okay. We won't tell him." I reached over to fix the mess Evan had just made of his hair. "But you need to talk to Marv. He's beating himself up over this."

"I'll talk to him." Evan leaned over and pressed a kiss to my temple. "Thank you for handling this so discreetly."

"Of course. I like Marv."

"Did you take some time to think about the offer?" Evan was doing his best not to look too hopeful.

"I've thought about it." I knew that he was disappointed I hadn't immediately accepted when he presented me with the job offer yesterday. I had wanted to say yes immediately. But I still had some concerns about accepting. "Ev, I can't just keep living at the cottage for free. If I'm going to be staying here long-term, I need something permanent."

"Fine. Move in with me."

I laughed. "That's not what I meant."

"I know. But it's an option. I plan to marry you someday, Lil. We'll have to live together eventually." He wrapped a strong arm around my shoulders. "How about I rent you the cottage for the next six months? When the time is up, I'll make you this offer again. If you're not ready to move in then, we'll extend it another six months until you are ready."

"I'll think about it."

"Good. That's all I ask." He pulled me tighter against him. "Em has been lobbying really hard for you to stay. She keeps texting me pictures of different engagement rings that she thinks you would like."

"You're kidding." I was equally horrified and touched.

"She has expensive taste, too." He put his lips to my ear. "I should probably let her know that I already have one picked out for you."

"What?" I gaped at him. "Why?"

He laughed nervously. "Do you really need an explanation?"

"It's too soon," I breathed.

"For you," he said not unkindly. "It's too soon for you. I understand and I'm not trying to pressure you or rush anything. You'll get there. We have plenty of time."

THE NEXT MORNING I was still thinking about that conversation as I helped Chase unpack boxes of new merchandise. Unlike Evan, he had been putting pressure on me to accept the job offer.

"Is it the money?" he asked in frustration when I wouldn't tell him why I was hesitant to accept. "Because I'm sure we can work something out."

"No. It's not the money." I had plenty of money and Tom's offer had been more than fair financially.

"Then what is the holdup? You love it here. Your best friend is here. Your boyfriend. Me." He smirked. "You have everything you could ever want."

"That's kind of the problem," I said, folding a t-shirt into a neat square. "What's that expression... don't shit where you eat?"

"And in that analogy, am I the shit or the food?" he asked with a laugh.

"You know what I mean. It's like mixing business with pleasure. Everything and everyone I care about is inextricably connected. What if I take the job offer and then end up quitting in three months? I would lose my home, my friends, and probably Evan."

"Over quitting a job? No way. Harper would never drop a friend over something like that and Evan isn't dumb enough to give up the best thing that's happened to him in twelve years. You are just making excuses because you're scared," he said confidently. "You aren't afraid that things aren't going to work out. You're afraid that they will."

Ouch. That was both blunt and accurate. I was used to

dealing with things going bad. I had no idea what to do with a happily-ever-after ending.

Chase turned away to answer his ringing phone. "Yeah?" His shoulders hitched up. "Where is he? I'll be right there." He glanced back at me, worry etched on his face. "She's with me. I'll bring her."

"What's wrong?" I demanded before he'd ended the call.

"Evan got hurt on the ranch. Nate is driving him to the hospital and Tom and Marv are on their way, too." He squeezed my shoulder. "I'm going to tell Kasey that we're leaving. Go wait in my truck."

"Chase." I felt like I couldn't breathe. "Is he okay?"

"He'll be fine." Chase forced a smile that was actually a grimace. "Can you call Harper and give her a heads up? Just tell her that we're headed to the hospital and I'll call her when we have more details."

I appreciated that he was trying to give me something proactive to do so I wouldn't start to panic. I called Harper on my way to the truck and after the initial shock, she responded with a surprising amount of optimism. "Evan will be fine. The boys are always getting injured on that ranch, but it usually just results in some stitches or maybe a broken bone."

I found that comforting. Even if he'd broken both legs and arms, at least he would be alive and able to recover from the injuries. I'd even sign up to give him a sponge bath every night. Just as long as he was okay.

We found the guys waiting for us in the emergency waiting room. Nate looked as calm as always, but Marv was bouncing his legs in his seat and Tom was too anxious to even sit.

"What happened?" I asked Nate.

"He was up on the barn roof repairing some rotted wood. One of the boards snapped beneath him and he lost his balance and fell. Tumbled right off the edge of the roof." Nate grimaced at the memory. "It knocked him out and fucked up his arm. He was lucky he didn't break his neck."

"Did he hit his head?" I was overcome with images of Evan smacking his head on the ground.

"I don't think so. At least not too hard. He was conscious when I got him into my truck and he wasn't slurring his words or anything."

That lifted a little of the weight on my chest. Nate grabbed my arm and pulled me toward the seat next to his. "Sit. Breathe."

"Someone needs to call Harper with an update," I said, sinking onto the plastic-covered seat. "And should we tell Naomi?"

"Let's wait until we know more details. We don't want the twins panicking over nothing." Tom gave me a reassuring smile. "We'll save the panicking for us."

"The doctor is coming." Nate nodded toward the hallway and we all quickly stood.

"Evan Sullivan's family?" she asked and we all nodded. "We've got the pain under control and I have reviewed the x-rays. He's got a broken arm and three cracked ribs. Very lucky considering the circumstances. It could've been a lot worse. The arm has a clean break so we'll be able to set and cast it. He'll need to stay overnight so we can keep an eye on him since he did hit his head during the fall. The tests don't show any brain damage or lung punctures, but he has a lot of bruising and swelling around his ribs and it could make breathing difficult for a while."

"But he's going to be alright?" Chase clarified.

"Yes. He should make a full recovery."

More weight lifted and I smiled when Nate hugged me from behind. "Sullivan men aren't easy to get rid of," he said, squeezing me tight around my chest. "You were worried for nothing."

"Yeah, yeah." I found Nate's embrace almost as comforting as having Evan's arms around me. "I'm so silly for being worried about my boyfriend falling off a roof."

"Didn't Chase tell you about the time he shoved Evan off the roof of that same barn?" Nate's arms dropped away as he shoved Chase's arm. "I honestly thought you were trying to kill him."

"He started that fight." Chase shrugged as if it was common to push your sibling off a roof.

"I don't know what I did to deserve the punishment of having so many dumbass sons," Tom grumbled.

It took almost two hours for them to get Evan admitted and moved to his room. I let the guys go inside first, preferring to hang back and let them swarm Evan with their exuberance. He laughed good-naturedly when his brothers gave him shit for being clumsy and Tom scolded him for not wearing the right shoes. It took almost five minutes for him to realize I was still lingering in the doorway.

"What are you doing? Get over here." He grinned and waved for me to come closer. "You're the only person I want to see right now. These assholes can all leave."

I awkwardly shuffled through the small space that had been cleared for me to approach the bed. One of Evan's arms was snug inside a cast tucked into a sling. I slid my hand through his non-injured hand. "You fell off a roof and scared the shit out of us."

"Sorry." He didn't look very sorry. "You're cute when you're worried, Lil."

"It would be wrong to punch him in the ribs, right?" I asked Chase.

"Probably. I'm willing to do it for you." Chase formed a fist.

"Hey now. I almost died." Evan let out a weak cough.

"I think we should let you get some rest, son." Tom patted Evan's good shoulder. "I'll get the boys out of your hair and Marv will make sure the ranch is still standing."

"Thanks, Dad." Evan kept a tight grip on my hand.

"I think I'll stay," I said. "Harper will be stopping by later and she can give me a ride home."

"Sure. If something comes up and you need a ride, just give one of us a call," Nate said.

They filed out of the room with a chorus of goodbyes and then we were surrounded by quiet as the door shut behind them.

"Damn, my family is so fucking loud." Evan laughed and tugged my hand. "Sit with me, sweetheart."

"I don't want to hurt you." Now that we were alone, I could focus on his injuries. The fingers peeking out of the cast were swollen and purple. His torso was wrapped tightly with medical tape and he wasn't wearing anything over it, revealing more bruising on his chest.

"It looks worse than it is," Evan insisted, tugging again. "Come on. This side isn't hurt and cuddling you will make me feel better."

Not for the first time, his smile had me willing to do whatever he asked. As I snuggled in next to him on the narrow hospital bed, the rest of the weight that had been pressing down on my chest finally faded away.

"I was really worried about you, Evan." I wrapped my arms around his arm and laid my head on his shoulder.

"I'm sorry." His hand was warm on my thigh. "I feel pretty stupid for making everyone worry. I've never lost my balance like that."

"What happened? Were you distracted?" I had never seen Evan be anything but sure-footed when he was working.

"I may have been reliving that thing you did to me in the shower this morning." He nipped lightly at my earlobe. "If I had died falling off that roof, I would've gone out on a high."

"Not funny." I wasn't ready to joke about his accident yet.

"Lil, I really am fine." He shook his arm free from my grip to wrap it around my shoulders.

"But what if you weren't? I could've lost you today, love." I blinked a few times to clear away tears that were threatening to fall. "I just found you. I can't lose you."

"Sweetheart, I'm not going anywhere. I'm right here."

"I'm not going anywhere either. I'm accepting your job offer. And the offer to stay in the cottage. I'm sorry I even needed to think about it." I snuggled closer to him. "I love you, Evan."

"I love you, Lily." He pressed a kiss to the top of my head. "I'm glad you're so obsessed with me because I'm going to need lots of help when they release me from this place."

"Help?" I smiled at the thought of Evan actually letting me take care of him.

"Mostly with bathing. Getting dressed. Styling my gorgeous tresses." He sighed extravagantly. "Are you sure you're still going to want to be with someone as helpless as me?"

I lifted my head and kissed his cheek. "For the rest of my life."

36

EVAN

Four Months Later

"Explain yourself, Sullivan."

I ignored the glare that Lily was shooting at me. "It's a horse. Surely you can recognize one after almost six months of living on a ranch."

"Don't be a smartass."

"But you like my ass." I turned to wink at her. "Ready to go for a ride?"

"On this horse?"

I waved her forward. "This is Daisy. She's a three-year-old mare with pretty hair and a sassy attitude. I bought her for you."

"For me?" Lily blinked in confusion.

"You need a horse, sweetheart. Everyone in the family has one."

"I'm not in the family." She reached up and stroked Daisy's nose. "You can't just buy me a horse, Evan."

"I absolutely can." I'd spent the last four months getting Daisy ready for Lily in secret. Lily had been riding Blaze on our weekly outings and she was ready for her own horse. "Blaze told me that he doesn't appreciate that you'd rather ride me than him."

"You and Blaze talk about our sex life?" She raised a skeptical eyebrow. "Have you considered therapy?"

"I got you a new saddle," I said, fighting a smile. "It should fit you better than the one you've been borrowing."

Lily was immediately suspicious. "Why are you giving me a new horse in the dead of winter?"

"You don't know what today is, do you?"

"It's Sunday."

"It's six months exactly since I first laid eyes on you." I shook my head at the memory of seeing her for the first time. "I haven't been able to stop looking at you since, sweetheart."

Lily held my gaze for a long moment. "I can't believe it's only been six months. I feel like I've loved you my whole life."

"Meanwhile I don't feel like I've loved you nearly long enough." I gestured to Daisy. "Check out the saddle and see what you think."

She approached the horse cautiously even though I knew she was perfectly comfortable around horses now. As she placed a hand on the supple leather, I fidgeted with the item in my pocket. Her fingers grazed the small design I'd had embossed on the side of the saddle. "Nice touch," Lily said, tracing the heart that had our names etched inside. "And a pretty ribbon, too?"

As she pulled taught the white ribbon tied to the pommel, the words stitched on it in blue became clear. "Ev?" Her voice hitched and she turned to me, but her gaze was too high because I was already down on one knee.

"Well?" I held up the block box and flipped open the lid, revealing the ring that I'd picked out for her months ago. "You read the ribbon. What do you say? Will you marry me, Lily?"

She dropped to her knees right in front of me, ignoring the ring as she reached for me. With one hand over my heart and the other on my cheek, she said, "I would be honored to be your wife, Evan Sullivan."

Check out the next books in the Crestwood Valley series.

ABOUT THE AUTHOR

Juliet Keane lives in Chicago where she surrounds herself with good food, great books, and fantastic friends. She is a contemporary and new adult romance author who also writes women's fiction and sweet romance books under the pen name Hunter J. Keane.

LONG HARD ROAD
MADISON

"This can't be right." I checked the map on my phone and prayed that I had made a wrong turn. After two days in my car, I just wanted a hot shower and a comfortable bed. When I'd randomly decided to leave home, I hadn't given a lot of thought to just how much I was going to hate taking a long road trip by myself.

"What the hell is this place?" With the map still directing me to turn off the highway, I quickly dialed my assistant.

"Are you there?" Kaylie asked.

"I don't know. I thought you had rented me a cabin."

"I did. It has two bedrooms and a beautiful view of the mountains."

I craned my neck in a futile attempt to see what was waiting for me ahead. "What can you tell me about Crestwood?"

"Not much. It looks like a really cute little town. If you

stay on the main road, it will take you right to the downtown area." Kaylie's computer chimed an alert and I could hear her typing. She was a queen of multitasking. "There's a café, bookstore, some boutiques, a few restaurants, and a couple of bars."

"I probably shouldn't start drinking until at least noon." I checked the clock and it was barely time for breakfast. "What time am I allowed to check in at my cabin?"

"You've got a couple more hours. Didn't you read the information I sent you yesterday?" Kaylie was annoyed. I wasn't great at paying attention to details. It was why I paid her so well.

"I'm going to find some food and coffee. Not necessarily in that order." The shower would have to wait. Now that I'd started thinking about food, that was all I could focus on. "I'll let you go, Kales. Thanks for getting this all set up for me."

"No worries. Drake has already called twice asking where you are."

"What did you tell him?"

"That you decided to take an impromptu vacation and when you are ready to speak with him, you will initiate a call."

"Perfect. Thanks." I owed Kaylie a very nice bonus after the work she'd done these last few days. She really was the best assistant in the business.

She hung up without a proper goodbye as per usual. I pulled off the shoulder of the road and headed in the direction of downtown. The roads were slick with some fresh, wet snow and I should've rented a more substantial car rather than drive my sports car all the way from Nashville. The giant red truck riding my ass seemed to agree.

I wasn't going to drive at an unsafe speed just to appease a man with a small dick complex. If he didn't like it, he could just go around me. I made a mental note to look into buying a truck so I wouldn't have to spend every drive into town worrying about someone else killing me with their supersized vehicles.

It wasn't hard to find the café since the main street of downtown Crestwood pretty much encompassed all of downtown. Before getting out of my car, I checked my reflection in the mirror. It was strange to see my hair bleached platinum blond and sporting a new style. The natural curl of my hair usually brought it to just past my shoulders, but straightening it had added several inches. Except for the hair by my face which had been chopped into long bangs that I had to push out of my eyes.

That was another big change. The irises were the same emerald shade, but they were no longer framed by fake lashes or highlighted by bright eye shadow. I wasn't wearing any makeup in public for the first time in a very long time.

"New me, new life," I mumbled.

That new life almost ended abruptly when my foot slipped out from under as I stepped out of my car. I was lucky that I was still holding the car door and I was able to keep from completely wiping out. The damn asphalt was too slick for my heeled boots. I made another mental note to look into ordering some appropriate winter clothing.

The bell above the door chimed happily as I pushed it open. I was met with a blast of warm air from an overhead vent and the smell of vanilla, cinnamon, and coffee. My stomach growled to make itself known. Never one to deny myself pleasure, I marched toward the counter.

"Hi!" The woman behind the counter flashed a megawatt smile. She was a pretty woman, probably not much older than me. Her nametag said *Amelia*.

"Hello." I pointed to the glass display case. "I'll take the biggest cinnamon roll and a large coffee."

"Coming right up!" She turned to grab a coffee cup. "You're not from around here, are you? What brings you to Crestwood?"

I was envious of the woman's energy and her genuine friendliness. This was a woman who actually enjoyed chatting with strangers.

"Just taking a little vacation," I said.

"Where are you staying?" Amelia put the coffee in front of me and slid open the display case.

"I've rented a cabin somewhere around here. I was looking for someplace remote to clear my head, but I was a little nervous about staying too far outside of civilization." In truth, I hadn't bothered looking at the information that Kaylie had sent me on the cabin she had selected. She was good at her job and I trusted her.

"My neighbor's aunt is renting out her dad's cabin. He had to go into assisted living last spring and she decided to fancy up the place and rent it out. I haven't seen all the new updates they've made, but it's a beautiful piece of land." Amelia added a giant cinnamon roll to a plate and placed that next to the coffee. She rang up my order and I paid, leaving a generous tip in the jar next to the register.

"Enjoy your time in Crestwood," Amelia said. "Maybe I will see you around."

"Maybe." I forced a smile. If things went according to plan, I would see as few people as possible. I hadn't come to Crestwood to mingle with the locals. I'd come to hide away in a remote area while my life went to shit.

When I turned to find a seat, I noticed a table with three teenage girls who were looking at something on their phones. I heard the light strum of a guitar playing a familiar song.

"Shit," I mouthed to myself, keeping my head down and letting my hair shield most of my face. It didn't just prevent them from clearly seeing my face, it also prevented me from seeing that a man at the table closest to me had just pushed back his chair and stood. I barely avoided sloshing my coffee all over him, but I did manage to splash it on my hand. "Ow. Fuck."

A large hand closed around my arm. "Sorry, miss. Are you alright?"

I looked up and nearly dropped my coffee along with my jaw. The man in front of me was staring at me with concern while I was staring at him in awe. He was gorgeous. Dark hair cropped close on the sides and a little longer on top. It had a perfect wave to it that was just begging for me to slide my fingers through it. He had equally enticing eyes, the color of a gray sky just before a storm.

"Um, yes." I somehow composed myself enough to

string together two sounds that passed for a confirmation. "I'm sorry. I didn't see you."

That was a laughable excuse considering this man was a few inches over six feet with broad shoulders that tapered to a narrow waist. Missing a man that large, and that beautiful, was impossible.

"No worries. I'm a bit of a wallflower. I tend to blend in with my surroundings." His smile was crooked, lifting higher on the right side. "Pretty much the opposite of you."

I just kept staring at him.

"You're sure you're okay?" His grip on my arm tightened.

"I'm good." I laughed awkwardly. "It's just been a long few days."

"Been there." He gestured to the table he'd just vacated. "It's all yours. Some food and caffeine will help clear the brain fog."

"That's the hope." I flinched when he stepped closer to pull out a chair. "Oh. Thanks."

"You've got your hands full." He winked at me and stepped back. "Enjoy. This place has the best cinnamon rolls in the state and the coffee is damn good, too."

I nodded and put down the plate and mug before sliding into the seat he'd pulled out. When I looked up to ask his name, he was already walking away. He chatted with Amelia quickly and she handed him some napkins. Then he returned to my table and handed them to me. "For the spill." Then he smiled his crooked smile and walked away.

In the haze of lusting after him, I had forgotten about the coffee that had splashed and burned my hand. Of course I had been a clumsy dork in front of the hottest man I'd ever seen. Not to mention practically mute. It was probably for the best since the attention of a hot man was the last thing I needed right now.

Check out Long Hard Road now.

Printed in Dunstable, United Kingdom

65334871R00190